They Laid Claim to a New World of Bold Challenge and Thrilling Opportunity. . . .

CAROLINE WICKHAM—As wife of the British Colonial Secretary, her future seemed secure—until she was forced to flee across New Zealand to escape the hurt, the scandal, the shame.

GRAYSON WICKHAM—Caroline's brother. He would risk his future to marry a beautiful Maori, only to betray his wife, his sister, his sons for the sake of his own savage ambitions.

SIR NEVIL HOLBROOKE—Intent on rising in the new colonial government, he prized his position. But desperate needs threatened to destroy his career, his marriage, his life.

JOCK MILSOM—Manager of a vast sheep-farming station in the High Country, he offered Caroline a marriage of convenience—a rugged, isolated life of simple satisfactions and unforeseen dangers.

GEOFFREY RUTLEDGE—Determined to succeed on his own, he hid his aristocratic heritage. When he embraced New Zealand as his homeland, only one woman could complete his happiness. But she was already bound, and only fate could set her free.

Now is the Hour

Joan Joseph

Weston, Florida
32136 - 701

This novel is a work of historical fiction. Names, characters, places and incidents relating to non-historical figures are either the product of the author's imagination or are used fictitiously, and any resemblance of such non-historical figures, places or incidents to actual persons, living or dead, events or locales is entirely coincidental.

EXCLUSIVE DISTRIBUTION BY
PARADISE PRESS, INC.

ISBN #1-57657-408-3

Printed in the U.S.A.

NOW IS THE HOUR

True lovers often must part;
Kiss me and leave me to sorrow!
Here, love, I give you my heart;
You will return some glad morrow.
But . . .

Now is the hour
When we must say goodbye;
Soon we'll be sailing
Far across the sea.

While you're away,
Oh, then remember me;
When you return,
You'll find me waiting here.

—Maori Farewell Song

Many people have assisted me in the researching of material for this book. I especially wish to thank Professor Keith Sinclair, Department of History, Auckland University; Professor Sidney Mead, Department of Maori Studies, Victoria University; David R. Simmons, Auckland Institute and Museum; Barry Skinner, Director of the Waitangi National Trust; Lawrence Nathan; Jean and Jacques Murchison; Mona Anderson; J. Blair Sheehy, Tourist Hotel Corporation of New Zealand; Lions Brewery; W. A. Coutts, Wilson Distillers Ltd.; New Zealand Airlines; Bill Narrhun, Air Pacific Limited; Patti Enting; the Reverend Alex Sutherland, Suva, Fiji; Dora Patterson, Levuka, Fiji; Suli Sandys, Levuka; Norman McGoon, Suva; Patricia Froomberg, London, England; and a special word of thanks to Fiona J. MacCuish for traveling with me throughout New Zealand and aiding me in absorbing the beauty and culture of the country, making it possible for me to impart these flavors to this book. My thanks, too, to Coleen O'Shea for encouraging me to write this novel, and to my editor, Marilyn Wright, for helping me to see it through.

Glossary

MAORI	TRANSLATION
haerera	farewell
haere mai	welcome
haka	war dance
hangi	earth oven
heitiki	neck pendant
hinau	Elaeocarpus dentatus—a tree
Hone	John
hongi	nose kiss
kainga	village
kawanatanga	governorship
kina	sea egg
Kua Pakeha	Maori who becomes Pakeha
mana	authority, prestige
Maori	Polynesian people

Glossary

marae	village common
moko	tattoo
Pakeha	European
Pakeha-Maori	European who becomes Maori
pa	fortified village
po atarau	now is the hour
raupo	bulrush
tangiwai	tear drop—greenstone
taniwha	ferocious beast
tarawhakairo	fertility tattoo
tena koe	hello
toetoe	feathery plumes of grass
tohunga	sacred priest
toa	wooden top made of wood from toatoa tree
utu	revenge, satisfaction
whare	hut

FIJI	TRANSLATION
bula venaka	hello
bure	temple
Cakobau	Name of High Chief of Fiji
Carloo	Great Spirit
eeo	yes
Kaivavalagi	European
lali	drum
liku	woman's dress
lobu	earth oven
maca	empty
meke	dance
neenee toma tah	you are an angry man
seengah	no
sinandrah	how do you do
solevu	feast
soro	ceremony of atonement to the chief

sulu	man's loin cloth
tui	chief
Tui Viti	High Chief (King) of Fiji
vaka singa	hair like sun
voi voi	native flax
yaqona	grog made from pepper plant

Fiji Islands

Vanua Levu

SOLEVU BAY

LOVONI   NAWAIDO

Ovalau

LEVUKA

Viti Levu

Bau

REWA RIVER   WAINIBOKASI

LAUCALA

SUVA   LAUCALA BAY

1140 Nautical Miles

New Zealand

N

W

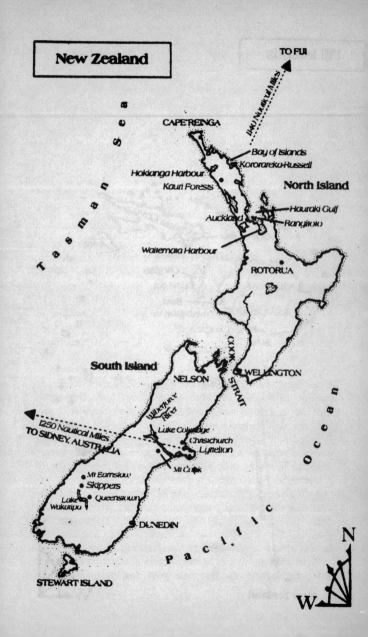

Chapter 1

1844

A HOLLOW, HIGH-PITCHED SOUND PIERCED THE RISING dawn. A single melancholy note from a nose flute, and then there was silence. The distant haunting tone awakened Caroline to her surroundings. At only seventeen years old, it was frightening to be twelve thousand miles away from home, yet, at the same time, it was mysteriously exciting. She stood near the bow of the ship, slowly watching land come into sight. The Bay of Islands was breathtaking—a combination of jagged rock and verdant land dotted the waters. There were one hundred and fifty islands, some large, some small, all rising out of a shimmering sea of brilliant green. A warm breeze filled the billowing sails, and the ship headed steadily toward Kororareka, New Zealand's most vital city.

At the stern of the *Rosanna,* a tall man of stalwart frame leaned against the rail, sketchpad and charcoal in hand. His dress was far less formal than most of the passengers, but then, Geoffrey Rutledge had not boarded the ship in England; he was already accustomed to the more casual colonial style.

From afar, the young man watched as the first streaks of dawn highlighted the few pale gold strands in Caroline's tawny hair. Dressed simply, in a full-skirted, high-necked blue muslin frock, she was an extravagant picture of loveliness. He wondered if she realized how beautiful she was. The magical spell of the moment was broken as Sir Nevil Holbrooke appeared on deck.

Returning to his work, Geoffrey quickly finished his sketch. The less he saw of Sir Nevil, the better. Three weeks at sea, traveling from Sydney to Kororareka, had been more than enough for Geoffrey. He thoroughly disliked Sir Nevil's arrogance. Yet, he reluctantly had to admit that the man was extremely intelligent and could be charming. Still, Geoffrey felt ill at ease in the Englishman's presence, completely unable to penetrate his mask of smug superiority.

A small blue penguin bobbed its head above the water, as if in search of a particular island. Caroline watched, fascinated as it pulled itself up onto a nearby shore. She laughed as she watched the pompous little bird waddle along the sandy shore toward a rookery of chattering penguins seemingly eager for their companion to join them. No more than twelve inches tall, the curious little creatures were quite different from what Caroline had expected—much smaller, and instead of black and white, their pelts were a gleaming teal blue.

"They're marvelous!" exclaimed Caroline.

"Yes," said Nevil delighting at her youthful exuberance. "It's rare to see them so late in the year. During the summer months they prefer the cold waters to the south, but they'll be back . . . in large numbers, I might add, as soon as the smell of winter is in the air . . . certainly by June."

Caroline smiled politely but made no comment. She knew in time she would grow accustomed to the reverse seasons, but now she was struggling with the fact that here, below the equator, it was colder in the south than in the north, colder in June than in December.

A series of doleful, hooting sounds distracted her.

"The Maoris have sighted our ship," Nevil explained. "That's their way of greeting us . . . a salute with conch-shell trumpets."

"I'm not certain I like that sound," said Caroline, looking up at him with a provocative smile.

They stood quietly, watching the shoreline come closer as the ship sailed slowly forward. Her thoughts drifted back to the life she had left behind. When her parents had died, and her brother Grayson had first told her he was going to New Zealand, her reaction had been one of fear. The thought of remaining in England without him had briefly crossed her mind, but he had always been her protector; she wouldn't, couldn't stay behind. Then, she had read about New Zealand and learned that it was called the land of promise, land of riches, land of hope, and her imagination had been fired. The thought of pioneering in a new world and expanding her horizons had excited her. And so, she had decided to join her brother in his quest for a better life. She had signed a three-year contract to work as a companion. Her voyage had been paid and her salary stipulated. Her friends in London had told her she would be no better than an indentured servant, but she had never looked at the contract in this way. To Caroline it was a good job, and more important, it was her passport to a new life in a new world.

She had dreamed of marrying a pioneer, a man who loved adventure as much as she, and had fantasized about how wonderful it would be to bring up children in the fresh air of wide-open country instead of the crowded slums of London's East End. But she had never expected a titled man to fall in love with her—she, who came from such humble beginnings. And yet, from the moment she first met Nevil, she had felt he cared for her. There was something about Nevil that drew her to him. He was twelve years older than she yet did not treat her like a child. He encouraged her aspirations and seemed to admire her spirit.

The usual boredom of sea life rarely gripped Caroline. Each day she spent with Nevil, she found him more and more fascinating. He seemed versed in every subject. As the days slipped by and weeks became months, she felt herself falling in love with him. Nevil Holbrooke was exciting. When he asked her to marry him, she felt she was living a dream. She could hardly believe that this man—the newly appointed Colonial Secretary of New Zealand—wanted to spend his life with her.

Now, as she stood at the rail of the ship, she found it almost impossible to believe her good fortune. Was it really true that at only seventeen she was betrothed to a man who would make her dreams come true, a man who answered her every hope and prayer?

Caroline was still looking into Nevil's soft gray eyes, silently admiring his gentle features, when her brother Grayson came up from behind. "We're almost there," he announced in his usual carefree manner. "I'll miss you when I leave for Auckland," he said, planting a kiss on Caroline's cheek. "These four months at sea together have been fun."

Caroline turned to face her brother. Ever since she could remember, his thick sandy hair was as untamed as it was now blown carefree by the wind from the sea. The thought reminded her of their childhood in London, and for a brief moment, she wished she were back home. His clear blue eyes met hers and he sensed her hesitation and feelings of trepidation.

"You'll stay for a few days, won't you?" she asked. "Until I'm settled, at least?"

"I'll be in Kororareka a fortnight," Nevil answered in Grayson's stead.

The look in Caroline's eyes thanked Nevil, and though she felt reassured, she was embarrassed by his answer to her youthful plea. Her gaze dropped from Nevil's eyes. For a moment she was distracted, noticing for the first time that morning that he was sporting a barrel-knotted tie. The rich green foularde was particularly becoming against his white silk shirt and sprigged mulberry satin waistcoat. She wanted to tell him how elegant he looked, instead, she just said "Thank you."

Grayson bristled. "I'll see to it that my sister's cared for and settled . . . even if it means staying in Kororareka an extra week or two," he put in sharply, resenting Nevil's intrusion.

Grayson, only twenty years old, was impressed by Sir Nevil, but still, there was something about him that he instinctively disliked. He could see that Nevil entranced his sister, and he understood why Caroline thought it would be a good marriage. Yet, he was in no way convinced that this aristocratic personage would bring his sister happiness.

Angry and frustrated, Grayson turned away. He caught a glimpse of Geoffrey at the far end of the ship, and relaxed at the sight of him.

Geoffrey, who had previously spent four years in this part of the world, appeared completely at ease. He had first come here as an artist employed by the New Zealand Company, commissioned to paint canvases that would entice Englishmen to settle in this new land. When his work was finished, he had gone to Sydney for a year and, to subsist, had worked in construction. But New Zealand held a magnetic charm for him, and at the first opportunity, he had decided to return. In his years away from home, he had slowly dropped the formalities of Victorian England. Now, instead of wearing finely fashioned brocaded waistcoats, he usually wore blue serge shirts and moleskin inexpressibles. Grayson thought he might enjoy wearing similar moleskin trousers, and wondered how long it would take him to feel comfortable in his new life.

He hurried his step as he saw Geoffrey turn toward the stairs to the lower deck. Grayson greeted him from afar and the artist stopped and waited.

"Sir Nevil's a bit of a blowhard," Grayson blurted out angrily.

Geoffrey nodded in agreement and reached for his pipe. "Ah, yes, a bit—and then some," he answered, barely concealing his sarcasm.

They both chuckled. Grayson sensed that Geoffrey was drawn to his sister, but the man was a poor struggling artist. What chance did he have competing with nobility?

A salute of exploding gunpowder attracted everyone's attention, and within minutes passengers and crew alike crowded the upper deck of the *Rosanna*.

"There she is," announced Captain Peter Nolan with a ceremonious gesture. "Kor-or-areka. That squalid little village is the lifeblood of New Zealand." He looked directly at Caroline. "There's no law here, Miss Wickham. You'd best be careful walking those streets."

There was a smirk on his ruddy face as he spoke. A chill of fear and dislike for the man made Caroline draw closer to Nevil.

"I'll protect you," said Nevil, putting his arm around Caroline's shoulder yet looking at Captain Nolan.

Grayson and Geoffrey walked up to the three.

"Here at last," said Geoffrey to Caroline. "Kororareka's not really the place for a beautiful young woman alone . . . it's a wild town, but I'll keep an eye on you."

"That's quite all right," said Nevil, his voice filled with hostility. "I'll take care of my bride-to-be."

Captain Nolan walked back to the bow, took the wheel, and began shouting commands to his crew. He alone would steer the ship into port. The *Rosanna* was nearing its destination.

"I really would love to see some of your paintings," Caroline said, turning to Geoffrey.

Geoffrey smiled. There was nothing he would have liked more than being alone with Caroline, but he knew that wasn't what she had meant—her statement had been made in innocence, connoting nothing.

Nevil, however, had heard enough. Ever since his first week aboard the *Rosanna*, he had known Caroline would be the perfect wife for him. He would let no one interfere with his plans. Politely interrupting, he said, "Caroline, my dear, do come here to the railing." He pointed toward the shore. "Look at the natives paddling out to meet us."

Just at that moment a long canoe drew up alongside the *Rosanna*. A Maori, apparently the paramount chief of the area, waved a greeting to Captain Nolan.

"*Haere mai,*" Captain Nolan welcomed his visitor in the Maori tongue, at the same time enthusiastically waving at him.

"*Tena koe,*" Chief Kawiti called back his greeting.

"Drop a ladder," Captain Nolan shouted to one of his crew. Within moments the chief was climbing the rope steps.

Caroline knew it was impolite to stare, but she couldn't help herself. Terror engulfed her and still she could not shift her gaze, unable to take her eyes off the grotesque tattooing on Chief Kawiti's face. As he came aboard, Caroline could see the deep furrows that had been carved into his flesh. And when he approached, she realized that the incised spirals covering his forehead and cheeks were permanently stained with a blue dye. Even his lips were tattooed. "Dear God, that must have hurt," she whispered, but her words went unheard.

The men standing next to Caroline were all engrossed in watching the traditional *hongi*—greeting—of Captain Nolan and Chief Kawiti. Clasping hands warmly, the two men let their noses lightly touch.

Nevil smiled. "It's difficult to believe they eat people." His voice was almost inaudible yet he took obvious delight in the shocking power of his words. "I've heard it said that human flesh is their favorite meat."

Caroline shuddered, but Nevil went on, "I've seen them . . . most are bloodthirsty cannibals whose greatest pleasure is the game of war."

"Now wait a minute," interrupted Geoffrey. "In the name of all the Maoris, I resent that description."

"Why you're a *Pakeha-Maori*," Nevil sneered.

Caroline looked from one to the other. She had never heard the word *Pakeha*—the Maori term for European. Before long she would learn, however, that *Pakeha* had become as much an English word as a Maori one, and that a *Pakeha-Maori* was a European who lived with Maoris, thought like Maoris, sided with Maoris or generally supported the Maori cause.

"You will soon see," said Nevil to Caroline, "that the Europeans accept the term *Pakeha*, which has already become a part of their language, but when they use the term *Pakeha-Maori*, it usually refers to a European who has become more savage than the natives themselves."

Nevil completed his curt explanation and then turned back to Geoffrey. "You may find painting their primitive costumes interesting, but what else could possibly attract you to those cannibals?"

"*Sir* Nevil," Geoffrey answered, "if you expect to make a

success of your position as Colonial Secretary, I suggest you learn to appreciate the Maori people. They're *not* like the Australian aborigine, you know. Culturally, they're very advanced. Just keep in mind that the Treaty of Waitangi was a compromise. The British came to terms with the Maoris, they never won the land from them. Tried to steal the land, yes; succeeded, no. The story here can't be compared to the British and the Indian in North America either."

Caroline spoke up, "For four months everyone has been talking about *that* treaty."

"The Treaty of Waitangi?" said Nevil.

"It gave New Zealand to the British," injected Grayson, proud of his knowledge of this country's history.

"I'm sorry to contradict," said Geoffrey, "but that's really not quite right."

"Of course it is," interrrupted Nevil. "By the Treaty of Waitangi, the Maori chiefs ceded their sovereignty to the Queen."

"That's not exactly true," said Geoffrey.

Caroline heaved a sigh. "I should never have asked," she said in whispered voice. The last thing she wanted was to start an argument between the men.

Geoffrey turned back to Caroline, his tone warm when he addressed her. "By the Treaty of Waitangi, the Maoris were tricked. And Nevil knows I'm right, because he was here in 1840 when the Treaty was signed and he understands the nuances of the Treaty. Don't you, *Sir* Nevil?"

"Now wait a minute—"

Nevil tried to defend the British stand, but Geoffrey didn't give him a chance. "There were two versions of the treaty, Caroline," Geoffrey continued, "the English version, and its misleading Maori translation. In the English version, the Maori chiefs ceded all the rights and powers of sovereignty over their territories and were confirmed only in the possession of their lands, forests, and fisheries. But the English didn't translate sovereignty by the Maori *mana,* which means authority as well as prestige." He paused for a moment, and drew deeply on his pipe. "There is a sense of justice and pride in the word *mana*—it's difficult to explain. Anyway, the English used the Maori word, *kawanatanga*, meaning governorship. The Maoris were led to believe that they had given the governorship of their land to Britain, they had no idea they were ceding their country to the Queen. And let me tell you, *Sir* Nevil," Geoffrey looked at the Colonial Secretary with disgust, "the Pakeha will rue the day they concocted their deceitful scheme. Even if it takes one hundred and fifty years, the Maoris will have their revenge. *Utu,* revenge or satisfaction, is too much a part of their culture for them not to exact their due."

Caroline was fascinated by Geoffrey, impressed by his sudden burst of passion. Throughout the journey he'd been so quiet, so elusive and unassuming. Was he really the shy simple artist he appeared to be? She looked into his midnight blue eyes, trying to understand this man who was such an enigma. She knew she should not stare at him, and forced her gaze upward to his wavy black hair. The question of who he really was continued to intrigue her, but she had no answers.

"It's true the Maoris can't be compared to the Australian aborigine or the North American Indian," Nevil conceded with an air of extreme boredom. "The Maoris have been traveling around the world for the past fifty years. They've not only been to Australia, but to Europe and the United States. Many of them speak English fluently. Nonetheless, they are still barbarians. They need to be taught the ways of the civilized world. And it's *our* responsibility to care for them."

"Talking to you is a total waste of time," Geoffrey said with disdain. He turned to Caroline. "I'm sure we'll meet in Kororareka. It's a very small town."

Grayson had remained quiet throughout the heated discussion. His impulse was to follow Geoffrey, but as a junior surveyor in the employ of Her Majesty's government, the last thing he needed to do was antagonize the Colonial Secretary. Anxious to change the subject, he asked, "Are you all packed Caroline, ready to disembark?"

Caroline nodded, but she wasn't thinking of her brother's words. She was confused by what she had heard. Was Geoffrey a daydreamer, a philosopher who envisioned that Utopian world there was so much talk of these days? Or was he just a fool? Was Nevil right? Was it the white man's responsibility to care for these savages? To civilize these people who tattooed their bodies and ate human flesh? These were questions that couldn't be answered lightly. Determined to draw her own conclusions, Caroline decided then and there to learn more about these strange people.

Nevil reached for Caroline's hand. "You look beautiful in the southern sun, my dear. I know we'll be happy here." He looked into her deep violet eyes as he spoke and Caroline felt a warm glow come over her. She knew, without hesitation, that she loved this man.

"Dear God!" exclaimed Grayson, intruding on the tender moment. "Look!" He pointed to the sandy beach.

Caroline thought her brother was referring to the anchor at that moment being thrown over the side of the ship. Nevil knew otherwise. He tried to shelter Caroline, gently covering her eyes.

"Don't!" she said, pushing Nevil's hand aside. "Let me see."

A young deckhand caught sight of the display. "Blimey! I don't believe my eyes! Look . . . right there on the beach that man . . . going at it with that woman . . . in front of everybody!"

Grayson roared with laughter at the sailor's shock. The lad, surely a runaway, didn't look a day over fourteen.

Caroline's face turned scarlet. She was too embarrassed to look at Nevil and didn't dare let her gaze meet her brother's. She had to turn away. She felt it was wrong to watch such a sight, but her entire body seemed paralyzed. Unwillingly she continued to stare, at the same time wondering what kind of country she had come to and worrying what life now held in store.

Chapter 2

Kororareka—Hell Hole of the Pacific. THIS DESCRIPTION, coined by the whalers of the South Pacific and now a popular phrase, echoed in Caroline's head, the unsavory words burning before her eyes. The Maori word meant sweet blue penguin, but it was impossible to imagine that Kororareka was once a wholesome, quiet town. As Caroline walked along the beach she wondered where Grayson had heard that this land —the sunny south as it was called in England—was a land of promise, a land of plenty, a land of hope. Why hadn't people back home told them the truth? Why hadn't she inquired further into what New Zealand was like, instead of listening to her brother, believing the pamphlets he had given her to read, imagining that life here would be idyllic—the answer to rising above the station into which they had been born. Nor could she fathom what or who had really enticed her brother into coming to this vile place full of wild, drunken men, released convicts, ships deserters, flotsam and jetsam, and lascivious women, both Maori and white. Four years older than she, he should have known better, she thought. A small smile played on Caroline's lips. Surely it wasn't the prospect of Grayson's job—Junior Surveyor to Her Majesty's Government—that had convinced him to emigrate. Though she had to admit it *was* an impressive title to someone whose father had been the minister of a small church in the poverty-ridden East End of London.

A light breeze swept across the bay, first reaching the far end of Kororareka then slowly drifting across the town, bringing with it the rank odor of whale blubber being rendered in large black try-pots along the beach.

Caroline coughed, choked by the foul smell, and her eyes began to tear. For a moment she almost wished she were back in London. She looked out to the clear green water, where twenty-four whaling schooners and two trading ships lay at anchor in the bay. The town would be wilder than ever tonight with all those seamen in port. The harlots would be kept busy; the grog shops could count on taking in a small fortune.

"Caroline! Caroline!" Grayson called from down the beach. He was not ten yards from the man-made jetty of the busy port and he sprinted to greet his sister, his sandy hair bobbing rhythmically over his eyes.

Caroline looked at him with amusement—in just two weeks he had transformed himself into a New Zealander, casually dressed and carrying himself with the confident air of one quite at home in familiar surroundings.

Their greeting was warm, their embrace one of genuine affection. "I'll miss you terribly," said Caroline, a single tear rolling down her cheek. With a casual gesture she wiped it away as quickly as she could. She had promised herself she wouldn't cry. For some reason it suddenly seemed important to her that Grayson not feel he was leaving a baby sister behind, not believe he had an obligation in Kororareka, not be burdened with the responsibility that she was still his charge. She forced a smile and compelled herself to strike a cheerful note. "You excited about sailing tomorrow?"

Grayson hesitated. "Excited, but a little scared," he answered truthfully. "You know I've never worked as a surveyor. I faked my experience to get this job."

Caroline's fears dissipated in laughter. "And I wrote my

own references. But I'm luckier than you. Mrs. Weatherby's in a wheelchair. She can't see the mistakes I make, has no idea how inexperienced I really am . . . at least, I don't think she does."

"Well," said Grayson with more bravado than he felt, "if I can help it, no one will find out the truth about my past either.

"Now tell me everything. This is the first chance we've had to talk since we landed, and it may be the last we'll have for a long time. What are the Weatherbys like? How's their little boy? And Nevil, are you still set on marrying him?"

Caroline detected an uneasy note in her brother's tone. "I know you don't like Nevil, but you haven't given him a chance. He's so kind to me, Grayson, and though you don't believe it, he is interesting to be with and he's brilliant. Besides, he loves me. It will be a good marriage. You'll see.

"I've made one friend," she said, quickly changing the subject. "Milly. She helps the cook. And she serves. I don't know what I'd do without her. She tells me everything. She's a tiny Irish girl, with flaming red hair and blue blue eyes. And she certainly knows how to cook. You'd like her."

Grayson smiled, silently thinking how wrong his sister was. He would never like a maid. Servants were beneath him. "What about the Weatherbys?" he asked again.

"Oh, they're wonderful too. Mrs. Weatherby's had a terrible time of things. Her two little girls and her mother were in a freak boating accident . . . she was with them. Mrs. Weatherby was the only survivor. It was a miracle that she didn't drown too."

"What happened?"

"I'm not exactly certain. They were out in the bay, on the way back from the mission in Paihia . . . you know, across there." She let her gaze indicate the opposite shore. "Apparently, a storm came up unexpectedly. Their boat capsized and struck her spine. She hasn't walked since. Dr. Weatherby says his wife could still regain the use of her legs. Spontaneous recoveries have been known to happen, but I can't believe she will. Her legs atrophied . . . there's nothing left but flab and skin."

A quiet descended, both so filled with questions about tomorrow, neither able to voice their apprehensions.

Grayson studied the beach—it was not a bed of sand like the beaches in England, instead it was a narrow expanse of tiny colorful rocks—pebbles of pink, gray, magenta, sand, and black. "Volcanic minerals," he said, sifting the softly shaded specimens through his fingers.

Caroline nodded, not bothering to ask about volcanic minerals, for her thoughts were miles away. She watched the sea gulls swooping into the bay, but her mind was fixed on the uncertainties before her. "I'll be sorry to see you sail tomorrow morning. However little we'd have seen each other, it would have been nice to know you were nearby."

"Auckland's not so far, Car—"

Before he could finish, loud shouts distracted him.

"Come here, you little hussy. I ain't finished with you yet," a deep, raucous voice bellowed.

Hilarious laughter could be heard from inside a nearby grog shop.

"But it's just past noon," the woman cackled. Coming out into the glaring sunlight, she picked up her long red satin skirt, exposing her ankles as she backed away.

"I paid my guinea for now, not for when the sun goes down . . . now, not tonight, you hear? And you ain't getting away," he shouted, reaching out to grab her. He reeled through the doorway but his hand clutched only air.

Within a minute the owner of the grog shop appeared. Gently but firmly he put his hand on the young man's shoulder, and with a well practiced move turned him around. "This way, Matt. There's a pinochle game inside. Come join it."

A small boy ran along the waterfront, calling Caroline's name. She heard and turned to see six-year-old Bradley Weatherby frantically motioning to her. "Mama needs you," he called. "She says, you've been gone too long . . ." He was panting as he stopped in front of Caroline. ". . . had no right to go in the first place."

Caroline's face flushed in anger. "That's not fair," she seethed. "I have every right to say good-bye to my only

26

brother. Sometimes, working for his mother is worse than being a slave," she muttered under her breath to Grayson.

"Calm down," her brother replied in whispered voice. "It's not forever. You're getting married soon, remember."

"Not for at least a year. Nevil says he has to get settled first —build a home, learn what's expected of him in his new post—"

"Mama says if you don't come . . ." the small redheaded boy interrupted.

Caroline lifted her chin and gave her brother a quick kiss. "Take care," she said, "and write. God go with you," she called over her shoulder, already holding Bradley's little hand and heading up the Grand Parade back to the Weatherby home.

Dressed in deep purple silk, Priscilla Weatherby sat regally in her custom-built white wicker chair, waiting impatiently for Caroline to wheel her along the Grand Parade. It had become almost a ritual for Mrs. Weatherby to have her daily outing, and she took particular pleasure in her short journey through the teeming town, past the saloons, the doss houses, and the trading rooms stocked with stolen goods pirated from foreign lands.

As a rule the two women said little during this promenade, but today Mrs. Weatherby was more talkative than usual. Her voice had a vitriolic sharpness as she asked, "Just when do you plan to marry *that* man?" And before Caroline could answer, Mrs. Weatherby continued, "Remember your contract with me is for three years. I'll see to it that you're put in gaol if you break the contract by even one day."

Caroline was thankful she was standing behind Priscilla Weatherby. There was no way the woman could see the look of secret delight on her face; Nevil had promised her that he would arrange to pay for the contract, buy it back. After several moments of quiet, she said simply, "You needn't worry, Mrs. Weatherby. The wedding won't take place until the time comes for me to leave."

"You're a sweet child," Mrs. Weatherby said, relaxing into

her chair. "Far too sweet to be promised to a rough, uncouth sailor lad."

Caroline debated silently—should she tell Priscilla Weatherby how very mistaken she was? No, her personal life was her own private affair.

"We'll have pikelets with tea," Mrs. Weatherby announced. "Last week you said you could prepare them. Well, Milly's out today, so now you have your chance."

Caroline had dreaded this moment for days. When asked last week if she could make tea, she had readily said yes; then, Mrs. Weatherby had told her to note the pikelets. "They're my favorite," she had said. "I'll expect you to make them just like Milly does . . . nice and thin." Now the moment was upon her. Caroline didn't have the faintest idea of how to make the thin little guinea-size pancakes which seemed to have become a colonial favorite.

Nervously, she walked outside to the kitchen. She was glad the cooking was done in a separate house—if she lost her temper, no one would hear her. Caroline was actually shaking as she entered the well-stocked pantry, wondering, worrying, terrified of what she should do.

"Oh, Milly, Milly, bless you. I'll never forget this," Caroline exclaimed, and tears of joy filled her eyes. There, on the large wooden table, was a plate of neatly stacked pancakes. Next to the pikelets was a note: *Serve cold and don't forget the butter, jam, and whipped cream.*

By the time Caroline returned to the main house, Lucian Weatherby had arrived.

"An extra cup for the doctor," Mrs. Weatherby said stiffly. "He'll join me for tea today."

Dr. Weatherby, a tall man of spare frame, with wire rimmed glasses and balding hair, sat down beside his wife. He seemed a mild gentleman, with his soft voice and easy manner, but those who met him quickly learned that no one stepped in his way. He had firm ideas of how the natives should be cared for and was adamant in his belief that their *tohungas*—holy men, he called them—must be schooled in the ways of the *Pakeha*, for only if the practices of the *tohungas* changed, only if they began accepting the advances of medicine and science, would the Maori people survive the European influx into their land.

Caroline had just started to pour tea when there was a loud knock on the front door.

On Sunday afternoon Caroline was the only one in help at the Weatherby residence. The other servants—the cook, Milly, the upstairs maid, and the liveryman—all had the afternoon off.

Bradley, a lively, spritely child, ran to see who had come. Moments later he returned, subdued and obviously very impressed, even at his tender age. "Mama, Papa, it's *Sir* Nevil Holbrooke. He told me *he's* the new Colonial Secretary." Now, large blue eyes widened in Bradley's tiny, freckled face, and his voice became almost a hushed whisper. "The gentleman wishes to say good-bye to you, Miss Caroline." Bradley had never before prefixed Caroline's name with the title of Miss. "Sir Nevil says he's leaving at dawn, sailing for the new capital."

Caroline smiled widely. "My, my, listen to the little tyke." She had already put down the teapot. She ruffled his curly red hair affectionately and said, "You certainly learned a great deal in only a few seconds. Please tell him I'll be there in a moment." She turned to her employers. "May I say good-bye to Sir Nevil, Mrs. Weatherby, Doctor? He really is sailing for Auckland at dawn."

"Yes, of course," replied Priscilla Weatherby. "Do ask him to come in," she said insistently, duly affected by the importance of the visitor and not quite understanding why he should come to call on Caroline, who was little better than servant to her.

Buffie, the Siamese cat, followed Caroline from the room, stalking proudly, as if she knew nobility awaited at the door.

Caroline greeted Nevil shyly, knowing her every movement was under surveillance from behind the curtained doorway to the large sitting room. After a few brief words they walked back inside to join the others.

"May I present Sir Nevil Holbrooke," said Caroline.

"Won't you join us for tea?" asked Priscilla Weatherby, delighted at the opportunity of entertaining such a prestigious guest.

"I am sorry," he answered, "but I'm leaving early in the morning and I haven't started to pack. Another time, perhaps. I'll be back to see Caroline in a few months."

He turned to Caroline. "I really must go." He politely said good-bye to the Weatherbys and turned to leave.

"I'll try to be back before long," he said, once he and Caroline were alone at the door, "but if not, I'll send for you as soon as I possibly can." He put his hands gently around her shoulders. "I wish there were some place to go where we could really be alone, where I could kiss you good-bye."

Caroline could feel her face flushing with desire. She tilted her head, but ever so slightly, lest her action seem forward.

Nevil's lips brushed hers, then he took her hands and held them tightly. "It won't be long until we're together again, I promise. Take care and be well."

"God go with you. I love you," she said softly. "I'll miss you." She turned away quickly, tears now streaming down her face. She had to go back inside, but not to join the others. She needed time to compose herself. Nevil was leaving. By morning her brother, too, would be gone. She was completely alone, alone in a foreign land.

Chapter 3

IT WAS WARM IN THE BAY OF ISLANDS THAT DECEMBER 1844, wispy clouds overhead only scantily patterning the clear sky. Caroline still found it difficult to comprehend the seasons, the complete reversal of what she had always believed to be the natural order of things. Yet, she now felt at times she belonged in this new colony, even viewed herself as a New Zealander. She marveled at the way the stars looked. She was even beginning to think of the Big Dipper as being upright in the skies, rather than upside down. And she took special delight in easily recognizing the Southern Cross, the constellation that could only be seen below the Equatorial Line.

She was standing on a small wooden ladder, carefully cutting down soft, spiky scarlet flowers from a Pohutukawa, when Geoffrey Rutledge unexpectedly appeared.

"Greetings," he called up to her. His deep, mellow voice startled her and at the same time sent a glow of warmth through her.

"Hello," she answered, her voice mirroring her pleasure and excitement at seeing him. "I'll be down in a moment," she said, giggling with delight like a happy child. "I promised to fix a bouquet for Mrs. Weatherby. She's sleeping now, so I have some time." Caroline was talking too quickly, rattling on in nervous speech. What was it about Geoffrey that made her react this way? She had asked herself the question dozens of times but couldn't find any answers.

"Let me help you," he offered, reaching up to take the branches she had already cut. "The blossoms are brilliant, aren't they?" he said, then asked, "Did you know the Pohutukawa is called the Christmas Tree?"

"Because it flowers at Christmas time?"

He nodded. Her happy tone of voice sounded so young, Geoffrey always found it difficult to remember that she was here in New Zealand on her own.

"The Pakehas believe that if the flowers bloom early it will be a long, hot summer," he told her.

"Is this early?" she asked, totally confused by the heat in December.

"Very," he answered. "The flowers always remind me of the poinsettias at home," he continued, laughing a soft warm chuckle. "Funny how I still refer to England as home. Even after all these years, somehow I can't think of myself as a New Zealander, yet I know I'll never return to the Motherland to live . . . perhaps for a visit, to see my family, you know, but I'll always come back here. I love this land," he said. He took her hand and helped her descend from her height.

"I've a wonderful surprise for you," Caroline said excitedly as soon as she was down on the ground.

Geoffrey looked inquisitively at the beautiful young woman who stood before him. If only her surprise was that she had broken her betrothal. If only he could tell her how she felt. But he had no right. She was promised to Sir Nevil. Geoffrey truly felt he would be less than a gentleman if he spoke of his feelings.

"I've persuaded Mrs. Weatherby to commission you to do her portrait. And," she paused for effect, proud of her achievement, "at the same time, to give Bradley drawing lessons. If she likes the portrait you do of her, she promised me she'll have you do her son, and her husband too."

"How did you do it?" Geoffrey asked. He was completely taken by surprise. This was the last thing he had expected Caroline to do.

"I showed her the sketch you did of me on the ship . . . and the one you drew of Grayson. I don't know if you realize how gifted you are," she said innocently, having no idea of the many prizes Geoffrey had won in England for his art.

Geoffrey had told no one that by the age of eighteen he had already earned an impressive reputation as a portraitist, that his portrait of the late King William IV now hung in the National Gallery in London alongside works by Thomas Gainsborough; and that before leaving England he had been commissioned to paint the young Queen Victoria. It was his secret because he had promised himself that nothing and no one could make him use his father's name. The mere sound of that name brought bitter bile to his mouth. His cruel father had never accepted him. The Earl of Pembroke had neither approved of his son's art nor sanctioned his way of life. Geoffrey was adamant in feeling that he would never capitalize on being the Earl's son. He was determined to make it on his own in this new land.

"That's wonderful," Geoffrey replied with real enthusiasm. "A few pounds will certainly find a welcome place in my empty pockets," he said, smiling broadly. "You most assuredly are a lady of many talents. I would never have thought you could persuade that crabby woman you work for to do anything."

"She's not really as irritable as she seems," Caroline replied. "You'd be morose, too, if you'd lost a mother and two children all in the same day . . . and been left crippled besides. And she's really quite good to me. I have to take her for walks, help her dress, see to it that her things are cared for, but other than that I'm left to do what I want. Sometimes, when Bradley's alone, she asks me to play with him, but he's a good little boy and I never mind that. As a matter of fact, I'm afraid next year will come too quickly. I'll really be sorry to leave the family."

These were the first encouraging words Geoffrey had heard

from Caroline. Was she having second thoughts about marrying Nevil? Could this really be? "You don't have to go away," Geoffrey said softly, almost sorry the words had escaped his lips, for even with all his former acclaim he was basically a very shy man. He quickly turned the conversation: "Thanks so much for arranging the commission, and the lessons. When do I start?"

"I think right after Christmas . . . after Boxing Day, that is," Caroline answered.

Neither spoke for the next few minutes, but they both felt a communication between them. Caroline stared into Geoffrey's inky blue eyes, totally unaware of the ardor that shone in hers, while he looked at her with equal feelings of love.

Priscilla Weatherby's shrill voice abruptly shattered the precious moment. "Caroline, come here at once. You have not been hired to chitchat with strangers. You're here to care for me. Now quickly, carry those blossoms into the house . . . put them in water and then take me for my walk."

"Yes, Mrs. Weatherby," Caroline replied politely and without a second's hesitation. Barely nodding a good-bye to Geoffrey, she ran back to the house.

"That was Geoffrey Rutledge," Caroline said to Mrs. Weatherby as she pushed the wheelchair down the Grand Parade. "He's the artist I told you about."

"You should have introduced him to me," Mrs. Weatherby said, not realizing that her harsh voice had intimidated Caroline.

Caroline did not reply. The few brief moments with Geoffrey had left her with an inner glow, a calm she had not known since her departure from London. She began humming the strains of "Rock of Ages," happily thanking God for her good fortune. Without realizing it, she was softly, sweetly vocalizing the lyrics.

"You've an exceptionally beautiful voice," Mrs. Weatherby said, turning in her chair and looking at Caroline. "Perhaps, tonight you'll sing that for us . . . a perfect selection for Christmas eve."

Caroline was speechless. The sudden request flooded her

mind with thoughts of other Christmases—family and friends so far away, merrymaking in another land where snow upon the ground hindered travel yet the welcome of roaring fires, mistletoe, and holly made braving the elements well worthwhile. How incongruous was the summer sun here, the flowers in full blossom and myriads of chirping birds—it was almost a mockery of the day of the Nativity. But this was her new home and she was determined to become comfortable with the unfamiliar surroundings.

"Thank you," she finally said, choked with emotion. "I would consider it a great privilege."

The attention of the two women shifted from thoughts of the holidays to the pier. The brig *The Marianne* had just anchored.

"Mail from home," shouted William Davis, the schoolmaster's son. He had only been in the colony for three weeks—his father would take over duties in Kororareka's small school as soon as the term began in February.

Suddenly, as if a great magnet were drawing everyone to the harbor, children, women, and men all came running, faster and faster, shouting with joy in anticipation of what was on board for each of them.

"Boxes galore this time," called Tyrone Whisker, *The Marianne*'s captain.

The children began jumping up and down with a glee that was contagious. Both Caroline and Mrs. Weatherby found themselves smiling—Mrs. Weatherby expecting Christmas gifts from those at home; Caroline, for no real reason, since she knew that there would be no mail for her. Still, she hoped that maybe someone would remember. After all, Aunt Penelope Swainson, her father's sister, couldn't forget how she had loved the Christmas cakes Penelope used to bake so very, very long ago.

"Buttons will collect the mail later," Mrs. Weatherby said abruptly. She was tiring from all the noise and excitement. There was no reason to be jostled and shoved about in this crowd when she had a liveryman to do her errands.

The rest of the day went by in a flurry of activity, and

Caroline was inwardly pleased that she had little time to reminisce, to think of her exquisite young mother, taken from her on Boxing Day just one year ago.

Laying out Mrs. Weatherby's clothes, waiting for her to finish soaking in the lilac-scented water in her copper tub, Caroline remembered Reverend Jonathan Butler's words: "We are gathered here today to pay tribute to Dianne Wickham, mother of Caroline and Grayson, beloved wife of the late Reverend Milton Wickham, minister of this very church. Those who knew Dianne loved her, for she was truly a child of God. . . ." Caroline could barely control the wave of grief and sadness that swept over her.

"Caroline! Caroline where are you? Come here! Help me out of this bath. It's late. I must get dressed at once." Mrs. Weatherby's sharp, impatient cries shattered the silence.

"I'm coming," Caroline called. "I'm coming," she repeated, wiping her eyes as best she could.

"As soon as you've taken me downstairs, I want you to tend to Bradley. He listens to you better than anyone else. See to it that he's dressed in his white satin shirt and red silk tie. He can be with the company for starters. Just be certain to impress upon him that when the guests go into the dining room, *he* goes to bed."

"Yes, Mrs. Weatherby," Caroline answered politely, glad to be busy again. She would write to Grayson tonight. And as she thought of her brother, she wondered if he was finding these few days as difficult as they were becoming for her.

Twelve people attended the Weatherby Christmas Eve dinner party—eleven guests and Caroline. Caroline was more than just a little surprised when she was asked to join the company first in the drawing room, then at the table. She was a servant. It was true that the official description on her documents read *Companion to Mrs. Priscilla Weatherby,* but that title didn't elevate her position. She was, nonetheless, a servant. She was speechless as Dr. Weatherby escorted her to her place and held a chair for her.

Bradley entered gleefully, hoping to go unnoticed as he took a place at the table. His face seemed to shine, it had been so well scrubbed.

"Let me take Bradley to bed," Caroline offered, pleased at having an excuse to leave the table.

"Bradley, to your room at once," stated Priscilla Weatherby firmly. "You were told that dinner was for the grown-ups, weren't you?"

"Yes, Mama."

"Then off to bed. If I have to say one more word to you tonight, I'll see to it that Father Christmas leaves you nothing."

This time Bradley scampered off without a word, not to return.

"Caroline, my dear," Mrs. Weatherby said, initiating the conversation. "Why don't you tell us something of your life in London. We're all so interested in your past."

But before Caroline could utter a sound, Mrs. Weatherby added, "Perhaps Mr. Bailey knew your father. He's our minister," she explained. "Your father was a minister, wasn't he?"

"Yes," answered Caroline. Now she was no longer embarrassed, just uncomfortable. Why was Mrs. Weatherby questioning her about her family now, in the midst of company? What was the sudden interest in her past?

"Was Milton Wickham your father?" Mr. Bailey asked.

"Why, yes," Caroline replied.

"Ah, yes, I knew of him. Not personally you understand, but he certainly made his voice heard in our Church."

Caroline's eyes twinkled. She was thoroughly amused by the description of her late father, the man the Methodist Church would have gladly excommunicated had he not died before it had its chance. His peers had called him a radical, ever preaching on the need for biblical criticism, always holding forth on the stupidity and backwardness of taking the Bible literally. "The Bible is not infallible," he would say. "It was written hundreds of years after the events occurred and should be interpreted, not adhered to line by line. It should be reexamined and its teachings applied to contemporary life." Caroline smiled as she remembered how her mother used to encourage her father. "He's a man with vision," she would say. "His name will be remembered, you wait and see."

Stanford Bailey continued, "I was sorry to hear that he passed on . . . he was so young."

The focus in the room shifted to Polly Domett, a prickly little woman, impeccable in blue satin and ecru lace. She had been closely studying Caroline since the moment she walked into the drawing room. With an air of conscious superiority betraying itself in every look and gesture, Polly asked, "And just how were you, of all people, able to sink your teeth into our new Colonial Secretary?"

A sudden silence descended on the room, like a shroud covering the entire table.

Caroline clenched her teeth and her nails dug into the palms of her hands. How dare that woman! she thought. She wanted to lash out at her, but she wouldn't act like a child—adults controlled their tempers. She took a deep breath and then, with total composure, she said simply, "Sir Nevil found me, Mrs. Domett, not the other way around."

A titter of embarrassment punctuated the air.

Suddenly it was all clear to Caroline—the change in Mrs. Weatherby's attitude toward her, the invitation to dine with the guests and to sing later in the evening. Though she was extremely embarrassed, she smiled. She refused to let anyone belittle her. She had come to New Zealand to begin life anew, to rise above her impoverished background, and if, at this moment, she would only be received because of her relationship with Nevil, so be it. One day she would make a name of her own, be accepted for herself.

To Caroline's left sat Colin Nugent. A wealthy merchant, he had not forgotten his own humble beginnings. The portly, jovial gentleman put a warm arm around Caroline, drew her closer and whispered, "Tittle-tattle is part and parcel of colonial life. You mustn't let it get to you. Be above it, my dear."

Dr. Christopher Relph, an old friend and colleague of Lucian Weatherby's, spoke up: "I trust you will sing for us this evening, Caroline? Priscilla says you have a splendid voice."

A grateful look shone in Caroline's eyes. "Thank you," she

answered, relieved to find that all the Weatherbys' acquaintances were not like Polly Domett. But she could not bring herself to agree to sing. She felt as if she had been on view long enough for a lifetime, let alone one evening.

It was Lucian who had the good sense to turn the conversation to his friend. Ignoring the question Christopher had just posed, Lucian asked, "How long will you be able to stay in Kororareka?"

"I sail for Nelson the day after tomorrow," Christopher answered. "I'm badly needed. From what I understand, the town doesn't have a single physician at the moment. Old man Eaton died last month."

The chat continued as two servants began serving the elaborate Christmas dinner. First the roast beef was passed around, then boiled turkey, green peas, and a delicious kumara pie. Though most of the guests thought the pie delicious, Caroline didn't like kumara—to her it tasted like mushy, watery sweet potato.

She felt a sense of relief when the conversation stopped and everyone began concentrating on the food. She had already decided that as soon as dinner was over, she would retire. On any pretense.

"It's a great treat not to have any pork tonight," said Polly Domett.

There was a general nodding of heads, everyone else at the table also having had their fill of New Zealand's staple meat.

While the party was resting, between the main course and dessert, Colin Nugent turned to Madeleine Fitzroy, the Governor's recently widowed niece. "I understand Torrance Hankin escaped from prison. . . ."

Caroline and all the other guests glanced at Colin, then eagerly awaited Madelaine's reply.

"Yes, but they'll catch him, and he'll hang," Madelaine said. "Have no fear."

"What did he do?" Caroline asked, her interest in the conversation making her totally forget her discomfort of moments before.

Dr. Relph answered offhandedly, "Hankin traded in stolen goods."

"Hardly," said his host.

Caroline's gaze shifted to Lucian Weatherby, but it was Stanford Bailey who explained, "Hankin stole tattooed heads and sold them."

"How inhuman!" Caroline gasped, truly shocked at the image her mind immediately conjured. She felt queasy at the mere thought of touching the preserved heads of dead Maoris.

"They say he's left New South Wales," Colin continued. "I hear he's headed here."

Everyone smiled at the pun.

Madelaine Fitzroy spoke next. "Governor Bourke had expected Edward Doyle's hanging would serve as an example, a warning to all in his penal colony—"

"I hope your uncle has more success," said Mr. Bailey.

"My uncle is Governor of New Zealand, *not* New South Wales," she replied with disdain, thinking little of the post of governor of a penal colony.

"Shall we toast the health of our family and friends in England?" said Priscilla Weatherby, hoping to change the grisly subject before the plum pudding was brought to the table. To her relief, her guests all lifted their glasses of grog and heartily toasted Queen and country—the land they still called their own.

The partying mood had returned and no one noticed the faraway misty look that clouded Caroline's eyes, for she was thinking of yesterdays and wondering what Grayson was doing on their first holiday away from home, their first Christmas Eve apart.

Chapter 4

AUCKLAND IS A CITY OF EMERALD-CLAD CONICAL MOUN-
tains and dormant craters—thirty rolling mounds lining the
Waitemata Harbour and stretching onto the isthmus that lies
in the Hauraki Gulf. Not far from the shoreline rises the
stark, sweeping silhouette of Rangitoto.

Grayson sat at the window of the small bare room he now
called home and stared out at the impressive sight, musing
about the possibilities of the island volcano erupting again.

He was particularly melancholic on this Sunday afternoon.
An unseasonably southerly gale had made going to church
impossible this morning. He had been sitting in his room for
the past two hours brooding, asking himself why he had come
to this godforsaken land, wondering how he had believed the
New Zealand Company's stories that this "land of promise,"
as they called it, would one day be a great empire. As far as
Grayson was concerned it was an uncivilized country overrun
by speculators and opportunists. The only positive thing to its
claim was the magnificence of the land itself. Everyone, in-
cluding his boss, Surveyor-General Felton Mathew, seemed to
be engaged in land speculation—cheating Maoris of what was

41

rightfully theirs, paying them trifling sums for large tracts and adding colorful blankets, well-honed knives, and other inexpensive items to the bargain to distract people from the fact that they were being robbed. Then these Pakeha thieves turned around and made up to five hundred percent profit on their sales.

The site of Auckland was strikingly beautiful but the city was a nightmare of natti wood houses, unformed roads, and stocks for criminals. Grayson's own tiny room, which he rented for thirty shillings a week, didn't even have a fireplace. He hated cooking at the back of the house in the cast-iron kettle which hung suspended from a hook on the outdoor hearth. Since his arrival in Auckland three months ago, his diet had consisted almost entirely of pork, potatoes, and kumara, which he thoroughly despised. He longed for a Cornish pastie or a hot sausage roll. Oh, why had he left England?

A letter from Caroline sat on the little table in front of him. He knew he should answer it, but what could he say? That he despised Mathew? That he couldn't believe he had come twelve thousand miles to measure angles of land, chart coastlines, determine suitable sites for settlements, and decide where to build access roads? Roads, he might add, that were already there, though they were little more than tracks of dirt. But still, he knew, and his boss—the cocky Felton Mathew—knew, exactly where the roads would be built.

Tomorrow they would supervise the laying of a metal road over the well-worn trail from Auckland to Orakei. Why did they call it a metal road, he reflected, instead of a macadamized road, as in England, or even a tarred road? He answered his own question. It was like everything else here. People changed in this land. Once a European became a Pakeha, he was never the same.

In disgust, Grayson decided to go for a ride. He smiled as he thought of Dobbs, his horse, the one good thing the government had given him since his arrival.

The winds and rains had stopped but it was still a damp, gloomy day. Grayson let his horse trot slowly toward Orakei, enjoying the expanse of beach and water as he rode eastward.

As he neared Orakei, a lonely figure, sitting on a hillock away from the beach front, caught his attention. She was leaning against some manuka brushwood, so completely absorbed in her sorrow that she did not hear him coming. He dismounted and approached her on foot. Even before he saw her beautiful face, he heard her sobbing.

"Are you all right?" he asked.

She looked up, her deep, velvety black eyes meeting his. She nodded but did not answer.

"Is there anything I can do?" he asked. He was overcome by her beauty. As he gazed at her, the sun-bleached flaxen cape tied across her shoulders held him with more alluring appeal than the most elegant satin gown. Her rich ochre-tinted skin glowed with silken softness, her luxuriant black hair, with the slightest wave, cascaded to her waist.

She smiled at him warmly through her tears. "No," she said. "I'll be fine."

The small tattoo on her upper lip and the unusual spiral design tattooed on her chin did not repel him or strike him as strange, but only seemed to enhance her perfect features. "Are you hurt?"

She nodded, and now he was not certain how much English she spoke.

"It is not that I am hurt," she said clearly in perfect English, "it is that I am the worst of cowards," she admitted softly. "I have come here to get away from my *kainga.*"

Grayson cocked his head inquisitively.

"A *kainga* is our word for village," she explained. "I did not want any of my extended family to see me. They would have laughed and ridiculed Amiria's lack of braveness."

"Then you are Amiria?" he asked.

"Yes," she answered.

"I'm Grayson Wickham. Why do you say you are a coward?"

"Because I cry with pain. I was brave when Rewi put the *moko* on my face," she said, pointing to the tattooing. "But when he did it this time, when he performed what we call the

43

tarawhakairo," shyly, she looked down to her private parts, "I could not keep from screaming."

Grayson's own eyes inadvertently gazed down at his crotch. "Dear God! That's where he tattooed you. How?"

She looked at him innocently and without shame as she explained, "Rewi slices the skin into a circular design, then he puts black coloring into the flesh . . . like on my face," she added.

"But why!"

"It is our way. A woman who has a *tarawhakairo* always is able to bear children. It is a sacred ceremony. It is a time of endurance, not a time to be weak and cry." She suddenly began weeping. "Everyone will hear," she sobbed. "Te Kawau will not want me to marry his son, and Te Hira is the bravest, the most handsome man in the world."

"Who is Te Kawau?" Grayson asked, not knowing what else to say.

"Chief of the Ngati Whatua," she answered.

There was a long silence as they both sat staring out at the still expanse of cerulean water in front of them.

"I must go," Amiria said suddenly. She rose and the dried flax coils of her skirt rattled as she moved.

"No . . . wait . . . don't go. . . . Will I see you again?" Grayson was touched by Amiria in a way he had never been by another. She was so open in the way she spoke, so honest, and there was a warmth about her that drew him to her. The very way she looked at him had an enchanting quality which captivated him, and he knew he must see her again.

"Tomorrow," she answered, an enigmatic smile on her lips. "I will come at dusk," she said, and turned toward home.

The following morning, Grayson left his room at dawn. For the first time since he had begun work in Auckland, he was looking forward to the day. He was glad John Tole would be with him today. John, who had just been given the title of Auckland Surveyor, was an easygoing man of about thirty. He had taken an immediate liking to Grayson and had quietly taught him how to use a theodolite to measure angles and a staff to measure height. He had then taught him how to use the long roll of wire they called a chain, to calculate distances. He had taken great pains to explain to Grayson how to rough plot a coastal survey with a compass and a patent log, and today he was going to teach him the main skills needed in plotting the course of a road.

As Grayson left his boarding house he whistled a cheerful tune, delighted that today they would begin projections for the road from Auckland to Orakei. He was thinking about Amiria, hoping he might have a glimpse of her before dusk, when John Tole's call diverted Grayson's attention.

"Glad you're on time," John said. "We've a lot to accomplish today." Tole was a tall, rugged man with well-bronzed skin from a profession that for years had kept him in the open air. "Now that we're starting the road, I think you'll find the work more interesting," he continued.

"I'm sure," answered Grayson.

John at once noted the new optimism in his young colleague's voice. "By the way," he said as the two rode side by side up Queen Street, "I spoke to Mathew over the weekend. He said, as soon as I think you're ready he'll send you south . . . to Rotorua and down the Wanganui."

"No, no. I'd much rather stay up here."

"But I thought you hated this area . . . and the Wanganui River's one of the most beautiful in New Zealand."

"Yes, I know, but . . ."

"But," laughed John. "But you've met someone and want to stay nearby."

Grayson's face flushed and he stumbled for words. "How could you tell?" he asked at last.

"How? By your eyes, by the way you were whistling when you met me, by the happy look on your face. I was young once, too, remember?"

They talked until they reached their destination, and Grayson told John about Amiria. "I've never felt this way about anyone."

"Careful, Grayson. You've just met her. Walk away now while it's easy. Be smart. Don't get involved."

"But why?"

"Because you have a government post . . . and she's a Maori."

"So?"

"So? So you want a promotion. You don't want to stay a junior surveyor forever."

"What does Amiria have to do with my work?"

"I can promise you that if you're living with a Maori, Mathew will look the other way when it comes to your advancement or to sending you on a choice assignment. Government personnel all take one stand where the Maoris are concerned, and it's a prejudiced one. You know that."

"What about you?"

"I'm smart enough not to get entangled with a Maori woman. It's asking for trouble."

Grayson did not answer. He hated Mathew and everything the man stood for. He refused to let him dictate the social mores that had to be adhered to for advancement.

By seven o'clock the two men began setting up their station-pointer. Shortly afterward, they were ready to start the topographical plotting necessary to survey the projected road.

The day passed quickly for Grayson, as he was concentrating on measurements and complicated calculations. He had little time to let his mind wander. But as dusk began to fall he said to John, "It's been a long day, don't you think we can stop now?"

"Sure, Grayson. I didn't think you'd listen to my lecture. What time are you meeting her?"

"Dusk," he answered. There was no apology in his tone.

As soon as they parted, Grayson rode to the point of yesterday's encounter. He went directly to the manuka tree and waited. He waited and waited. He stayed until the waning moon was high in the sky, but no one came. Then, filled with disappointment and desolation, he rode slowly home.

Throughout the following week Grayson's spirits were as low as he could remember them being. He did his work but spoke little. John Tole assumed what must have happened, but he did not pry. By Saturday, Grayson decided that John had given him good advice—the further he stayed from a Maori woman, the better off he would be. But on Sunday, following church, Grayson could not keep himself from returning to the spot where he and Amiria had met.

He was sitting on soft fern, gazing out at the Gulf, when he heard a rustling from behind him.

"I'm glad you came," Amiria said.

Grayson was speechless, overcome by her beauty. The thought flashed through his mind that he had misunderstood her—when she had said she would be here tomorrow, she had really meant this day next week—Sunday. "I'm glad you came too," he answered. He reached up, took her hand and pulled her to the ground beside him.

"I could not come on Monday," she began. "I was punished."

"Punished? Why? By whom?"

"By the gods. The spirits were not pleased with me. I was not worthy of my ancestors. It was Tane who caused my sickness."

"Who's Tane?"

"He is the god who produced women. He fertilized the earth."

"A god of fertility?"

"Yes, that's it."

"What happened?"

"It was very bad. I had much pain and high fevers. I did not think I would ever be forgiven."

Grayson did not know what to say—he could not understand these strange beliefs, so different from his own.

"Our *tohunga* took pity on me . . . cured me."

"A *tohunga* is a doctor?"

"No. A sacred priest."

"I thought the Maoris around Orakei had been Christianized?"

"We have." She chuckled. "We go to church. Your God is the same as our Io. And we like Jesus. But we know that Tane took red clay from the puke of the Earth-mother and molded

47

a woman. Not Io. Tane lay with her and breathed life into her. It was Tane who gave her the first sneeze of life, not Io."

"Have any of you given up your gods?" he asked.

"No. How could we? They are a part of us."

A bee buzzed overhead and the two were still. Then, carefully, they moved to another spot.

Grayson found Amiria's ways intriguing. And he was amused at how the Pakeha all believed they had converted these people. The Maoris went to Church to conform, or maybe because they liked the ritual, not because they believed in the concept of one god.

As the afternoon wore on, Amiria told Grayson stories of her extended family—her parents, grandparents, brother, sisters, cousins, uncles, and aunts. And the more he listened to her, the more he knew he did not want to turn from her. John Tole was wrong.

"I must learn Maori," he said without prompting.

"Perhaps."

"Will you teach me?"

"If you would like me to."

Grayson could not bear the distance between them, feeling emotions that he wasn't certain he could handle. His heart was pounding so rapidly, he was positive that Amiria could hear its every beat. He put out his arms to draw her to him and enclose her into the warmth of his being. He was almost afraid to kiss her, for fear that the magic between them would be broken, but his rising passion would not be held back. He needed to feel his lips on hers, to satisfy himself by tasting the sweetness of her mouth. If no more were ever to happen between them, at least there would be this to treasure. At first he held her tightly to him, but then, leaning slightly back, he released her and gently framed her face with his hands. Her polished skin gleamed in the sunlight, her dark eyes beckoned him until he could bear it no more. Their lips met. Grayson felt his life had changed, and unwittingly his tenderness gave way to a savagery he didn't know he had.

Amiria, too, was overcome by his passion, yet she was afraid. She didn't understand the meaning of his kiss, but she could not push him from her. Her hands met at the nape of his neck, her fingers becoming entangled in his hair as she pressed her body against his until they were both lying on the sweet-smelling fern. And as she kissed Grayson with an ardor equal to his, the safe world she had always known slipped away from her forever.

Much later, when the sun had already set, Amiria knew she must return home. "I will be here tomorrow," she whispered.

He nodded, staring helplessly into her intense eyes.

She rose and slowly moved away.

As Grayson rode back to town he felt he was riding in a dream. He at last knew the meaning of love. He had always been a cynic when he spoke of love—to him one married for position, for money, and to move up in society. Amiria had changed all his thoughts. He didn't care about the repercussions of his actions, he wanted to be with her and to live with her. The question was: Dare he tell her how he felt? But by the following morning Grayson's joy had turned to panic. What about the son of that chief? He couldn't remember the boy's name. Was Amiria still planning to marry him? Did the fact that she had screamed when that barbaric *tohunga,* or whatever he was called, tattooed her private parts, mean that the marriage was off? He felt powerless and confused by her strange world, whose beliefs and customs eluded him, a society that had created this woman he couldn't live without. He wished he understood the emotions pulling him to her, attracting two people together from alien worlds. But all he knew was that he could hardly wait until the next evening, when they would meet again. But when they did, he decided it was too soon. He did not want to rush her, for fear she would disappear again. Not to return.

More than a week passed before Grayson felt the time had come when he could no longer keep his thoughts to himself. Shortly after they greeted one another, he said, "Amiria, you know I love you."

She smiled but did not reply.

"Will you come and live with me?" He felt a twinge of guilt.

Why was he not asking her to marry him? Had John's words impressed him so?

She hesitated.

"You're not going to marry that chief's son?"

"No," she answered, and he couldn't tell by her tone if she were pleased or sad. "Te Kawau will not let Te Hira marry me. I am not worthy of him."

"That's wonderful!" Grayson said, clasping her hands in his. "Then there's nothing stopping you."

"My extended family will not be pleased," she answered. "They will not like me to go with you."

"But you aren't marrying Te Hira. You've disgraced your family—" He bit his lip, sorry he had said the words. "I mean . . . they should be glad that I want you to come away with me . . . that I love you."

"It is not you. It is because of my sister, Mihi."

Grayson looked puzzled.

Amiria continued. "Mihi was married to a great whaler, Brian Thompson. When they were together, they were very happy. But Brian only said he married Mihi so that my people, the Ngati Whatua, would be friendly . . . trade with him. He used all of us. Then he went back to England . . . to his Pakeha wife."

"You mean he was a bigamist?"

"Bigamist?" It was a word she did not know.

"It means being married to two women at the same time."

"Yes, that is what he did. But their union was blessed by one of our *tohunga,* not in your Church, so the marriage was not legal by your people."

Grayson held Amiria close to him. "I don't want anything from your people but you," he assured her. "Please, Amiria, come with me. I'll never hurt you. I love you."

"Yes, I will come. But not now. I need time to prepare my things, tell my family." She paused before asking, "Would you like to come home with me tomorrow afternoon? Have the evening meal with my family? If they meet you, it will be easier to explain why I am leaving them. Also, when there is a guest, we make a feast. You will enjoy it."

"I'll come," he answered, though he had no desire to be put on exhibit. But he loved Amiria and he was certain her parents would never give even their tacit consent to her leaving without first meeting him.

Fifty-seven people stood on the *marae*—the large area, like a village common, in front of the village meeting house— waiting to greet Amiria's new friend. Grayson was astounded by the number. Was this her family? She had told him he would meet them, she had even said her extended family would receive him, but he had never expected to be confronted by so many people. He was overwhelmed.

Amiria began by introducing Grayson to everyone. He felt totally lost. He would never remember their names, the sounds were all so unfamiliar to him. Every adult there had a tattooed face—how could he tell one man from another, or one woman from another? Except for their ages and sexes, they all looked alike to him. More than anything, he wanted to mount his horse and gallop away.

"My sister Mihi," Amiria said, interrupting Grayson's thoughts.

"How do you do," he replied. He was glad he didn't have to say more, for Amiria continued introducing her brother to him and then the younger cousins in the family.

"Do you all live together?" Grayson finally asked.

Amiria's hand swept from left to right, pointing to the eleven small, low sleeping houses in the *kainga.* "We all have our own cooking houses too," she explained, "but when we have a feast, we have one big *hangi.*"

Grayson knew that the *hangi* was the earth-and-stone oven the Maoris used. But he had never seen how they cooked in the ground, and had never tasted food prepared in this manner.

Amiria's father, chief of this village, held up his hands to quieten the crowd. First he spoke in Maori, then he translated into English. "The *hangi* is ready now. Perhaps our guest would like to see it opened?"

"Oh, yes," said Grayson to Amiria. He had forgotten how

uncomfortable he was moments before. He nodded to the chief, then let Amiria lead him to the *hangi*.

Grayson was mesmerized by the sight, so different from anything he had seen. On the ground was a large split-flax, closely plaited mat covered with dirt. Two men, one on either side, each took hold of the overlapping edges of the mat and, with the dirt in place, carefully lifted it off. Underneath this were several more mats. As the men flicked these off one by one, great floods of hissing steam rose from the ground. It was impossible to see even inches around the *hangi*.

As the steam slowly drifted away, Grayson saw a hole about three feet wide and one foot deep, filled with hot stones and food. "What's in there?" he whispered to Amiria.

"Everything," she laughed. "Pork, pigeon, eel, fish . . . whatever's around. Then there'll be potatoes, kumara, maybe some thistle, it's difficult to know."

"How long does it cook?"

"Two to three hours."

"And where do we eat?"

"Right here, around the *hangi*."

A smoky aroma wafted by and Grayson realized how very hungry he was. But when it came to actually eating the food, he felt extremely self-conscious. He was handed a basket of food, but there were no utensils. He soon saw that a stone served as a knife, and that everyone was using their hands instead of forks.

A vivid image of Grayson's childhood came into focus—memories of his mother and father telling him and Caroline to hold their forks and knives properly.

"Do you like the taste?" asked Amiria, bringing Grayson back to the present.

"Yes," he answered, not entirely truthful. "It's a combination of a smoky, steamed flavor . . . it's very interesting."

"You don't have to like it," she told him. "You will not hurt our feelings."

Grayson looked at her lovingly but did not reply.

Amiria's brother Kani interrupted the tender moment. Speaking rapidly in his Maori tongue, he addressed his sister.

"What has happened to you? Has your intelligence fled with the wind? Did you learn nothing from our sister? A Pakeha will never stay with you."

"Enough," said Amiria with quiet strength. "I am not making the mistake of Mihi. My Pakeha is different." She turned to Grayson. "Come, it is time we leave."

"Must we say good-bye to everyone?" he asked, rising from the ground.

"Just my father and my mother," she answered. And once she and Grayson reached them, Amiria saw to it that the parting was brief, without unnecessary conversation.

As they were leaving, Grayson noticed the many children spinning their *toa* tops. He lingered to watch them, again recalling his early childhood.

The noise of laughter and conversation suddenly stopped as Amiria's entire extended family began singing *"Po Atarau."* The melody was enchanting, and Grayson stopped to listen. "That's beautiful," he said softly.

"Yes," answered Amiria. "It's our farewell song."

"What does it mean?"

"Now is the hour, when we must say good-bye. . . ." She continued translating the melancholic words as they slowly walked from the *kainga.*

The strains of the music faded as they mounted their horses. Grayson had no idea that according to Maori tradition such a feast was a wedding celebration and that Amiria was now considered to be his wife.

The air was still as they rode back to Auckland, and although the noise of the youngsters was behind them, the couple did not speak. They rode slowly, side by side along the dusty trail, looking at each other from time to time but saying nothing. When they finally reached Auckland the tension between them was as great as any conversation could have made it.

Grayson entered his room and quickly lit his whale-oil lamp. Amiria stood with quiet calm in the doorway. The light of the lamp cast a soft shadow on her bare shoulder and outlined the voluptuous limbs beneath the thinly coiled flax strips of her skirt.

Grayson's excitement mounted as he watched her, more certain than ever that he had made the right choice. He held out his arms and like a vision she came to him. At first he was almost afraid to touch her, lest the apparition fade away. But as she reached him, the sweet scent of her aroused in him an unquenchable desire. Gently, he drew her to him, his eyes never leaving hers, and as their lips touched they both knew their love was all that mattered now.

Chapter 5

GOSSIP TRAVELED RAPIDLY FROM AUCKLAND TO THE BAY of Islands and within ten days of Grayson's bringing Amiria to live with him, Caroline was privy to the news. A surge of anger rose within her as she read Nevil's letter. She was furious at him. How dare he criticize her brother! And certainly, Nevil had no right to lecture her on Grayson's behavior.

Caroline finished reading the letter with watery eyes, hurt that Grayson hadn't been the one to tell her about this woman. But she was also worried about him, fearing that maybe Nevil was right, that taking in a Maori woman could jeopardize her brother's civil service career.

She stood on the upstairs verandah of the Weatherby home, debating the question over and over. No, she decided at last. Grayson hadn't acted irresponsibly. He wasn't throwing his future away. He had every right to fall in love with any woman he wished—regardless of the color of her skin.

Feeling satisfied with her resolve, she walked back inside to write to her brother. But Caroline was not really at ease. As she picked up her pen, she saw her hand quivering. She was not thinking of Grayson, but of who and what the Maoris really were.

Ever since her arrival in Kororareka, there had been trouble with the tribes in the area. They were now beginning to realize how they had been tricked by the Treaty of Waitangi, to understand just what the British had done to them. In the past the Pakeha had been dependent upon the Maoris—whalers and traders had come to them for food, land, flax, and timber —but once customs regulations were imposed by Britain, whalers went to free ports elsewhere in the Pacific. The Maoris had no recourse but to stand by helplessly as the dependency shifted. Furthermore, once the capital was moved to Auckland, the tribes around the Bay of Islands watched the commercial significance of Kororareka evaporate before their eyes. Rapidly, the Maoris were discovering that their power and influence had waned. Their land had been taken from them—the Pakeha ruled.

"Caroline," called Bradley from the doorway. "Will you play ninepins with me?"

Caroline wanted to refuse, she was in no mood to play.

"Mama said you could," Bradley continued in his usual exuberant way. "She said she's going to rest awhile. She doesn't need you now."

"How can I say no to you?" Caroline asked, putting out her hand to let Bradley lead her downstairs.

As they reached the front door, Geoffrey Rutledge was also leaving. "I've just put the final touches on Mrs. Weatherby's portrait," he said to Caroline.

"You mean it's finished? Does Mama like it? Can I see it now?"

"Your mama loves it," Geoffrey said, smiling with satisfaction. "You can go and see it, but you must promise not to touch it. The paint's not dry yet."

"I promise," said Bradley. He scampered away.

Caroline and Geoffrey walked down the garden path to the picket gate. They stood in the shade of the brightly blooming Pohutukawa as they spoke.

"I'm leaving at dawn," said Geoffrey.

"Where are you going?"

"Across the island to Waipoua . . . to the Kauri forest."

"Where's that?"

"About fifty miles from here. I cross over to Paihia and from there I'll ride to the west coast . . . it's just south of Hokianga Harbour."

She looked at him inquisitively, wondering why he wanted to go there.

He read her thoughts. "I want to see the gum diggers, paint them in action. You know, Caroline, you can find gold diggers all over the world. I think New Zealand's the only country that has gum diggers. They're unique here, and they've become a part of this land."

"What do they use the gum for?"

"We use it primarily for resin and as a gloss in paints. The Maoris chew it. They also use it to light fires and, I think, for tattooing." He paused to brush an insect from his nose.

"Why are they called gum *diggers?* I thought the gum came from the Kauri tree."

"It does. It oozes from cracks in the tree's bark and then forms lumps which eventually fall to the ground. The hardened resin is usually buried in the swamps of the bush." When he said *bush,* he was using the New Zealander's word for forest; and what he had once called bush in England he now called scrub. "Some of the resin's been lying there for thousands of years," he continued. "You just have to find it."

"I think the portrait of Mama is wonderful, sir," called Bradley, bouncing down the three steps from the verandah to the garden. "Can we play now, Caroline?"

"You set up the ninepins. I'll be with you shortly."

She turned back to Geoffrey. "I'll miss you," she said. "I know the Kauri trees are some of the biggest in the world, but I wish you'd stay and paint some of the smaller trees around here."

He threw back his head with laughter. "It's not quite the same," he said. "There's a whole way of life in the bush that I want to catch. And anyway, once I'm gone you won't even miss me, you'll be so busy."

"That's not true, and you know it."

"I won't be gone forever. Just a few months."

"Can we play now?"

"In a moment," said Caroline without turning away from Geoffrey.

The bright crimson legs of a sea gull landing on the garden fence attracted Bradley's attention. "I'll be back in a minute," he called, but he was running toward the bird as he spoke and no one heard his words.

"You've been a real friend to me, Geoffrey. I'll never forget these days, the talks we've had. . . ."

"You've been a friend to me too. You've put money into my pocket," he said with an engaging, forthright smile. "This commission from Mrs. Weatherby was just what I needed."

Another sea gull landed next to the first one, and then the two flew off, soaring and swooping down the beach, fishing near the shoreline for their dinner. Bradley ran after them, enchanted by the graceful birds.

The birds landed for a moment on the tip of a point of jutting rocks. Bradley could not resist following them. He looked back to see if Caroline was watching and was relieved to see that she was still deeply engrossed in conversation. Carefully, but as quickly as he could, he began picking his way across the slippery rocks. The birds flew around the point. Bradley increased his speed, intent on following them. As soon as he turned the corner, completely out of Caroline's sight, he slipped and fell.

"Help! Help!" Bradley screamed, but the wind swallowed his cries. "My ankle," he sobbed. Helplessly he watched it swell. He tried to stand and could not. His head was aching. He put his hand to his temple. It was wet with blood. Bradley emitted a howling scream. Still, no one heard. He hated the feel of the slimy rocks. There was a pool of water not ten feet from him—if he could pull himself to it, at least he could wipe the blood from his face. But he couldn't. The jagged rocks cut into his tiny chest. He was helpless, trapped. He could only pray that Caroline would come.

"Where's Bradley!" A sudden wave of panic engulfed Caroline as she looked around and saw that the child was nowhere in sight.

"Don't get all upset," said Geoffrey. "He can't have gone far. Maybe he saw a rabbit and decided to follow it."

"Into the scrub!" exclaimed Caroline, looking over at the thick brush adjacent to the next house. "He wouldn't do that. He wouldn't. He knows he's not allowed in there."

"Then maybe he's chasing a pukeko. You know how he loves to run after those long-legged little birds."

"How fast can a pukeko run? For that matter, how fast can any bird here run? You know the birds here don't fly much. None of them do. They walk everywhere they want to go. And Bradley can certainly outrun their walking."

Geoffrey hesitated a moment. Caroline was right. One of the first things he had noticed when he came to New Zealand six years ago was that, with the exception of the sea gulls, the birds here rarely flew. Historically they didn't have to, he'd been told, for until the white man came to these islands, New Zealand was a land devoid of predators—birds had no reason to fly. Not only were there no animals on any of the three islands that made up this country, but the only mammal to be found was a small bat that lived in caves of the South Island.

"Let's walk along the beach to the pier," he said, trying to sound as calm as possible, for Bradley was certainly not in sight.

"Don't you think we should split up? You go along the pier, I'll go over to the scrub."

"I think it should be the other way around. That dense scrub isn't any safer for you than it is for Bradley."

"Caroline," called Mrs. Weatherby from the verandah. "Would you come and help me downstairs. I'd like to sit in the garden until teatime."

"Dear God! Now what do I do?" Caroline muttered under her breath. "I'll be right there," she called up.

"Tend to her," said Geoffrey. "I'll go see if Bradley's playing near the scrub. I'll meet you back here in ten minutes. If he's not over there," he pointed, "we'll go to the pier together."

"What will I tell Mrs. Weatherby?"

"Nothing for the moment."

"But she'll want to know where Bradley is."

"I'll be back before she realizes he's not here. Just pray I find him."

Caroline was trembling as she walked into the house. She hoped Mrs. Weatherby wouldn't notice how nervous she was.

"I was just saying good-bye to Geoffrey," Caroline said to Mrs. Weatherby in as cheerful a tone as she could muster. "He's going across to the Kauri forests in the morning. Wants to paint there."

"I know," Mrs. Weatherby muttered. "He told me." She was not happy that Geoffrey was leaving. She had wanted him to do a portrait of her husband and had hoped he would continue giving her son art lessons. "But he'll be back," she said emphatically. "He'll never stay once he sees what those Dalmatians are like. They've taken over the North, you know. They should have stayed in Dalmatia where they belong. Instead, they've monopolized one of this country's leading industries."

They had barely reached the garden when Mrs. Weatherby asked, "Where's Brad? I thought he was out here playing with you."

Caroline swallowed hard. She could feel the beads of cold sweat running down her forehead. She looked toward the scrub, silently praying that Geoffrey had found Bradley.

"I said, where is Bradley?"

"I'm not sure."

"You're what!"

"I don't know," Caroline answered.

Geoffrey ran from the scrub. He was panting as he reached the Weatherby garden. "He's not there," he said. "I looked everywhere."

Now it was Mrs. Weatherby who felt the stranglehold of panic. The memory of the boating accident was instantly resurrected. Both daughters had been killed. And now her only son! Her face blanched and she looked as though she was going to faint. Caroline was afraid the news had been too much for her.

"We'll find him," said Caroline, trying desperately to sound reassuring. "He's probably just down the road . . . searching for shells, or following a rabbit."

"If you'll be all right, Mrs. Weatherby," said Geoffrey, taking command of the situation, "we'll start looking at once."

"I'll be fine . . . once you bring Bradley home."

Caroline was not certain she should leave Mrs. Weatherby. The woman seemed in shock, barely able to speak. But Geoffrey urged her on.

"We've no time to lose," he said softly, so that Caroline alone could hear his words. "It'll be dark soon."

"Please try not to worry, Mrs. Weatherby," Caroline said as she wheeled the woman back to the verandah. "I'm sure we'll find him."

Mrs. Weatherby did not answer. She just sat staring down the Grand Parade, watching to catch a glimpse of her son's curly red hair.

Bradley had cried and cried until at last, thoroughly exhausted, he had let the warm sun cradle him to sleep. Now that dusk was falling, a chill came into the air and Bradley awakened. No sooner were his eyes opened than he wished he were still asleep. But he was awake—the woman in front of him wasn't a nightmare. In total terror, afraid to make a sound, he watched the Maori woman searching in the shallow pools of water at the edge of the rocky point. His gaze was firmly fixed as he watched her put something into her basket. Then she looked up and saw him.

"Tena koe," she said.

Bradley knew she was saying hello but he could not reply.

"That means hello," she said with a broad grin, her stained teeth making her tattooed face more frightening.

As she came closer, Bradley cringed. He was terrified. All he could think of were the stories he had heard of how the Maoris ate people. His friend Willie had told him that the

Maoris put live Pakehas—children especially—into earth ovens. Then they sliced off the top of their skulls with greenstone clubs, so they could see when the brains began to boil.

"Are you hurt?" the woman asked, seeing that the child did not move.

Bradley continued to stare at the deeply incised spirals on her face, but he remained speechless.

She came a little closer to him. She was a grandmother herself and understood the fears of children. "Have you ever seen a *kina?*" she asked, holding up the green-and-white spiny striped sea egg.

Bradley did not move.

The elderly woman saw the cut on Bradley's head and wondered if his fall had made him unable to speak. Then she saw his ankle, by now not only swollen but badly discolored. "Where do you live?"

Bradley wanted to tell her. Oh, how he wanted to go home to his mama and papa, and to Caroline, but he couldn't find his voice.

"I'll take you back to the *pa,*" she said.

Bradley pulled back, every muscle in his body taut. He knew the word *pa.* That was a fortified village. The fortified village that everyone in Kororareka was afraid of. "That's where the trouble will begin," he had heard his father tell his mother this very week. If this woman took him to her *pa,* that would be the end—they would burn him alive. Eat him. He scrunched his eyelids together, hoping that when he opened them again, she would be gone.

The Maori woman put down her basket of eggs and lifted Bradley into her arms. "I'll carry you back," she said as gently as she could. "Our *tohunga* will make you walk again. Then we will find where you live."

"Please don't eat me," Bradley tried to say, but the words caught in his throat.

The westering sun was quickly disappearing behind the horizon and still Caroline and Geoffrey had no idea what had happened to Bradley.

"I think I've knocked on every door in town," said Caroline, thoroughly exhausted. "He's nowhere. Just disappeared."

"We may as well go back," said Geoffrey. "He's certainly not in town."

They walked back to the Weatherbys' slowly, silently.

"You don't think he's been kidnapped?" Caroline said at last. She had been thinking this for the past hour but had not dared to voice her thoughts.

"I'm afraid you may be right."

"But why?"

"Money," Geoffrey answered. "Or, maybe . . . maybe revenge."

"What do you mean?"

"If a patient Dr. Weatherby treated died, somebody might want satisfaction. The Maoris are big on revenge, you know."

"I know. *Utu* was one of the first words I learned in Maori. But why would anyone want to exact *utu* by kidnapping Bradley?"

"Can you think of a better way of hurting the doctor?"

"No." She paused, then asked, "What are we going to tell Mrs. Weatherby?"

"The truth. We looked everywhere and we can't find him. What else can we say?"

Caroline could feel the cold sweat returning, and again she began to tremble.

Dr. Weatherby, waiting impatiently for Caroline and Geoffrey to return, walked down the road to meet them as he saw them approach. He listened to their story quietly and then turned to Caroline. "How could you be so irresponsible? We trusted you."

"But—"

"I'm not interested in excuses, Caroline. I'm only interested in getting my son back."

The three reluctantly joined Mrs. Weatherby. They avoided conversation, restlessly pacing instead. Only Mrs. Weatherby sat, nervously tapping her fingers on the arm of her chair, silently glaring at Caroline. There was nothing to do. There was no place else to look. There was nothing more to say. The only thing left was to wait. Wait and pray that before long Bradley would return.

Bradley laughed and laughed as he watched the Maori boy make his little dog do tricks. For the first time since he had fallen, Bradley began to relax. He was no longer afraid. These people were being too nice to him—they wouldn't eat him. At first the heavy tattooing on the faces and around the midsection of the men frightened him, but as he watched the men his fears began to evaporate.

He looked around the *pa* and was surprised to see that he was the only youngster who was clothed. As the day waned and the air cooled, the boys and girls put blankets or cloaks around themselves, but none of them wore clothes. The older children, dressed like the adults, wore brown-and-beige striped flax skirts. Bradley liked the way the dried strips of coiled flax rattled as they walked. He thought it would be fun to wear one of those skirts. Almost seven, he had just gotten his first pair of breeches. They were hot and uncomfortable, and he hated them.

"This is our chief, Hone Heke," said the woman who had brought Bradley to the *pa*.

"Tena koe," Hone Heke said, smiling warmly at Bradley.

Bradley shrunk back. Even at six years old he knew the name of Hone Heke. Everyone in Kororareka knew that name. This was the man who had cut down the flagpole. Not once, twice. Bradley wasn't certain why this was such a terrible thing, he just knew it was. He had heard everybody talking about it. An insult to the Queen, or something like that. Anyway, one thing he knew—Hone Heke was a bad man.

"You won't shake my hand?" said Hone Heke.

"No. I want to go home."

"Well, at least he's talking again," said the woman to her chief.

Tears came to Bradley's eyes. She was speaking in Maori. He was certain they were planning to boil him alive.

"If you tell us where you live," she said, "we'll take you home."

"Not him." Bradley looked directly at the man. "You," he said.

"I'll be glad to go with you," she told him, "but I'll need help. You're too heavy for me to carry all the way back to town."

Bradley's eyes pleaded as he looked from Hone Heke to the woman. He would go with anyone, but not this man.

"I see even the Pakeha children are afraid of me." The chief laughed. "And so they should be. I am a very fierce warrior." He pretended to do a *haka,* the traditional Maori war dance. He let his tongue hang out and rolled his eyes to the back of his head as he jumped up and down shouting the first words of their war song.

Bradley was more terrified than ever as he watched the horrid grimaces on the chief's face, the white eyes, the foaming mouth, the gestures designed to appear fierce. "I want to go home," he said to the woman. "Please take me home."

"Do you know where you live?" she asked.

"Next to Bishop Pompellier's house, at the end of the Grand Parade."

"Then you must be Dr. Weatherby's son," said Hone Heke, by now having stopped his display.

Bradley nodded.

"Your father's a good man," the chief said. "He has brought good medicine to my people."

Bradley had a cautious look in his eyes as he listened to the chief. He did not speak.

"Let me take you home," Hone Heke said. "I know your father well. I will bring him greetings from our *pa.*"

Bradley shook his head vigorously.

"I won't hurt you," the chief said. "I give you my word." He stroked Bradley's head. "Always remember, the word of a Maori is sacred, never to be broken."

Bradley listened to the chief skeptically. Then he let a small smile creep onto his face. For some reason he believed this man. "All right," he said. "You can take me home."

Chapter 6

A FULL MOON LIT UP THE DESERTED BEACH IN FRONT OF the Weatherby home, and everyone inside kept walking back and forth to the window, glancing at the lonely strip of sand, praying Bradley would return.

Priscilla Weatherby's vigil, however, was not interrupted. She refused to move from her perch, her sight glued to the lonely stretch of shoreline, watching and waiting for her son to appear in the night.

But it was Geoffrey who first spotted people emerging from the thick scrub. "Look! Near those trees! See them! They're carrying someone. I think it's Brad!" he said excitedly, running from the house.

Lucian Weatherby and Caroline followed close behind.

"Oh, God, thank you, thank you," Caroline whispered. Reaching Bradley before his father, she took the child from the chief and cradled him in her arms. She held him tightly, kissing his soft cheeks. Tears of joy flowed from her eyes; she did not bother to wipe them away.

Lucian Weatherby took Bradley from Caroline. "You scared us all, you little tyke," he said. He held his son close to him, and he, too, silently thanked God for returning his only child.

"Tena koe," the chief said to Lucian Weatherby.

"Tena koa," Dr. Weatherby answered, then recognized Hone Heke, chief of the Ngaphui tribe.

They greeted each other warmly, pressing noses in the traditional Maori way.

"How did you find Bradley?" Dr. Weatherby asked.

As they walked back to the Weatherby home, Hone Heke explained. "Perhaps you should look at his ankle," the chief said after he had finished relating the details of the past few hours. "Our *tohunga* tended him, but you may wish to do something else."

Priscilla Weatherby began to weep when she saw Bradley, crying so hard she could barely utter a word. She had been sure she would never see him again, certain he was dead.

"Mama, Mama," he said, holding out his arms to her.

Lucian put his son into his wife's lap. It was a touching scene to watch the two hug each other. For a few moments everyone in the room had the feeling that Bradley would never let go of his mother. Suddenly he began talking, spilling out the events of the day with such speed that it was almost impossible to understand what he was saying. "I told Caroline where I was going," he said innocently. "But when I fell and she didn't come, I knew I should have told her better." He had said enough. He was exhausted. Then, as if someone had magically blown out a lamp, his head drooped and he fell off to sleep.

The strain of the day had taken its toll on everyone, and they were all glad when Hone Heke and the woman departed.

"I think I should say good night too," said Geoffrey. "I hope to leave tomorrow at the break of dawn."

"You'll be back," insisted Mrs. Weatherby.

"Indeed I will. I promised you a portrait of the doctor, and you shall have one." He turned to Lucian. "Good-bye, sir. It's been a pleasure getting to know you and your family."

Lucian replied graciously.

Then Geoffrey turned to Caroline. He bid her farewell

quickly, not wanting her to see how he felt, and yet in his mind's eye he hastily sketched her, trying to capture a moment that he could recall when he was alone. He was sad to be leaving her and knew if he looked directly at her, his face would betray him.

Caroline's good-bye was said only with her eyes, for words would not come to her as she looked at this dear friend, knowing somehow that she would feel a terrible loneliness once he was gone, and not understanding why.

"Now, Caroline," said Priscilla Weatherby in an icy voice, as soon as the door had closed behind Geoffrey, "take Bradley to bed. I'll speak to you in the morning."

"Yes, Mrs. Weatherby," she answered. She was too tired to worry now about the consequences of the day—tomorrow would be time enough. She lifted Bradley into her arms and slowly walked away. Yes, she thought, looking down at the peacefully sleeping child, tomorrow will be time enough.

"She leaves tomorrow," Priscilla told her husband.

"You can't just throw her on the street. You have to give her a few days to find a place to live."

"Why? What did she do for me except cause me anguish, anguish worse than any I've ever known."

"Priscilla, it wasn't really her fault."

"What!" It was a shrill, piercing scream, and she began to tremble with rage.

"Calm yourself, Priscilla," Lucian said, gently patting his wife on the shoulder. "Even Brad said he should have told Caroline better."

"She should have been watching him, not flirting with that painter. She's nothing but a hussy."

"She was just saying good-bye to Geoffrey. They're friends, Priscilla. I'm certain there's no more to it than that."

"Hmm!"

"As for Brad," Lucian continued, "he started chasing sea gulls. From here to the rocks isn't more than two minutes. If he hadn't fallen, none of this would have happened. You can't expect Caroline to have been watching him every second he was in the garden."

"What are you paying her for? To talk to any man around?"

"Priscilla, be fair."

"We won't discuss this further, Lucian. You hired her as a companion for me and I don't want her around. She leaves tomorrow."

"Then let her stay and work with me. The few times she's assisted me, I've found her most helpful."

"Are you mad? You mean you'd trust her with your patients? Never. I wouldn't be a party to that. It's just not fair. She leaves tomorrow."

"No. She leaves when she finds a place to go. She doesn't have to be around you, but I will not let you throw her onto the street. She's a decent young girl, not a tramp."

"All right. I'll give her a week, but not a day more. Now please take me to bed, I'm tired."

But Mrs. Weatherby could not sleep, and at six o'clock the following morning she had her husband call Caroline into the sitting room. The doctor, still garbed in his dressing gown, stood quietly at the side of his wife's chair.

"Caroline," Mrs. Weatherby began, "you are a totally irresponsible child. You're not trustworthy, you're unreliable, and you're certainly not the person I want as a companion for me . . . nor for that matter, as someone to look after my son.

"I will give you the rest of the week to find a place to live." She paused a moment. "In all fairness, I must tell you that I will *not*, under any circumstances, give you a reference. You don't deserve one. If I were you, child, I'd go to Auckland. Stay with your brother until you find work—at least no one will know you there. And you'd best be careful how you tell Sir Nevil that you've been sacked or that will be over too."

She turned to her husband, "Lucian, do you have something to tell Caroline?"

"I'm sorry this didn't work out Caroline, but you understand, Mrs. Weatherby feels she just wouldn't be able to trust you anymore. Bradley's the only child we have left. It would be unfair to everyone to let you stay."

"I understand," said Caroline, fighting back the tears. She would not break down in front of these heartless people. They had no idea of what the word fair meant. Neither of them had even asked her what had happened. They listened to the tale of a six-year-old . . . and even he had said he should have told her better.

"May I go now?" she asked, keeping her voice as steady as she could.

"Is that all you have to say, 'I understand,' and 'May I go?' Aren't you going to try to exonerate yourself?" Mrs. Weatherby asked. She couldn't believe Caroline was walking away without a fight. She had been certain the girl had more gumption than that.

"I didn't think there'd be any point in arguing with you. It seems to me that your mind is made up. It's better that I leave now," Caroline said. She suddenly felt she had the upper hand, knowing Mrs. Weatherby would be alone with only Milly to help her, and that Mrs. Weatherby couldn't stand Milly's talkative ways for more than a few minutes at a time.

Without waiting for a reply, Caroline excused herself and went outside. The sun was just dawning. Geoffrey had said he was leaving early, maybe he was still there. She'd walk by his room, hope he'd been delayed. But when she arrived at the house where he had stayed, she was not surprised to find him already gone.

Caroline walked toward the waterfront. She always found it restful to watch anchored ships in the harbor, rhythmically swaying at rest. When she came to the main pier, she leaned against a wooden post, staring out at the peaceful scene, trying to decide if she should go to Auckland and wondering if Nevil would marry her now. Was it too soon? Did he want to be more established before taking on the responsibilities of a wife? She knew he wouldn't care that she'd been fired. He had never thought the job good enough for her anyway.

Her thoughts shifted to Grayson. She could hardly turn to

him, not the way he had described his tiny room. Having Amiria there would be crowded enough.

Maybe she should stay in Kororareka, just to spite Mrs. Weatherby. Caroline was certain she could find work teaching at the school. She knew they were short of teachers. She smiled at the thought of having Bradley as a pupil. "I wonder how that would hit Mrs. Weatherby?" she asked herself.

A loud explosion made Caroline jump. Suddenly, muskets were being fired from all sides. Caroline stood paralyzed. Where should she go? What should she do? The grog shop at the end of the pier was in flames. She couldn't go back to the Weatherbys'. The way was blocked.

She turned and saw soldiers everywhere, and masses of people running toward the pier—the whole town seemed to be heading in this direction.

"This way, miss," said a man in a naval uniform.

"What's happening?" Caroline asked, finally taking hold of herself.

"The Maoris have decided to attack. Hone Heke's mad. He's behind this. Just come with me . . . right this way," he said, leading her to the first dinghy to leave the pier.

"But why?"

"The faster you get out of town, the better." He helped Caroline into the boat. "Good luck to you," he said and turned back to the screaming, hysterical mob.

Caroline was one of the first to seek refuge, but by noon, British soldiers were evacuating all the women and children in town.

Kororareka was in the hands of the Maori.

Caroline was talking to the captain of the *Anna Watson* when two sailors approached.

"He's done it again," chuckled Tommy, a young lad of slight frame with platinum hair and deep brown eyes.

"Who's done what?" asked the burly captain.

"Heke's cut down the flagpole again."

"He's a clever little bugger," said the other sailor, a strapping Scotsman about the same age as his friend. "Waited till

Kawiti attacked this morning. When the soldiers guarding the flagstaff heard firing, they went down the hillside to see what was going on below. Damn fools left it unguarded."

"So," laughed Tommy, "Heke cut it down again. Third time now. Got to give him credit for perseverance."

"I still can't see why that flagpole's so important," said Caroline.

"Heke's a madman," answered the captain. "He thinks the staff is the source of all evil. The natives all seem to believe the pole has powers. If they cut it down, their troubles will be over."

"So why do we keep putting a pole back up there?"

"Because that's where the Governor wants the flag to fly, so that's where it's going to fly," the captain answered.

Another explosion distracted them. The ship-of-war had opened fire on the Maoris now plundering the town.

The Maoris were furious. The Red Coats had no right to fire now. The fight was over. The town was being evacuated. The Maoris had the right to plunder. Those were *their* rules of war. Now they wanted satisfaction, and *utu* they would have.

"Look," called someone Caroline didn't know. He wasn't calling her, just drawing everyone's attention to the burning town.

From afar Caroline could see the Weatherby house in flames. Briefly she wondered what ship they were on, curious to know where they would now go.

As the sun was setting, the burning of Kororareka lit up the eastern sky. Soon the town would be nothing but a heap of rubble and ash. The Hell Hole of the Pacific was going up in flames.

"Hoist the anchor! Haul the sheets!" shouted the captain. And looking down at his compass, he set the *Anna Watson*'s course for Waitemata Harbour, Auckland.

Chapter 7

THE HEADLINE IN *The Southern Cross* READ: KORORAREKA and Caroline Sacked on the Same Day.

Caroline woke up smiling. What a crazy dream! Yet it did seem ironic that Hone Heke and the Maoris had been connected to both events.

She patted down her hair and straightened the folds of her full skirt. She knew she must look a sight, but there was nothing she could do. All her possessions, even her comb and brush, had burned to the ground. It was a little frightening to know she had nothing and had to start completely afresh, yet the mere thought of beginning life in a new town was exhilarating to Caroline. She could hardly wait for daylight.

She left the uncomfortable paillasse where she had been resting and walked up on deck. The sky was a myriad of stars, and as always, she enjoyed looking at The Southern Cross—it was such a bold constellation, so easy to locate overhead. She wondered what she should do when she got to Auckland. She couldn't let Nevil see her looking like this; and Grayson, she hated to barge in on him, especially now. No, she decided, the thing to do was to find a room and a job. As soon as she could afford some pretty clothes, or at least one new gown, she would go to Nevil. She realized how foolish she was being. Everybody in Auckland would learn about the sacking of Kororareka, if they hadn't already heard about it. Nevil would know she had no place to go, he would be expecting her. Unless . . . unless he thought she was still with the Weatherbys. All this debate was ridiculous. When she got to Auckland she would go to Nevil, and with his help she would decide what to do.

Having reached what seemed a logical solution to the immediate problem, Caroline went back to her straw mat and lay down to sleep.

Gray skies and a soft drizzle greeted the *Anna Watson* as she sailed into Waitemata Harbour. Caroline stood near the rail of the ship, trying to glimpse the town. The nearer to Auckland they sailed, the more surprised she was. Both Nevil and Grayson had described the capital in their letters, but neither had told her that Auckland was a city of rolling hills, and neither had emphasized the mass of closely packed, small wooden houses and thatched homes built of reeds, rushes, and raupo along the water's edge.

There must be a better neighborhood, she thought, not wanting to believe that this was what she was coming to—from afar it appeared primitive and overcrowded. It was difficult to believe that there were only four thousand people living in the capital.

By two o'clock that afternoon Caroline was standing on the shore. She looked around, having no idea where to go, not knowing if she could walk to Nevil's or if she had to hire a coach. She put her hands in the pockets of her disheveled skirt —there was a small white lace handkerchief that had been her mother's and a sweet Caroline always carried in case Mrs. Weatherby felt ill, and that was it. Caroline was more conscious than ever of her unenviable situation. She hated being dependent on anyone, and the thought of having to go to Nevil because she didn't have the wherewithal to go elsewhere bothered her immensely. However, she knew she had no alternatives so she bottled her pride and walked over to the first man who looked safe and presentable.

"Excuse me, sir, could you tell me how I might find O'Connell Street?"

The man looked at her for a moment before answering. His dark probing eyes made Caroline feel most uncomfortable, though he was fine-looking and dressed as a gentleman, hardly the sort to harm a woman.

"Queen Street's right over there," he pointed. "You walk down it until you come to Shortland Street. Have you got that?"

"Shortland Street?"

"Right. Go up Shortland . . . it's quite a steep hill . . . until you come to O'Connell. Who're you looking for there?"

"Sir Nevil Holbrooke."

"The Colonial Secretary?"

"Yes, sir," Caroline said.

"He lives in the second house on the right. It's a good-sized house, you can't miss it. Say hello to him for me. Name's Fitzroy."

"Governor Fitzroy?"

Fitzroy tipped his hat.

"I certainly will," she said. "And thank you," she added.

Caroline was properly impressed as she turned from the Governor. But the momentary elation vanished as quickly as it had come. Her step slowed as she turned up Shortland Street. What would she say to Nevil? How would he react to her unexpected arrival?

But a renewed surge of excitement washed over her as she approached the front door of Nevil's home. They had been away from each other for almost five months, she could hardly wait to see him again. She knocked on the door, then waited. Slowly the minutes passed. No one came. It seemed as if she had been there for hours, though she knew it had probably been less than ten minutes since she mounted the few steps to the front door. She thought she heard sounds inside. Still, no one came.

A light rain was falling now, but Caroline was oblivious to

the weather. A feeling of panic came over her and she had difficulty thinking logically. What if Nevil were away? Where would she go? She lifted her hand and knocked again, this time with a forceful fist.

"Caroline!" Nevil exclaimed as he opened the door. "Come in, come in," he said, taking her hand. "I can't believe you're here. What happened? How did you get here?" he fired questions at her with such rapidity that she had no chance to reply. There was an edginess, a nervousness about him—or was it excitement?—that Caroline had never seen before. Were her worst fears realized? Could it be he was not happy to find her drenched and disheveled at his front door?

"Oh, forgive me," said Nevil, turning to the man to his right. "Let me introduce you to Mark Watson, Captain of the *Queen Charlotte.*"

"How do you do," said Caroline politely. Instantly, anxiously, she turned back to Nevil, but before she could say anything he was talking again.

"Captain Watson, I'll have the final order sent to you tomorrow. Thank you for everything. Good day."

"Good day." The captain made a curt bow to Caroline. "Pleased to meet you, Miss Wickham. Good day."

Nevil looked relieved as the door closed behind Watson. Caroline was overjoyed that at last they were alone.

He led her into a small sitting room. Caroline could barely restrain her delight to find herself in a Victorian parlor transplanted from England, deep burgundy curtains and a muted oriental carpet conveyed a feeling of warmth and richness in the room. How wonderful to be here with Nevil, safe and welcome. She let herself relax, sitting next to him on a comfortable sofa, totally absorbed for a moment by the well-tended fire's comforting glow.

"Now, tell me how you came and why."

"Haven't you heard? Kororareka's been sacked."

"A rumor reached our office this morning. What happened?"

Caroline recounted all the details, omitting the story of

Bradley's disappearance and of her sudden dismissal by the Weatherby family.

"The government will certainly build a new town there," Nevil told her. "And I know the Weatherbys will go back. He's the only qualified doctor in that area. For the time being you'll have to return with them, Caroline. I couldn't even try to negotiate to buy back the contract until you've been there at least a year."

"You don't have to buy it back." She hesitated for a moment. "I've been let go," she said, then proceeded to tell him exactly what had happened.

"That means we can be married at once," said Nevil, taking both of Caroline's hands in his. "That's wonderful."

"Are you sure? I can wait if you'd rather. I'm certain I can find some kind of work here."

"Why wait? I'll speak to the minister at once."

Caroline could not believe how wrong she'd been. He had not been unsettled by her sudden arrival. It was all her own upset and anxiety, the disturbing events that had led to her dismissal, the shock of being forced to flee Kororareka, the terrible uncertainties that had plagued her during the journey —all the events that had contrived to land her penniless and distraught on his doorstep. Of course he had been . . . not nervous, but surprised. She had no idea of what important official business she might have interrupted. But now she was here and they would be married. Married at once.

"And Caroline," Nevil went on. "I know that your father was a Methodist, but Richard Churton is a good friend of mine. Would you mind being married in the Anglican Church?"

"No, of course not," she answered, but the surge of elation she'd felt was tempered by a touch of sadness and the wish that the ceremony could take place in the Church to which her father had devoted himself with such fiery zeal.

"Is Sunday next all right?" Nevil asked. "If I can arrange it, that is."

"Oh, yes," Caroline said, then hesitated. "Is there somewhere I can stay until then?"

"I suppose it wouldn't be proper for you to stay here; there'd be too much talk. And Grayson could hardly take you in . . . not with that girl there. Besides, if I'm not mistaken, he left for Rotorua last week. As a matter of fact, I think he took Amiria with him. Perhaps we shouldn't wait at all. We should get married tomorrow."

"That would cause even more chatter." Caroline giggled. "Everyone would be speculating why we married so quickly."

"Then I guess it's the least of two evils. I say we marry at once."

Caroline moved closer to Nevil and rested her head on his shoulder. Looking up at him lovingly, she asked, "What about this afternoon? That would answer all our problems."

He leaned over and kissed her forehead. "Wonderful," he said, and started to stand. "Shall we go, Lady Holbrooke? I'm certain the Reverend will make time for us."

But Caroline hesitated. She looked down at her drying clothes. She had not only slept in her gown, but it was further mussed from the rain. "How can I be married in this?" she asked, despondently holding out her wrinkled skirt. "I look—"

"Shh," he said. "I've a wonderful blue wool cape you can wear. It might be a little big, but I'll wrap it around you and you'll look just lovely. Now, let's be on our way."

It was a simple ceremony at Auckland's first Church of England, and as soon as Caroline said "I do," she was more certain than ever that she had made the right choice. She was sorry that her brother had not been at the wedding. As her only family, he belonged with her today. But she would explain things to him when he returned. They would celebrate this day then, and all the happy years to come.

She let Nevil take her hand, and radiating with contentment, she walked back to her new home. At the door he lifted her and gallantly carried her over the threshold, and Caroline felt her every wish was about to come true.

"You must be hungry," he said as soon as they were inside the house. "Wouldn't you like something to eat?"

78

The question upset Caroline. Somehow, Nevil's actions were discomfiting. How could he think of food now? This was the time for him to sweep her passionately into his arms and claim his prize of love. Ever since she had arrived, she had felt uneasy, as if something were awry. Caroline struggled to conceal her own impatience, her disappointment. "Yes, please," was all she could bring herself to say.

Teatime was a long drawn-out event. Caroline felt restless and uncomfortable as Nevil talked on and on of his work and of what she would do. But she was delighted when he pointed out that her first chore must be to buy some clothes and other personal items. At last Nevil rose and suggested a tour of the house.

"The servants live out there," he said, indicating a small thatched building. "They're off today . . . some Maori feast is being held at their *pa*, so I told them they could have the afternoon." Upstairs there were two bedrooms and a small library. "This will be yours," he told her, leading her into a charming room papered in pink-and-white floral design with matching silk curtains. A brass rail bed with flounces of pink and white lace stood there, luxurious and inviting, the sheet turned down as if the bed were awaiting her, welcoming her home.

Caroline was speechless. As beautiful as the appointments were, there seemed to be no reason why she should have a bedroom of her own. Alone.

She looked at Nevil, her surprise apparent. "I don't understand—" she began.

"Nobody of station who can afford two bedrooms lives in one," he stated matter-of-factly.

With some dignity, he took out his pocket watch. "It's nearly eight o'clock. Surely you must be exhausted. Wouldn't you like to rest?"

Was this an invitation, Caroline wondered, or was he asking her if she wanted to lie down? She gazed at him longingly. "Whatever you'd like," she answered, afraid to show herself immodest, too forward.

Much to her relief, Nevil led her into her bedroom and

closed the wooden shutters. Without a word he took her in his arms. His lips found hers and a simple kiss became one of such passion that Caroline actually felt giddy, her head whirling rapidly.

He began fumbling to undo the buttons of her blouse. "Let me," she whispered, and with practiced skill she flicked them open.

He did not want to wait to undress her slowly. Suddenly, he wanted her now, but he restrained himself. He did not want to frighten her. He took her blouse from her and let his hands caress her soft, creamy skin. Then he turned his back to her while he disrobed.

Now it was she who wanted to feel her body next to his. But her modesty made her feel restrained. She was glad the curtains were drawn and no lamps were lit. She undressed quickly and before Nevil turned back to her, she was lying between the cool linen sheets.

He slipped into bed next to her, gathered her into his arms and gently kissed her. The feel of her body was soft and inviting. He began exploring her mouth with his tongue and despite her shyness her body began to tremble with desire. As he caressed her supple skin, she began to respond to his touch. But suddenly she felt his passion change—the prelude was over. And though he continued to fondle areas of her body she didn't know existed, she felt excluded from his world. He took her quickly, without caring whether she was ready to accept him, and then, when he was spent, he abruptly turned from her and fell into a heavy sleep.

Caroline lay in the darkness unhappy and distressed, yet not understanding that her own desires had been aroused, her passions unsatisfied.

A long time later, while Nevil was sleeping peacefully, Caroline was still awake. She lay beside her husband, quietly staring into the night, but now her frustrations had eased and optimism had taken their place. A map of romantic dreams unfolded as she imagined Lady Holbrooke and the life she would lead.

The sun's rays, streaming through the window, awakened Caroline. Nevil was gone. Downstairs she found his note. He had an early appointment and hadn't wanted to awaken her. He would be home in time for tea. She should ask the servant, Aroha, to show her about town. She should not tire herself, and he looked forward to seeing her later.

Caroline was disappointed but at the same time elated—She was married. And to such an important and busy man!

She would ask Aroha about the shops and their whereabouts, but she would wander through the streets and savor the sights of town alone. She was a married woman now, she no longer needed a chaperone.

Caroline left the house in high spirits, but as she walked along Queen Street she was almost overcome by the foul smell. Why, upon her arrival, hadn't she noticed the putrescent entrails of slaughtered animals which lay rotting in the streets? Perhaps because yesterday had been cool and wet. As she reached the lower end of Queen Street and the Horutu Creek, the odor intensified. She was afraid she would be ill right there. The creek was a noisome sewer, more noxious than any cesspool she had ever encountered. But the contrast of rolling hills and sweet-smelling fern that surrounded the town compensated for the ugliness of the growing city, and the tranquil sight of sailing ships with naked masts swaying peacefully at anchor seemed to calm the loud and bustling new capital.

By the time Caroline returned home, she was exhausted. She had enjoyed the day thoroughly, but she could hardly say she'd had a successful shopping spree. She had managed to buy a change of clothes, and tomorrow she would engage a dressmaker to style her wardrobe.

Nevil was sitting in the parlor when she returned, deeply engaged in conversation with Alexander Shepherd, the Colonial Treasurer.

"I don't know how you expect to do something with the postal system," said Shepherd, angry frustration reflected in his voice. "The treasury's in a mess. There's no extra money for anything."

"Take it easy," said Nevil. "Our problem is to find a source of revenue, not let the system fall apart. The postal system must be put in order. It's ridiculous as is. You know as well as I that it's faster to send a letter from Auckland to Wellington via Sydney than direct, and that takes several months. Letters should go back and forth to Wellington within a few days."

"What do you propose?"

"To get the money through land. Fitzroy wants to issue Government Debentures. I think we should back him." Nevil spoke with firm resolve.

"Maori land sales are controlled by the Home Authorities now, not by the Colonial Office."

"Everything we do is controlled," Nevil said. "What does London know about what's happening out here? The only way we're going to get out of the financial mess we're in is to buy land from the Maoris cheaply and sell it at a substantial profit. The treasury's bankrupt. What other choice do we have?"

Shepherd was against doing something totally in contradiction to orders from London. He shook his head in dismay and as he did so he noticed Caroline standing in the doorway. He quickly stood up. "How do you do," he said. "Lady Holbrooke, I presume."

Caroline was delighted. It was the first time anyone had called her by her new name.

Nevil made introductions then swiftly brought the meeting to a close, suggesting that Shepherd think over their discussion. They would meet in the morning at Nevil's office; they would reach a decision then. With a few parting words, Alexander Shepherd left the house.

At half past eight that evening Caroline and Nevil were called to dinner by Aroha, but it was Tomika, the houseman, who served their meal. He was a young man, not more than twenty years old, and Caroline was surprised to hear his English was perfect.

As Tomika passed the food, Caroline barely looked at what she was serving herself. She was more intent on taking in the splendid room, her senses touched by the soft green walls and contrasting forest-green damask curtains. "What kind of wood is this?" she asked Nevil, indicating the highly polished table that filled the room.

"Kauri," he answered.

For a brief moment her thoughts drifted to Geoffrey, and she wondered how he was enjoying life in the Kauri forest.

"Saturday evening the Governor has invited us to dinner," Nevil said, not realizing Caroline's thoughts were elsewhere. "It will be a formal evening, my dear. Make sure you have an appropriate gown."

"What kind of gown?" she asked hesitantly. She had no idea how one dressed for such an occasion.

"Just tell the woman who's making your gown that it's for an evening at the Governor's. She'll know what to suggest. Actually, you'll need a number of gowns, Caroline," said Nevil, and then continued with her week's schedule: "On Tuesday, the Swainsons—he's the Attorney General—are entertaining for us. Also dinner. I imagine that during the week the wives of the Council members will come around to introduce themselves. You must prepare yourself for luncheons and teas, that's all part of the world of government."

Caroline listened attentively without comment. Was this what life held in store? What had happened to her dreams, her fantasies of leading an exciting pioneer's life? Nevil's description of her days sounded like a total bore. There had to be more to her existence as a government official's wife. Surely there were things she could do to help in the community. There was so much that needed to be done in Auckland, how could these women do nothing but entertain at lunch and teatime, day after day?

"And remember, Caroline, anything you hear in this house is strictly confidential. The women you'll be spending your days with like nothing better than to gossip. That seems to be what keeps them happiest."

Caroline nodded. She liked the sound of this less and less.

"Is there anything you want to ask me?"

"No. It's all very clear. But I'm not certain I'm going to

enjoy this kind of life." She wanted to kick herself when she saw the look on Nevil's face. But the words had slipped out. Now what could she say?

"Caroline, I thought you loved me. I thought you wanted . . . what I wanted."

"I do, Nevil. With you, not with gossiping women." She forced herself to think quickly. "I don't know any of them. Give me time. It's just all so new to me. I'm certain I'll find a place for myself."

"That's my girl," he said, clearly relieved. He bent over and kissed her gently. "Let's go upstairs," he whispered. Without waiting for an answer, he lifted her into his arms and carried her away.

Chapter 8

THE SITE OF KORORAREKA WAS RENAMED RUSSELL, AND the new town seemed to spring up overnight. Russell, however, was different from the wild city of vice it replaced; it began and remained a quiet village, little more than a pleasant resort. However, the problems with the Maoris in the area did not change. The British were infuriated by the sacking of their former colonial capital, and they were determined to subdue the natives.

Shortly after Caroline's marriage, Nevil was sent to Russell to evaluate the situation. While he was away, Caroline felt a loneliness more intense than she could have believed possible. For weeks she seemed to talk to no one except the servants in the house. She had no desire to accept invitations to dine without her husband, and though she did occasionally lunch with the ladies and play whist, she felt an outsider, totally alone in a crowd. Today, at last, her melancholy lifted. Nevil was coming home.

Caroline dressed carefully, wanting to look her best for her husband. She put on the gown that Mrs. Phipps, the finest dressmaker in Auckland, had made for her—a muted blue padded dress trimmed with passementerie and set off with a white lace fichu. She pulled back her long hair tightly, accentuating her high cheekbones and well-formed features. As she stood before the long mirror in her bedroom, she was pleased with her appearance.

She was in the sitting room when she heard a carriage draw up in front of the house. She pulled aside the heavy velvet drape and looked out the window. It was Nevil. He entered the house quickly and by his step she knew at once he was in an elated mood.

"Caroline, you look beautiful. I love you," he said, taking her in his arms and holding her tightly. He kissed her ebulliently. "I've the most exciting news," he said before she could even say hello. "Fitzroy's been recalled and I've been made Acting Governor."

"How wonderful. What happened?"

"The settlers have had enough of him. They want a man who considers their interests first. Everything Fitzroy did was for the Maoris. He should have realized that this is a Crown Colony. We come first, not the natives."

"Is there any chance that you'll be appointed Governor?" Caroline asked, and Nevil could see how proud she was of him.

"Not this time round." He smiled. "But who knows what the future will hold? From what I understand, the Colonial Office has sent for Captain George Grey."

"Who's he?"

"An Irishman who became Governor of South Australia. They say he did an extraordinary job there, really put that colony back on its feet. But he won't be here for several months, and until then, I'm in charge. It won't take long for London to see what I can do. I couldn't have wished for better luck."

Caroline gazed at Nevil with adoration in her eyes. "You'll be Governor yet," she said with assurance. "I just know you will."

Their eyes met in a warm embrace. Almost simultaneously

they glanced at the stairway. Nevil put his arm around Caroline's shoulder and led her from the room.

The winter sun was flirting with dusk, but still its light filtered into Caroline's bedroom. For the first time since she had been with Nevil, she didn't care if the room was not dark. She felt beautiful today and no longer feared her husband's eyes feasting upon her.

They both undressed quickly, each wanting to touch the other, to lie in each other's arms, to know again the meaning of love. Their month apart would make today's union special, an afternoon of lovemaking she would remember for many years to come.

Caroline felt an overwhelming desire to have Nevil hold her, take her, smother her with his weight.

Sensing his wife's passion, he responded fully and carried her in his arms to the bed, his face buried in her silky hair. He laid her on her stomach and mounted her from behind. Suddenly realizing what he was doing, he stopped. Gently, he turned her over and seeing the frightened look in her eyes, leaned down and kissed her softly. Now he caressed her with a tenderness she didn't know he had, and for the first time since she had married Nevil, Caroline felt the exquisite sensation of desires satisfied.

It was well past eight o'clock when the two relaxed their embrace and got out of bed. Caroline's face was flushed and Nevil could not help but see his wife's deep contentment. He was pleased that he had turned down a dinner meeting. There would be other evenings with his friends, tonight was for his wife.

The following morning, as was his habit, Nevil left the house at the break of dawn to take his morning constitutional before going to Government House. Caroline was sorry he hadn't waited to breakfast with her but she knew he was a man of habit, difficult to change. She was having a cup of coffee and reading *The Southern Cross* when a loud knock startled her. She looked up at the large mahogany clock standing majestically on the white marble mantelpiece. It was not yet half past seven. Who would come round this early?

Aroha answered the door.

Grayson pushed the servant aside and bounded into the dining room. "Caroline! You really are here! I'm so excited!"

"Grayson!" Caroline exclaimed, throwing her arms around her brother. "I can't believe it. When did you get back?"

"About an hour ago. I found your note and came immediately. What happened? How did you get here? I thought you weren't getting married for another year."

"One question at a time," said Caroline, delighted with her brother's youthful enthusiasm. Apparently, New Zealand hadn't changed his zest for living. "You heard about Kororareka?"

He nodded.

"Well, that's it. That's how I got here. You were out of town, so I came to Nevil. For obvious reasons we decided to marry at once."

"And the Weatherbys?"

"That's a long story. But tell me about Amiria. I heard you were married."

"No, not really." He hesitated. "Her people say we are, but it's not legal."

Caroline was surprised by her brother's attitude.

"But Amiria's going to have a baby," he said proudly. "My baby."

"That's wonderful. When?"

"Any day. Get dressed and we'll go to my place so you two can meet. She's wonderful, Caroline. I know you'll like her."

Caroline kissed her brother affectionately and ran upstairs to change. She couldn't believe he was back, that at last they were in the same city again. Now, even if Nevil had to leave town, she would have family at her side. She would no longer be alone.

They walked hand in hand to Grayson's room, Caroline not wanting to let go of her brother for a minute. Grayson talked incessantly and Caroline knew he was nervous, apprehensive about her reaction. "She's the daughter of a chief," he said.

"Her face is tattooed, but you'll get used to it. After a while you'll even think it's pretty. But don't *you* go out and get your face tattooed."

"Don't worry." She laughed at him. "I like my face just the way it is . . . without the freckles on my nose, that is."

Amiria was fixing breakfast at the back of the house when Caroline and Grayson arrived. *"Haere mai,"* she said with a warm smile.

"That means welcome," Grayson translated.

Caroline tried unsuccessfully to repeat the words and then added, "Hello."

Amiria responded demurely, then turned back to preparing biscuits and tea. The uneasy quiet that followed did not last long, for as soon as the three sat down to eat the conversation began to flow with ease.

"Tell Caroline about Rotorua," Amiria said to Grayson.

"It's the most impressive sight in the world," Grayson began. "The earth is black and bubbles, and geysers spout up to tremendous heights."

"What makes the earth bubble?" Caroline asked.

"Thermal pools in the ground. They're almost like tiny volcanoes."

"And the scenery is so beautiful. Wonderful mountains," said Amiria.

Caroline loved the musical lilt of Amiria's soft voice. There was something so sweet and wholesome about her that Caroline could well understand how her brother had fallen in love with this woman.

"I hope we will go back soon," continued Amiria. "As soon as the baby is born."

"You mean you're not staying here?" Caroline said to her brother.

"I go where I'm sent," he answered. "But you can join us when the time comes."

"Go to Rotorua? You must be mad, Grayson. You know Nevil would never let me do that."

"Why not? He travels, why shouldn't you?"

"His trips are for business. My place is here at his side."

"Maybe he'd object to you going to Rotorua, but he couldn't criticize your wanting to see the Pink and White Terraces," Grayson said with conviction. "They're one of the wonders of the world."

"Where are they?" Caroline asked. "And what are they?"

"The most beautiful sight in New Zealand," interjected Amiria.

"They are," Grayson continued. "They're like seeing poetry come to life. It's almost mystical to watch the cloud of vapor rising above them. It's like seeing a staircase of glistening pink rock spreading over the slope of a hillside and disappearing into the soft mist that meets the sky . . . about twenty steps form the Terraces, and they rise up at least a hundred and fifty feet. And if you stand at the top, you can see the most magnificent crater below, with crystal-clear azure water." He took a deep breath and then added, "If Nevil won't let you go alone, maybe he'll come too . . . we'll all go down together. You have to see them, Caroline. You'll never see anything like them anywhere in the world."

Caroline nodded, making Grayson feel she would certainly go, but she knew Nevil would be against her taking such a trip. In the short time that she had been married, she had come to see clearly that Nevil believed a woman's place was at the side of her husband, nowhere else.

"Now tell me about you," Grayson said.

Caroline dismissed her life briefly. She resisted her temptation to complain to Grayson—what would have been the point? She turned to Amiria, wishing to find out more about this woman. But Amiria was so reserved that Caroline had difficulty in drawing her out. There was something so very deep and intriguing about her—Caroline hoped that one day they would know each other better.

The noon sun had long since started its descent into the horizon when Caroline realized the time. Startled, she jumped up. "I promised Nevil I'd be home by one," she said. "Dr. Philson is coming for lunch. I must go." She was trembling as she took her black wool pelerine and put it over her shoulders, worrying about what Nevil would say. She turned to Amiria. "Perhaps we could meet tomorrow," she said.

"Yes, I would like that."

"See you soon," Caroline said to her brother, and kissed his cheek quickly before leaving.

Caroline ran nearly all the way home, but as she approached the front path she slowed her pace. She was afraid, nervous about Nevil's reaction. She was late. He would never understand that she had forgotten the time, been carried away by the excitement of seeing her brother after all these months. Finally, there was nothing to do but to go in and face him, feeling, all the while, like a child—a very naughty child.

"And just where have you been?" Nevil greeted her icily.

Frank Philson was extremely embarrassed. "It's quite all right," he said, but Nevil did not hear his words. His own anger was too intense.

Caroline tried to explain, but it was useless. Nevil's dark eyes glared at her with an anger almost sinister. His teeth were clenched, his voice hardly more than a whisper. "Don't you ever do this again," he hissed.

Frank Philson tried to alleviate the tension. "I understand you used to work for Dr. Weatherby," he began.

Caroline at once liked this man. He had a kind face and his soft gray hair reminded her of her father. "Yes," she answered, her voice still unsteady. "I was a companion to his wife, but I assisted him, too, from time to time."

Nevil gave Caroline another fierce look. He felt it demeaning for her to tell people she had been a companion; the woman he married should be above that servile station.

"I wish you'd give us some help for the hospital we're proposing," Dr. Philson continued. "We could certainly use it."

"I'd be delighted to do anything I can," she answered, averting her husband's eyes.

Before the conversation could develop further, Nevil interrupted. "Frank and I have business to discuss, Caroline. I'd appreciate your leaving us alone."

Upstairs, Caroline closed her bedroom door. Why was Nevil so difficult? So moody? So uncompromising? Must she meet his every whim? How could she ever fulfill his ideal of the perfect wife? Somehow, her feelings didn't matter. She lay down on her bed sobbing. Would she never really please him? Would he ever love her as she loved him?

Caroline heard the front door slam shut. When her tears had subsided, she went downstairs to make some hot cocoa, hoping to soothe and comfort herself with a drink that reminded her of her childhood. But the moment she set foot in the kitchen, she was greeted with a new barrage.

"Lady Holbrooke," said Mathilda, the cook, "you've been told before that I do not allow a mistress to come into my kitchen more than once a day. You were here this morning to give me the evening menu. Now, please leave."

Caroline had had enough of this domineering, impudent cook. With the temper she would have liked to have lost when speaking to her husband, she said sharply, "Mathilda, you work for me, not the other way around. If you wish to keep your position here, you'll mind your tongue. This is my home, not yours. I'll come into the kitchen as often as I please."

"I'll speak to Sir Nevil this evening," Mathilda said haughtily.

"It's me you work for. One more sassy remark and you're fired."

"It is your husband who hired me, Madam, and *he* who pays me." She turned back to the stove and ignored Caroline.

Caroline returned to her room in a state of fury. How dare that fat little woman declare the kitchen was hers? Was that the way all servants acted in this country? Caroline wished she'd had more experience in running a household. If only there were someone, other than Nevil, whom she could ask.

Later that afternoon Mathilda thought better of her actions. Knowing it was not her place to go into the main house, she had Aroha call Caroline back to the kitchen. "Lady Holbrooke," she began politely, "here in New Zealand the kitchen is the cook's domain. No one who works for you will like you coming into the kitchen. I'm a fine cook and there is nothing I can't do. I'm good at dinner parties and ball suppers and have been used to milk seven cows twice a day, and bake and cook for ten men as well. If you leave me to do my work, I think you will be well satisfied."

Caroline was impressed as she listened to Mathilda enumerate all her accomplishments, and at the same time amused by the way she bragged. "Very well, Mathilda," she said. "Dinner will be at eight." She paused. "And I'd like some hot cocoa now. Would you have Aroha bring it when it's ready." Without another word Caroline walked back inside.

At eight o'clock that evening dinner was ready to be served, but Nevil had not returned home. Caroline waited an hour before sitting down at the table. Mathilda had outdone herself, but when the food was put before Caroline, she couldn't eat. She toyed with the roast of pork, took one bite of kumara, then left the table. She knew how angry Nevil was. She had displeased him but she had not been purposely late. She felt a sense of failure, not knowing how to apologize to him. She retired to her room and lay down on her bed without undressing. She did not even light a lamp. Miserably unhappy, she just lay there staring into the cold darkness until she fell into a restless sleep.

Caroline awoke several times during the night. The absolute silence of the house disturbed her. Finally, she got up and went to Nevil's bedroom—empty; he had not come home. Filled with anguish, wondering where he was, worrying that something terrible might have happened to him, she could not go back to sleep. She went back to her own room and sat by the window, watching and waiting. And still Nevil did not return.

It was not until noon the following day that Nevil entered the house. He made no explanations nor did he comment on Caroline's tardiness at lunch. Instead, he kissed her warmly, as if nothing had happened. "This is for you," he said, taking a small black velvet box from his pocket.

"For me! What's the occasion?"

"My love for you," he said. "Open it."

"Nevil, it's magnificent!" Caroline could hardly believe her eyes as she looked down at the cabochon ruby surrounded by tiny pink diamonds. "It's the most beautiful ring I've ever seen," she said, still disbelieving her eyes. Carefully, she took it from the box and placed it on the fourth finger of her right hand. She looked from the ring to her husband, hardly knowing what to say. "How can I thank you?"

He laughed. "With a kiss, for starters. And then how about lunch? I'm starved."

As the weeks passed and the sharpness of winter eased, the landscape seemed to take on new life. With spring in the air, Caroline felt renewed confidence. She was going to make a life in this land, going to become involved in something beyond the narrow confines of her home. She desperately wanted a child, but for some reason she did not conceive. Her only answer was to find something to do outside of the house. Nevil, however, disagreed. A wife of his was not going to work. That would be demeaning. He alone was the breadwinner in the family.

No man could have been more generous than Nevil. He showered Caroline with gifts, yet he could not fill her loneliness. Day after day she begged him to let her help Dr. Philson in starting the hospital. Nevil's answer was always the same: "It is for me to support you. I forbid you to work like a commoner."

The pain of Caroline's loneliness eased when Amiria gave birth to a son. John, whom Amiria called Hone, filled Caroline's days almost as much as he did Amiria's. Both women adored the child and Caroline found herself spending as much time as she possibly could at her brother's home. But this interlude did not last long, for the day the baby turned ten weeks old, Amiria and Grayson, with Hone at their side, returned to Rotorua.

Again Caroline was alone. She found she had little in common with the women with whom she came into contact, and most of her days were spent at home.

On the last Saturday in September she decided to take a stand. She and Nevil were having a leisurely noon meal, chatting about the imminent arrival of Governor Grey. "It will be difficult for me to go back to being just the Colonial Secretary," said Nevil.

"At least we'll be able to spend more time together." Caroline smiled at the prospect.

"I doubt that. With Grey's coming, there'll be even more changes in the government. The workload won't ease for some time."

"But you'll be home in the evenings. . . ."

"Caroline, my work day doesn't stop at six, it never will."

"Then I want you to let me work for Dr. Philson. I can't stand this solitary life."

"We've discussed this often enough. I won't have it."

"Then I'll volunteer."

Nevil ignored her statement. "Only one of us can make a name for ourselves in New Zealand, and I prefer it to be me." A wry smile crossed his lips and he rose from the table. "I'm going out."

"But it's Saturday night."

"I'm tired of arguing with you. This is a pointless discussion. I'll see you later," he said, and left the house.

Caroline was furious at her husband. She categorically refused to continue living like this. Her mother had worked and she would work, regardless of what Nevil said. She had to convince him that her volunteering on the founding of the hospital would be helpful to his career. But how?

They had lingered over their noon meal until dusk began to fall. Now it was quickly becoming dark. Caroline walked around the sitting room, lighting the oil lamps. Her actions were those of habit, her thoughts deeply involved with how to persuade her husband that her life counted too.

She did not hear the soft knock on the front door. But the visitor saw her from the window and did not go away. He knocked again, this time a little louder. The noise jarred Caroline, but not wanting company, she paid no attention to the sound. Now, loud knocking made her realize that she had no choice. The intruder knew she was at home.

"Geoffrey!" she exclaimed as she opened the door. "When did you arrive?"

"About an hour ago." His smile was warm and friendly and Caroline's mood changed at once.

"Come in, come in," she said.

They talked until after midnight, Geoffrey telling Caroline all about his experiences with the gum diggers and the wood cutters. "One of the most desolate, yet spectacular sights is Cape Reigna."

"Where's that?"

"It's at the northernmost tip of the island. You can actually see where the Tasman Sea and the Pacific meet. Their currents crash against each other . . . it's fascinating to watch. But the most interesting thing," Geoffrey continued, "is a huge, gnarled Pohutukawa which clings to the side of the rocks. It's amazing that it still stands . . . some people say it's more than seven hundred years old. I did a marvelous painting of it. The Maoris believe the tree to be the jumping-off place of the departing spirits of the dead on their journey back to their ancestral homeland, the mythical island of Hawaiki." He paused for a moment, drinking in Caroline's beauty. "One day you'll see my paintings," he added. "I think you'll like them."

"Why one day? How about tomorrow?"

"I sail tomorrow."

"For where?"

"England."

"England! Why?"

"It's time I visited my family. I'll be back soon, I promise."

Like a miracle Geoffrey had appeared, sweeping away all her loneliness, all her sadness and desperation. Was there no way she could keep him a little longer? Must he really leave? And so soon. Her eyes blurred as tears rushed to the fore. For a moment all she could think of were the words of the popular Maori farewell song, "Soon you'll be sailing far across the sea. While you're away, O, then remember me. . . ." But she did not voice her thoughts, for though she felt closer to him than ever before, she just couldn't tell him.

"Oh, Geoffrey," she sobbed.

"I promise I'll be back soon," he repeated. He took her in his arms and let her cry. "Caroline, don't let anybody live your life for you," he said, his own heart breaking at her misery. "Work for Dr. Philson. Do what makes you happy. Nevil will come around, you'll see."

A rush of air from the front door drew them apart.

As Nevil walked into the room, Geoffrey immediately sensed the tension between them. Even before Nevil could question his presence, Geoffrey said his good-byes and quickly departed.

Caroline looked at her husband sharply. Geoffrey was right, she had to take a stand. The time had come to confront Nevil, to tell him what she planned to do. But before she could say a word, Nevil spoke: "I'm sorry about this evening, Caroline. If you think volunteer work on the hospital will make you happy, well then, go right ahead."

Caroline was so taken aback, she was speechless. Nevil was completely unpredictable. Yet it was at moments like this, when he seemed so understanding, that her love for him blossomed and she carefully hid what she knew of the darker side of him in the recesses of her soul. A small smile crossed her lips, but she remained silent.

"By the way," Nevil asked, "what was Geoffrey doing here?"

"Saying good-bye. He's leaving for England in the morning."

"Come upstairs with me," Nevil said without questioning further. Taking her hand, he added, "Let me show you how much I love you."

A flush of color brightened Caroline's face, and she readily let Nevil lead her to her room.

Tonight her husband seemed different than he had in the past. There was no urgency in his actions. He undressed her slowly, caressing every inch of her body as he removed her clothes, kissing her tenderly until her own state of excitement was as great as his. He lifted her and gently put her on the bed, then quickly took off his own garments.

"Don't ever leave me," he whispered, his lips touching her earlobes. His hands began exploring her body, and as they moved across the length of her, his mouth followed the path he made.

Caroline moaned, the ecstasy almost painful, but Nevil did not stop. He pinned her down with his legs, torturing her with his kisses until she could bear it no more.

He turned his body so that his head faced her toes, and continued to let his tongue seek out her most sensitive parts.

He was lying on top of her but she did not mind his weight —it made her feel more a part of him. Now, every inch of her felt alive, burned with desire. She found herself kissing him as she had never done before. She could not believe what she was doing, how much she was enjoying his body. "I love you," she whispered.

Suddenly he turned around and his lips silenced her as he entered her with a passion beyond anything she had dreamed possible.

Warmth and love engulfed Caroline and she knew at last that everything would be all right. And as dawn broke, she fell into a totally untroubled, peaceful sleep.

Chapter 9

NOVEMBER IS USUALLY WARM AND SUNNY IN AUCKLAND, spring at its most beautiful. Today, however, the temperature had dropped to an unseasonable low.

Caroline lay in bed shivering. The brass warming pan had done little more than take the dampness out of the sheets. She pulled the blankets around her more tightly, wondering if she would ever be warm again. The tears welled up as her unhappiness engulfed her. Life in London had been idyllic compared to her existence as Sir Nevil Holbrooke's wife. She had come to Auckland with all her young dreams before her; she had envisioned a glowing future. Now her happy delusions were gone. After eight and a half months of married life, she thought of herself not as a wife but as a servant. She still had no life of her own. Nevil had said she could work with Dr. Philson, but as yet the doctor had not given her an assignment. And so Caroline continued to find herself doing only what Nevil expected, going where he wanted her to go, and entertaining the people he wished to be guests in their home. Even their sex life was totally at the mercy of Nevil's whim. She was locked in a marriage and there was no retreat.

She rose and dressed slowly. She had an appointment at eleven o'clock for the final fitting on her gown. Tonight was a welcoming party for the new governor, George Grey. She had been to so many parties since her marriage and still felt uncomfortable and out of place at every affair. It was not that the other women were better than she, it was that their entire lives revolved around what to wear and about whom to gossip. She was certain that when she wasn't around, she was the center of their vicious talk.

She picked up her silver filigreed hairbrush and began stroking her long blond hair, becoming more and more angry with each movement of her arm. "There must be more to life than this," she muttered aloud.

"Is something bothering you, my dear?" Nevil asked in a conciliatory tone.

Her husband's voice surprised her. She had thought he had long since gone to Government House. She turned to him and shook her head. She was silent for a moment, then suddenly her anger spilled forth, "It's just that we spend so little time together. If we're not at a party or entertaining your friends, you're working. You get home so late, and I'm always alone."

"Caroline, I'm amazed at you. These past four months I've been Acting Governor. I've had to work every night, I've had no choice. Fitzroy left the administration in a mess and the government bankrupt. That's why he was recalled. Now that Grey's arrived, the pressure should ease."

Caroline did not answer—she had heard these words so often before. She put down the hairbrush on her walnut dressing table and watched her husband in the mirror. But her thoughts were not with Nevil. She was remembering her mother, so involved in her own husband and his Church; her parents were so much a part of each other's work. Her mother may not have gone to fancy parties at Government House but she had a full, rich life. And her marriage was a partnership.

"Dinner will be at eight this evening," said Nevil, insensitive to his wife's misery. "Please be ready, it wouldn't do to be late."

"I won't keep you waiting," Caroline answered.

Nevil bent over and kissed her perfunctorily and without further conversation left.

"Damn him!" Caroline muttered under her breath. "Why can't he look at me as a person instead of just a possession, a pretty ornament to have on his arm. There must be a way that I can make him love me. If only we had a child!"

Garbed in a blue-and-white print Chinese silk gown, Caroline descended the narrow stairway. Her full flowing skirt set off her narrow waist and she looked more beautiful than Nevil had ever seen her. The gentle décolleté of the gown aroused him and he wanted to lead her back upstairs. Instead he took her arm and said simply, "You have outdone yourself tonight, my darling. I'm proud to have you at my side."

Caroline gazed up at him lovingly. He looked so handsome in his black dress coat and high-necked frilled shirt that she forgot her unhappy moments, only feeling the delight of pleasing him.

Their carriage awaited them in front of the house, and they rode the short distance to the Greys' stately home. A colorful array of flowers lined the Governor's front path, and a light rain made the leaves glisten. In the warm dusk light, the entire lawn had a fairy-tale appearance. It somehow made Caroline relax as she entered the house.

Tonight was to be an elaborate party for the Governor. Fifty people had come to greet the new couple, the women dressed in colorful ball gowns, the men suitably attired in well-cut tails. Tapering candles lit the chandeliers. They combined with the soft light of numerous oil lamps to give the ballroom an air of warmth and elegance.

It was a gala affair, yet Caroline did not feel that George Grey was enjoying the evening. From the moment she was introduced to him, she sensed an unhappiness about the man that she could not readily explain. He had greeted her stiffly and then immediately walked over to another guest.

"I'd like you to meet our new Governor's wife, Eliza," said Nevil, intruding on Caroline's thoughts.

"How do you do," said Caroline, noting at once that although Eliza was not beautiful, she gave the impression of being a stunning woman. Eliza had an open face and Caroline instinctively liked her.

"Have you been here long?" asked Eliza, and the two became engaged in conversation. Within minutes the commanding figure of George Grey loomed over them. "Eliza," he said, his cold blue eyes looking at her with disdain. "You are to mingle with our guests, not monopolize Caroline's attention all evening."

Eliza returned her husband's icy glare but did not reply. There was an emotion of deep hatred between the two that Caroline could not help but recognize.

"Perhaps we should dance," the Governor began. "Eliza, I would appreciate . . ."

The waltz took them out of earshot.

"They despise each other," Caroline said to Nevil.

"Gossip does not become you, my dear," he answered, and then added, "You, too, should mingle. Remember, you are the Colonial Secretary's wife."

A waiter walked by and handed Caroline a glass of claret. She felt unnerved by what had just happened and an uncomfortable chill came over her. She hoped the drink would warm her. She walked over to the fireplace and leaned against the wall. At the moment she was in no mood for small talk.

The Chinese paper lanterns hanging from the high ceiling gave the room a festive air, but they did little to alleviate the tension that permeated the room. The military band began playing a polka, and before Caroline had time to further contemplate the situation of the Governor and his wife, she found herself being twirled around the room by Dr. Frank Philson.

"You can start working with me whenever you like," the doctor said when the music stopped.

"How wonderful," answered Caroline. "Is Monday too soon?"

"Not at all. Is eight o'clock too early for you?"

"Oh, no," Caroline replied.

"Good. Then meet me at my home at eight and we'll put you to work."

Alfred Dommett, the Colonial Secretary of the southern district of New Munster, interrupted the conversation. He introduced himself and then said, "Your husband and I have much in common." The snide grimace on his face irritated Caroline. "I'm sure Nevil wouldn't mind me taking you into the supper room."

Caroline immediately disliked this overweight, overbearing gentleman—if he was a gentleman—but she had no choice but to allow him to take her arm.

"Did you know I'm a poet?" he asked.

"No."

"And Robert Browning's a dear friend of mine."

Why does he have to brag? she wondered. His position should give him the stature he needs. "When are you returning home?"

She had not realized she had asked the question aloud until Dommett answered, "I'll be here a week."

By his tone Caroline knew she had insulted the man. At a loss for words, she looked over at the apple-mouthed suckling pigs and baked hams, the platters of kumara pie, potatoes and salads, and she picked up a plate. "Shall we take some food?" she asked, hoping to change the subject.

Dommett served himself and they walked over to a table but said little as they ate. Caroline was relieved to see her husband coming. He held out his hand to her, a warm look in his eyes as he invited her to waltz.

"You're by far the most beautiful woman here," he said. "I'll spend more time with you from now on, I promise. I'll see to it that you're happy here."

Caroline thought her ears were playing tricks on her. Surely it was the music that was making her hear these tender words. The dance ended and Nevil took her by the arm to get some champagne.

"To us, my darling," he toasted.

Again Caroline felt the warm glow she had experienced when they first met, and her face reflected her inner contentment.

The following Monday morning Caroline was at Dr. Philson's before eight. It was exciting and exhilarating to know she was going to be associated with the beginnings of the first hospital in Auckland. "Good morning," she greeted Dr. Philson. "Where do I begin?"

Dr. Philson was delighted by her enthusiasm but he hesitated to outline his plans. He needed people to help him get his project off the ground but he knew nothing of Caroline's prejudices—what would she say when she learned she was volunteering to work on a Maori hospital?

"I'll take you over to the site we've planned for the hospital," he said, "and as we're walking I'll tell you what I propose."

They left the house immediately and started over to the site that had been set aside for the hospital. "We've decided to call it General Hospital," he began, then quickly added, "It will be for all natives, and those with a native ward."

"I think that's wonderful," replied Caroline. "The Maoris certainly need proper medical care."

Dr. Philson sighed with relief. "This is where it will be." He pointed to a small plot of land. "We hope to have a building erected by mid-July."

"And what can I do?"

"Well, for starters, you can begin to learn Maori."

"I already have," she laughed. "My brother . . ." she hesitated, trying to phrase her sentence most delicately. "My brother is married to a Maori woman. They've just had a little boy."

"Congratulations," Dr. Philson said, now certain that he had made the right choice in Caroline. "Then you can start by making a list of all the things you think we'll need. Try to remember what Dr. Weatherby used—mustard plaster, laudanum, thermometers, anything you can think of. In addition, we'll need beds, blankets, pillows, wooden tubs for bathing, dishes, pots and pans, and everything used in a dispensary."

"There will have to be a laundry," added Caroline.

"Definitely. Once the hospital is up, I'd like you to be in

charge of ordering medical supplies. I think you'd be good at that. Nevil tells me you have a talent for numbers."

Caroline smiled. Her father had always said she was good with numbers. He had wanted her to continue her studies but there had been no money. Then he had died.

"Well, what do you think?"

"That I'll do everything I can to make the hospital a success."

"Good. You can begin on those lists at once, because most of the things will have to be ordered from England, and that takes time."

Dr. Philson then told her about Frederick Thatcher, who would be the architect, and what the plans looked like to date. "And as soon as possible," he said, "I'll also introduce you to Dr. Johnson."

"I've met Dr. Johnson," Caroline said. He had been appointed Colonial Surgeon and was an acquaintance of Nevil's.

"Then I suggest you contact him. I'm sure he'll be of great help to you."

They parted company shortly afterward and Caroline returned home feeling happier than she had since her arrival in this foreign land. At last she was going to have a life of her own, to take part in creating New Zealand's future.

In the days that followed, Caroline spent most of her time making lists of equipment and supplies. She was busy and happy and Nevil couldn't help but notice the change in his wife. She didn't even mind when he was out late, since her evenings were filled with her own work. One morning at breakfast he commented on her mood.

Caroline did not reply.

"I just gave you a compliment, Caroline. What's wrong? Why aren't you talking?"

"I don't feel well," she answered.

"Have you told Dr. Philson?"

Caroline shook her head.

"Why not?"

"I'm sure it's nothing. I'm just queasy."

"You could be coming down with the fever."

Typhoid Fever was a serious problem among New Zealand settlers.

"No. I don't think so. I'm not feverish and I've none of the other symptoms."

"Then what is it?" he asked with genuine concern.

"I don't know."

"Please speak to Dr. Philson today. Let him examine you."

"All right," she answered apathetically. She just wanted to lie down and be left alone.

That afternoon Caroline was feeling fine again, and so she ignored her husband's request. But the following morning the nausea returned. As she sat at the breakfast table a wide smile crossed her face. "I think I know what's wrong," she said to Nevil.

"I hope so," he answered, "because you look positively green."

"I think I'm with child," she said softly, embarrassed to voice the words.

"Caroline, darling," Nevil said and went over to kiss her. "Really? That's wonderful. I've always wanted a little boy."

"And if it's a girl?" she laughed.

"You wouldn't do that to me," he said in all seriousness.

"Oh, don't be silly, Nevil. You know I have no choice."

"It will be a boy," he said with determination. He looked over at the clock on the mantle. "I have to be at the office in ten minutes," he said, and rose from the table. This was not a discussion in which he chose to participate. Caroline would have a boy and that was that.

Nevil's mood swings continued to puzzle Caroline. She wondered how a man so brilliant, so generous, so handsome, could be so irrational at times. She wished she knew how to handle him.

As soon as Nevil left, Caroline began to busy herself with preparations for her lunch with Eliza Grey. At first she thought of inviting some other women, then decided she would rather be alone with Eliza so they could get to know each other better.

It was a meeting Caroline would never forget. For the past two years Eliza had kept her feelings bottled inside of her, never believing she would have a friend in whom she could confide. Though they had just met, Eliza felt closer to Caroline than any woman she had ever known. Caroline was smiling happily when she told Eliza that she was with child.

Eliza answered by saying, "I had a son. He died four years ago." Her eyes filled with tears. "It was so fast, little George didn't have a chance. One minute he had a high fever . . . the next . . . he was gone."

"How terrible!"

"George blamed me," Eliza continued. "It wasn't my fault, but he wouldn't listen. He didn't care. He needs a wife for his career, for the sake of appearance. That's why he brought me here, not because he loves me."

"Are you certain?" asked Caroline, not knowing what else to say.

"Certain," Eliza snickered, "of course, I'm certain." She paused. "He stands before the world stating his mission is to bring together two races . . . and as proof, he has a Maori mistress."

"I can't believe it!"

"Oh, he denies it, but I know the truth. When he says he's working late, I know he's with her."

A sharp, painful light flashed in Caroline's head. Did Nevil also have a Maori mistress? Did he have any mistress? Is that where he was night after night? She had thought he was married to his work, but was it another woman?

"I wish I didn't love him," Eliza said softly.

Caroline's thoughts were with Nevil. She hardly heard Eliza say, "I'm glad you don't have such problems, Caroline. And the baby will bring you and your husband even closer together."

"Yes," she answered. "I hope so."

Their conversation drifted to the latest fashions in England and gossip of the Queen and her handsome German Prince Consort.

A lamplighter lit the Aladdinlike lamp outside the Holbrooke home, and the two women suddenly realized how quickly the afternoon had passed. Ever since Eliza had confided in Caroline, she had been thinking of Nevil's behavior. As she and Eliza were saying good-bye, Caroline could no longer control her thoughts. "Should I confront Nevil?" she asked.

"About what?" Eliza had no idea what Caroline was thinking.

"He stays out almost every night," she answered.

"The truth is painful, Caroline. Sometimes it's better not to know."

"But at least then I'd have some idea of what I was up against."

"Would that help any?"

Caroline shook her head in dismay. "I don't know," she said. "I just don't know."

For a long time after Eliza left, Caroline sat in the sitting room trying to decide what course of action to pursue. Deep shadows filled the room, but Caroline didn't bother to light the lamps. Somehow she just couldn't bring herself to believe that her husband was involved with another woman, but his pattern of late nights was so like the Governor's—was she being naive?

It was close to eight o'clock when Nevil arrived home. He was surprised to see his wife sitting in the dark room but he didn't question her. Instead he kissed her hello warmly and said, "Nathan, the Jew, had another auction today. When I saw this, I couldn't resist buying it for you."

Caroline knew that David Nathan was not only one of Auckland's leading business men, he also owned the most successful auctioneering house in town. It always irritated her when Nevil referred to him as "the Jew." But she had more important things to discuss with him than a man she barely knew. Reluctantly, she took the blue velvet box from her husband. She didn't want a gift tonight, not before she confronted him. She opened the box carefully and, as so often before, she was speechless. Inside was a magnificent necklace—three tiny clusters of emeralds, set off by myriad diamonds. "How can you afford this?" was all she could say.

Nevil answered her with a kiss. "Nothing is too much for you, my dear."

Caroline felt the muscles in her stomach tighten. How could she accuse him of being unfaithful when he had brought her such an extraordinary gift? Surely no man who expressed his love so generously could have another woman. And so she kissed him in return and thanked him graciously. She would ask about his evenings away from home another time.

Chapter 10

CAROLINE HAD BEEN IN NEW ZEALAND FOR JUST OVER A year and she found it difficult to believe that in such a short time her life had so changed. Last December she was helping Mrs. Weatherby plan a Christmas Eve dinner, tonight she was sitting with her husband, discussing the party they would have.

"I received a letter from Grayson this morning," she told Nevil. "He expects to be back in Auckland for the holidays."

"Then that makes twelve," said Nevil, making a quick calculation of the guests they had decided to invite. "If we include anyone else, we won't be able to have a sit-down dinner."

"That's fine with me," said Caroline. "In my condition," she looked down at the slight protrusion of her stomach, "I think more people would be too big a strain."

"You're still not feeling well, are you?" Nevil asked.

"I'm just fine," she said, dismissing the question lightly. She hadn't told him that she was staining, but she sensed he knew that something was not quite right.

"I had a long talk with David Nathan today," Nevil said,

changing the subject unexpectedly. "He came to me to discuss the new government ordinance that auctioneers have to pay a license fee of thirty pounds a year and a levy of ten percent on all sales."

"Thirty pounds does seem high," Caroline commented.

"Hmm. I suppose. Anyway, I told him I'd see what I could do. I give the man credit. His word is his bond and everyone knows it. Because of his absolute integrity there's not a Maori in the area who doesn't trust him."

Caroline chuckled. "Coming from you, that's quite a compliment."

"Well, it's true. And today I heard that he and John Montefiore—and if I'm not mistaken, Israel Joseph, as well—have all given large contributions to the building funds of the Anglican and Methodist churches. They not only have a deep respect for their own religion, but for other people's too." He paused for a moment, deep in thought. "The Jews who have come here are different from the ones I knew in England. It's amazing how people change, isn't it?"

Caroline didn't want to argue with her husband. She knew that people were people everywhere and any change was superficial. She also knew that Jewish families in England had donated large sums of money to all kinds of philanthropic and religious charities. But she saw no point in trying to explain this to Nevil.

Caroline watched Nevil pick up a cheroot from the humidor and light it. She was sorry he had started smoking the strong smelling cigars, because she disliked the odor. One more thing to get accustomed to, she thought, for she knew she would never mention a word to him of how she felt.

"I'll tell you who haven't changed," said Nevil.

Caroline looked up at him inquisitively.

"The criminals . . . the convicts from New South Wales who have escaped and flooded our country. You can't believe how much crime there is. Not a day passes that a store doesn't get robbed or someone isn't accosted in the streets. It's getting so that I worry about your being out alone."

"Oh, don't be silly, Nevil. Criminals don't frequent the places I go. They stay around the waterfront."

"Not anymore, Caroline. I mean it. I want you to be very careful when you're out alone."

"I promise," she replied dutifully, feeling more like a child than a wife.

"As a matter of fact," Nevil continued, "Clendon's house was broken into today. I told him I'd come round tonight to see the extent of the damage and theft."

"You mean you'll be out again tonight?"

"Caroline, I have to make a report to the Home Office at once. That's the only way we'll get funds to set up a proper, full-scale police department. What we call a police force at present is a farce and little more."

For a brief moment Caroline thought she should confront Nevil, but his excuse seemed so plausible, how could she say anything?

Caroline watched Nevil depart and then busied herself with recopying a final list of dispensary items for Dr. Philson. It was at times like this that she wished she had a crystal ball, wished she could see into the future and learn what was happening to her husband.

By the time she went to bed, it was well past midnight. She was used to Nevil coming home in the early hours of the morning and she no longer tried to wait up for him. This evening she was particularly tired and had no trouble falling asleep. It was a deep sleep, but not one that lasted very long. At about two thirty she awakened with a start. She thought she heard noises. If Nevil were home, she would love him to come to bed with her. She wanted his closeness tonight. She needed him to be near her.

She took her pink silk dressing gown from the closet and put it over her shoulders. Instead of going to Nevil's bedroom, something directed her into his library. It was a room she had been told to stay out of, actually forbidden to cross the threshold for any reason. Yet she felt compelled to enter. A heavy velvet drape at the far side of the room was open slightly. She had always thought it covered a window and was more than just a little surprised to see that it hid a door—a door connecting to Nevil's room. She was puzzled, not being able to understand the purpose of concealing the door. A voice startled her and she jumped in fright. If Nevil found her, he would be furious. Again she heard someone speak—it didn't sound like Nevil, but who could it be? Why would Nevil carry on a conversation in his bedroom? Why wasn't he downstairs, or at least here, in his library? On tiptoe she walked to the door and listened. Strange sounds she could not comprehend came from the room. The voices were muffled, and she had difficulty deciphering even the simplest of words. She stood there for what seemed a very long time, then, afraid of being discovered, she quietly returned to her room.

Caroline's hands were cold and clammy. Her head ached. She lay down on her bed and stared into the darkness. A feeling of desolation enshrouded her. She just could not grasp what was happening.

The following morning Nevil was having his tea when Caroline entered the dining room. He greeted her warmly, rising to kiss her as if nothing were awry. She wanted to tell him what she had heard, but how could she admit that she'd gone into a room she'd been forbidden to enter, that she'd eavesdropped at his bedroom door?

"Will you be home for lunch today?" Nevil asked.

"I expect Grayson and Amiria back this morning," she answered. "I'll probably have lunch with them."

A sharp pain shot through Caroline's stomach and she winced.

"Are you all right?" Nevil asked.

"Fine," Caroline answered as the spasm subsided. She must be crazy, she decided. His voice was so obviously filled with tender concern. There was no question that Nevil loved her. She was certain there was a perfectly valid explanation for the voices in her husband's room, and with this thought in mind she dismissed the entire incident.

It was good to have Amiria and Grayson back in town, even though they said it would only be for a few weeks.

"Next stop, the Wanganui River," Grayson told Caroline. "I understand the area's magnificent. I can hardly wait to go."

"You've become quite a traveler," Caroline said, trying not to let her brother know how much she missed him.

Amiria had been sitting in the corner nursing Hone when Caroline arrived. Now she stood up, the baby still in her arms, and came over to kiss Caroline.

With great pride Caroline greeted her in her Maori tongue, and then still conversing in Maori, asked her how she was.

Amiria laughed with delight. "You are studying my language. How wonderful, but why?"

Caroline told them all about Dr. Philson's plans for the hospital. "It will be a hospital for the Maoris. If I don't know the language, how can I work there?"

"The work agrees with you," said Grayson. "I see you've gained some weight."

Now it was Caroline who chuckled. "I'm going to have a baby," she said.

"How wonderful," Grayson and Amiria both said.

Grayson looked from Caroline to Amiria and then back to Caroline. This was the perfect time to ask his sister what was on his mind. "Caroline," he began with hesitation, "as long as you're going to have to take care of a baby, would you mind . . . would you mind taking Hone for a few months?"

"Taking Hone? No. But I don't understand."

"The Wanganui River area is very wild country," said Amiria. "There is often fighting among the tribes who live there. I do not think it is safe for Hone."

"Hone hasn't been well, Caroline," Grayson interjected. "At times he has terrible trouble breathing. I think he should be near English doctors, and Amiria agrees."

Caroline could not hide her surprise. She knew the Maori people believed in the power of their *tohungas* and were in general opposed to Pakeha medicine. It must have been very difficult for Grayson to persuade Amiria to think as he did. She looked from her brother, casually garbed in his work clothes, to Amiria, in her flaxen skirt and simple cotton top.

There was something incongruous about the two together, yet they looked so happy.

"Dada," Hone cooed, holding out his tiny hand, his little fingers opened and then curled as if wanting to be held.

Caroline took the infant from his mother and clutched him closely to her. "Of course, I'll take him," she said. "I'll have to ask Nevil, but I can't see why he'd object." But even as she said these words, she knew that her husband might not like the idea of a Maori child living with them. "I'll speak to him when I can and let you know as soon as I have an answer."

The conversation moved on to other things, and Caroline told them about the Christmas Eve dinner she and Nevil were planning. "You'll be there, of course," she added.

"Wouldn't miss it for the world," Grayson said cheerily.

Caroline was in high spirits when she returned home and fully prepared to ask Nevil about Hone coming to live with them. Much to her surprise, she found her husband in the sitting room, deeply engrossed in conversation with the Governor.

Governor Grey was angrily pacing back and forth across the room. He banged his fist on a table, his voice raised as he said, "We've got to quash Kawiti and Hone Heke. Those chiefs are nothing but trouble to us. The Northland will never be ours as long as they rule."

"But George," Nevil said gently, trying to calm the irate man, "Ruapekapeka is an impossible *pa* to destroy. It's more than just a fortification. From what we've learned, the Maoris have a whole underground system . . . our cannon balls destroy nothing and no one."

"Do you know what Ruapekapeka means?" asked Grey between clenched teeth.

Nevil shook his head.

"The Bat's Nest," Grey said. "Well named, wouldn't you say?"

Caroline could see that the Governor was seething as he spoke. She wanted to enter the room but thought better of it. She turned to go when Nevil saw her reflection in the window.

"Caroline," he greeted her, "do come in." She was his perfect answer to breaking the tension.

Grey greeted her perfunctorily and then turned back to Nevil. "We'll plan our final attack to take place right after the first of the year. That will give us time to come up with a foolproof strategy. You will go there, Nevil?"

"Yes, of course," Nevil answered. And the discussion came to a close.

In the days ahead Nevil seemed to be more involved in his work than ever. Caroline knew the attack was being planned and her husband's absences didn't concern her. What did bother her was that he was helping to prepare for the annihilation of the Maoris in the Northland. She couldn't understand why terms couldn't be reached with the warring chiefs, why war was the answer. What did that really solve? She wanted to apprise her brother of the situation and discern his reaction to the plan, but what was discussed in her home was said in the strictest confidence and she knew it wasn't her place to divulge government secrets. Besides, Grayson's loyalties were divided, how could he take sides?

When Christmas Eve came, however, Caroline realized for the first time just how her brother really felt.

Doctors Philson and Johnson and their respective wives arrived at the Holbrooke home punctually at eight o'clock. The Greys walked in several minutes later. The Dommetts had been invited, but Mrs. Dommett had sent word that morning that she was under the weather and had offered her regrets.

Caroline greeted her guests cheerfully, trying to let the Christmas spirit take hold of her, but something seemed amiss. Grayson prided himself on always being on time, why was he not here?

At eight forty-five Aroha entered the room to announce that dinner was served. Caroline looked over at Nevil, unsure of what to do. It was not polite to begin dining before all their guests had arrived. On the other hand, how could she keep the others waiting? As she was struggling with a decision, Grayson entered. He was alone.

Before going into the dining room, Caroline took her brother aside. "Where's Amiria?" she asked.

"I decided not to bring her."

"Why?"

"I didn't think it was her place to be here. I knew you were having the Governor and his wife. I thought it would be wrong."

"But Grayson you're—"

"Please Caroline, I know best."

Grayson turned from his sister and walked over to the Governor. "Good evening, sir," he said. "I'm Caroline's brother, Grayson Wickham's the name." He held out his hand to Grey.

Caroline was astounded by her brother's conduct. He was the father of Amiria's child, how could he treat her like this? Amiria believed Grayson was her husband; how did he look at their relationship?

Christmas, as always, made people think of home and times past. The table conversation seemed to revolve more around England than what was happening in New Zealand. Caroline was pleased about this—she hated to listen to discussions of war.

Eliza Grey looked particularly stunning this evening in her white muslin gown trimmed with pale blue ruching. She seemed more at ease than usual and was obviously enjoying the company of both Margaret Philson and Dianne Johnson. Perhaps she and the Governor had worked out their problem. But just as this thought passed through Caroline's head, George Grey addressed his wife in a harsh tone.

His dark eyes peered at her as he said, "We'll have to make this an early evening, I've work to do."

"You can't leave now," said Caroline. "We haven't sung any Christmas carols yet." As soon as she had uttered the words, she was sorry she'd spoken. The tension she had felt when she first met the Greys returned. "Of course," she added politely, "if you have business to attend to, Nevil and I will certainly understand. Perhaps Eliza can stay. The evening's still young."

"I'd be delighted to take your wife home," said Nevil.

"As you wish, my dear," George Grey said to his wife. "As you wish." He excused himself from the table and said his good-byes.

Caroline saw Eliza sigh with relief as her husband left the room; she also noticed the watery glaze that now covered Eliza's eyes as the young woman did all in her power to hold back her tears.

The two doctors were so engrossed in the discussion of a patient, they were oblivious to the domestic drama that had just transpired. It was Margaret Philson, sensing Eliza's difficulty, who said, "Let's sing 'Joy to the World,' it's my very favorite carol."

With this suggestion they all moved into the sitting room and began harmonizing. For the next hour they sat around the fireplace singing and telling Christmas tales. Several dozen candles lit the room, flickering warmly, inviting all to partake in the yuletide cheer, but the mood of the evening had been marred and time passed slowly.

No one seemed to mind when Dr. Johnson rose and announced that he had to leave. "Christmas time means drinking, and you know that brings accidents. I'm afraid tomorrow will be a very hectic day. You'll forgive my leaving so early, Caroline."

"Of course," she said. "I understand."

"I think we should be going too," said Frank Philson, taking his wife's hand.

Grayson immediately rose. The last thing he wanted was to be left alone with his sister. There would be time enough for her questions. "I'd be delighted to take Mrs. Grey home," he offered, knowing there was no way Caroline could object.

"Thank you," said Eliza. "That's very kind of you."

When the six guests had left, Caroline sank into the nearest chair. "I'm exhausted," she sighed. "The Greys always make me so tired. I find it uncomfortable to be around them. He fooled no one at the table . . . everyone knew he wasn't going to work."

"Nonsense," said Nevil. "The Governor was busy. He had

a great deal to do tonight. He's leaving in the morning for Ruapekapeka. There was nothing more to it than that. Eliza just doesn't understand the great responsibility of his position." Nevil went over to the fireplace and took a small package from the mantel. Holding it out to his wife he said, "Merry Christmas."

Caroline could tell by the box that it was another piece of jewelry. She tore off the wrapping excitedly. Then her mouth dropped open. Nevil had given her one beautiful piece of jewelry after another, but nothing compared to this. Deep blue sapphires were sprinkled among a bed of perfect diamonds, forming the most exquisite brooch she had ever seen. Was she really deserving of his generosity when at times she so doubted him? "Nevil, it's . . . it's . . ."

"Shh," he whispered. "Come into my arms and let me hold you."

She went to him without hesitation and in a sweep of passion they fell to the floor and made love in front of the fireplace.

Chapter 11

TIME SEEMED TO EVAPORATE DURING THE NEXT TEN DAYS for Caroline, for as hard as Nevil was working, he was always home for dinner and spent every evening with her. She chastised herself for ever having thought he had another woman and made a silent vow never to question her husband's absences again.

She was feeling relaxed and happy on the evening she asked him if he would mind if Hone came to live with them while Grayson and Amiria were away. "When our son is born, it will be good for him to have a little boy to play with."

She had chosen her words well and the minute Nevil heard her concede that she was going to have a son, his entire face lit up. "Of course, Hone can stay here," he answered. "You didn't even have to ask me, Caroline."

"We've been invited to the Philsons for New Year's Eve," he said a few minutes later, "but I'd rather be alone with you. I'm leaving the following morning."

"I agree," she smiled, and then asked, "You're going to Ruapekapeka, aren't you?"

"No, to Russell. It's twenty miles north."

"For how long?"

"Not long, I promise."

"How can you tell?"

"I know. The way we've planned things, it should be a one-day war and that's it."

Caroline nodded. "I'll miss you," she said softly, tears rushing to her eyes.

"Come here," he said, holding out his arms to her.

"You'll be careful."

"I won't be anywhere near the fighting. Now relax." He held her to him, gently kissing the nape of her neck as he stroked her back. "I'll miss you too," he whispered into her ear. "Let me take you upstairs," he said, lifting her into his arms.

In the soft light of evening, Caroline looked more lovely than ever to Nevil. Her body had rounded just enough and still she had not lost her exquisite shape. He lay her on the bed and sat beside her, savoring her beauty. He caressed her stomach gently and then put his head to his hand and smiled. "That's our baby. The gift of our love."

She pulled him to her and their lips met in the tenderest of kisses. She did not know it was possible to love any man so deeply. With this thought in mind she gave herself to him without reservation.

New Year's Eve was anything but festive in the Holbrooke home. Caroline had seen to it that a special dinner was prepared. She and Nevil toasted in the new year with champagne yet their mood was somber.

"Ruapekapeka is one of the most heavily pallisaded *pas* in the country," Nevil told Caroline. "And, I understand there is a system of trenches around it that's almost impossible to cross. The Maoris are a clever bunch," he continued. "They've invented what we're now calling trench warfare. The only good thing about it is that we'll be able to use it on other fronts."

"Like where?"

"India, Ireland, everywhere and anywhere the British fight."

"Nevil, I don't understand. If it's so difficult to break into their *pa*, how do you know it will be over so quickly?"

"I told you, we have a foolproof plan." He bent over and kissed her lightly. "Now come, let's go to bed. I have to be up at dawn."

There was sadness on Caroline's face as she rose to go upstairs. In the past two weeks Nevil had seemed so close to her, she could not bear the thought of his leaving in the morning.

There were no good-byes the following day because Nevil departed long before dawn. When she opened her eyes, sun streamed into her room and she sensed, at once, that Nevil had already gone.

Caroline tried to get out of bed but sharp sudden pains forced her to lie back down. She wanted to call for Dr. Philson but was afraid of what she might hear. She knew that something was very wrong—childbearing should not be so painful in the fourth month. It took her almost an hour to be able to cross the room and pull the bell cord for Aroha. Caroline decided that if she stayed in bed all day, she would be better in the morning.

But the following day Caroline's pain only intensified. Finally, she could brave it no longer. She knew she needed a doctor immediately.

Sobbing softly, she again called Aroha. "Send for Dr. Philson," she told the young girl. "Tell him it's urgent that he come at once."

"Yes, Madam," said Aroha. She looked at her mistress for a long moment and could see that Caroline was suffering greatly. Then she quickly left the room.

"Caroline, my dear," Dr. Philson greeted his favorite patient. "You look ghastly. Why didn't you call me sooner?"

"I knew there was nothing you could do."

"Just because you're working on hospital supplies doesn't make you a diagnostician." He smiled warmly. "What is a doctor for if not to help his patients?"

Caroline tried to answer but another sharp contraction made her unable to speak.

Dr. Philson lifted her nightdress, felt her abdomen, then placed a stethoscope to it and listened carefully. He shook his head in dismay. "I'm afraid you're right," he said. "I think you're having a miscarriage, Caroline."

"Oh, no!" Caroline cried, bursting into tears. "I want this baby more than anything in the world. It's taken me so long to be with child. Can't you do something?"

"There are some things that only God can do," he said soothingly.

Caroline made no comment. The contractions were coming at regular intervals now, only a minute apart. The pain was so intense, it was all she could think about.

Suddenly she let out a piercing scream, then lay back and broke into tears. "It's over," she sobbed. She was lying in a pool of blood, too exhausted to move. The pain was still there, but the intensity had lessened.

Dr. Philson called for Aroha to fix a bath for Caroline. "The warm water will take all the pain from you," he said gently. "But you mustn't soak in it too long. I'll be back in a few hours to make certain everything is all right."

Caroline nodded. She wiped the perspiration from her forehead then lay back on the soft down pillow.

"There'll be other babies," Dr. Philson said. "This doesn't mean you can't have a child."

"But—"

"Don't try to talk now. Lay back and rest until your bath is ready. We'll discuss this later."

"I want Nevil," Caroline said softly. "Could you send for him?"

Dr. Philson knew where Nevil had gone; he was aware that there was no way he would come home. "We'll talk about Nevil later," he said.

"But what will I tell him?"

"Your bath is ready, Madam," Aroha interrupted.

Dr. Philson lifted Caroline and carried her to the copper

tub. He sat her down on a nearby chair. "Bathe and then go to sleep. . . . I'll see you later."

As soon as the doctor had left the room, Caroline began to sob. She had never been so depressed. All she wanted was to die.

During the next few days Caroline refused to see anyone except Dr. Philson. She stayed in bed and insisted that the wooden shutters of her room be tightly closed. She would not allow Aroha to light a lamp; she only wanted to stare into the darkness. She did not eat and barely slept. Over and over in her mind she composed the letter she would write to Nevil, rehearsed the words she would say to tell him that she had lost their son. But no matter how hard she tried, she could not find a way to inform him of what had happened the day after he'd left.

News traveled quickly in Auckland and the following day Eliza Grey came to visit Caroline. Caroline agreed to see Eliza but would not talk to her friend, and nothing Eliza said seemed to comfort her.

Amiria and Grayson also came. But Caroline refused to see them. She wanted to be alone. She felt inadequate next to Amiria, who had given her brother a son.

Dr. Philson did all he could to distract his patient. She listened to his talk of war but had little interest in the Northland. And when she did focus on the doctor's words, she thought of Nevil, which upset her even more. The news from Ruapekapeka was not good. All the guns and rockets of the 58th Regiment seemed useless against the Maori trenches. The Pakeha were being killed; the Maoris appeared invincible.

On Tuesday, January 13th, Caroline again felt that life had meaning, that spring would come again. For the first time in almost two weeks, she wanted to get well. She sat by the open window, reading and rereading Nevil's note:

My darling,
    The war is over. We have won. I'll be home very soon.

Let's try to have another son. Don't worry, next time is not so far away.

I love you. Get well quickly.

Your husband always, Nevil.

Caroline was ecstatic. Nevil knew she had lost the baby. Dr. Philson must have written to him, that was the only way Nevil could have learned of their loss. And he understood—he wasn't angry at her.

No longer fearing her husband's reaction to her miscarriage, Caroline's strength returned quickly. Within a week she was back at work on the hospital and again began seeing people. She found it difficult to apologize to her brother and Amiria, and was delighted to discover that they understood.

Caroline had told Grayson that she would take Hone but was surprised on the morning of the twenty-first of January when he and Amiria arrived with the baby.

"We're leaving at noon," Grayson said.

"I thought you weren't going for another few weeks," Caroline replied.

"So did I," said Grayson. "But Mathew decides when and where I go, and yesterday afternoon he told me I leave today."

"Is it all right?" asked Amiria with her usual concern. "With all that's happened, is it still all right? Are you strong enough to take Hone?"

"Of course," said Caroline. "You know I wouldn't let you down. And it will be good for Nevil, too, to find a baby in the house."

Amiria looked from Caroline to Grayson. She was not convinced that Nevil would like the idea now that Caroline was no longer going to have *his* child. But she kept her thoughts concealed.

Caroline took the baby from his mother. "Grayson, you can put the crib into my room. That will be the nursery until Nevil returns. Then we'll decide what room to fix up for Hone."

Grayson bent over and kissed his sister. "Call him John

once we're gone," he whispered into her ear. "I want him to grow up to be one of us."

Caroline pulled back from her brother. She didn't understand his attitude. He appeared to be pulling away from the Maoris, yet still seemed to be in love with Amiria. But how could he hurt her by changing the baby's name? There was no way that Caroline was going to listen to Grayson. She just wouldn't do it. She smiled at him, letting him know that she understood his wishes, but promised nothing.

"You both be careful in that wild country," she said cheerfully.

"The cannibals won't get us, I promise," chuckled Grayson.

Amiria looked at Grayson with fury in her eyes. "They only eat the enemy . . . they don't eat surveyors, and you know that," Amiria said in her Maori tongue.

"Grayson, how can you talk like that?" asked Caroline, understanding every word Amiria had said. She glared at her brother with a look that was even more livid than Amiria's.

"It was just a joke," said Grayson defensively.

"You've a perverted sense of humor, my dear brother."

"That's enough, Caroline. I'll live my life my way, without my baby sister's interference."

They were stinging words, but Caroline did not try to argue.

Grayson turned to Amiria, his anger imprinted clearly across his face. "Let's go," he said. "We haven't finished packing and it's getting late."

Amiria kissed her tiny son good-bye and then hugged Caroline. *"Haerera,"* she said.

"Farewell," Caroline repeated.

The days ahead were easier for Caroline. Hone took up a considerable amount of her time and the separation from Nevil didn't bother her nearly as much as it had in the past. She did, however, spend long hours worrying about her brother. New Zealand had changed him. A once ambitious, happy boy, Grayson had become a ruthless man. He was using Amiria. He wanted her companionship when he was out in the wilds. He certainly couldn't love a woman whose child he wished to bring up as his—not hers, not theirs. Caroline wished she had had time to speak to Grayson, to tell him how abominable his conduct was. But what would have been the point? She knew he would never listen.

By the time Nevil returned home three weeks later, Caroline was feeling well and happy. But when she saw her husband, she was shocked. Nevil had lost at least fifteen pounds since his departure. His face was gaunt, his body emaciated. The war had certainly taken its toll on him.

His walk was stiff as he slowly entered the sitting room, tracking dirt across the floor. His boots were sodden, his usually well-pressed trousers wet and filthy, clinging to his sweaty legs. He dropped into a chair, so tired he could barely speak. But there was victory in his dark eyes.

"We did it, Caroline. We won," he said after several moments.

"You're limping. Are you all right?"

"Fine. It's nothing."

"Oh, Nevil, I'm so glad you're back," she said, hugging him tightly. "You'll never know how much I missed you." She paused and then asked, "Would you like some port?"

It was only ten o'clock in the morning, but the thought of alcohol sounded good to him. "A whiskey, perhaps," he said. He rubbed his thigh and Caroline could see he was in severe pain.

"You have been hurt. It isn't nothing."

"Just a small musket wound." He tried to smile. "It really isn't serious."

"Have you had it tended to?"

He nodded.

"Are you sure? Should I call Dr. Philson?"

"No, I'm fine. Just some whiskey . . . it eases the pain."

Nevil drank two shots and heaved a sigh. "I'm all right now," he said, then asked, "Do we have any laudanum in the house?"

"I'll get some right away," she called as she dashed upstairs to find the opiate. Minutes later she returned.

Nevil didn't take the time to pour himself a spoonful. He grabbed the bottle from her and took a swig. "That's better," he said. He inhaled deeply before adding, "Not to worry, my dear. It's just a small wound . . . to be expected in battle."

They looked at each other for several moments, each savoring their reunion.

"Hone's living with us now," said Caroline, breaking the silence.

But Nevil didn't seem to hear his wife. "Let me tell you what happened," he began enthusiastically. The combination of whiskey and laudanum had taken the pain from his voice. "The Maoris think they're smart, well, we're smarter. We bombarded their *pa* for days, but with their internal tunnel system, it was impossible to make a dent. But I told you we had a plan, and we did." He grinned smugly.

"What did you do?"

"We waited until Sunday. We knew the natives would all go to church. And they did. Their *pa* was almost empty. We hardly fired a shot. We just walked in and took over. They never expected us to fight on the Lord's day." He chuckled. "But God was on our side. We won."

"That's sacrilege!" Caroline was aghast. Her father was a minister. Everything her upbringing stood for was against such action. How could Nevil have been party to a plan that ordered an army to fight on the Sabbath. "Nevil, how could you?"

"Don't be so naive, Caroline. This is war." He paused and took another deep breath. The pain had not altogether subsided. "Kawiti's made peace and Hone Heke's alone now. There's no way he'll wage war again. The Northland's ours."

Nevil let his head rest on the back of the chair and closed his eyes.

"But Nevil?"

He began snoring softly and she knew he would not discuss the action further.

Chapter 12

THE ROLLING COUNTRYSIDE REMINDED GRAYSON OF SCOTland. He had been there once, when he was seven, and he was certain it had looked like this, and yet, the vegetation of this landscape was quite different. Clumps of tussock lined the trail he and Amiria were following, the golden grass blowing gently in the soft breeze. Manuka scrub was in bloom, its tiny, starry white flowers giving life to the hills, its sweet scent permeating the air. They stopped on a narrow precipice to enjoy the scenery. When Grayson looked over the side of the ravine to the Wanganui River below, he thought he would be sick. He turned his head quickly.

"How will we ever get down there?" he asked Amiria.

"We ride to Pipiriki, then there is a trail."

"How do you know?" Grayson asked.

"A cousin many times removed from me married a Wanganoui. From the time I was a little girl, I heard talk of Pipiriki. When my people come up the river, that is where they leave their canoes."

Grayson smiled at Amiria. He always found her stilted speech charming.

As they rode down the narrow, winding road toward the riverbed below, Grayson said little. He was entranced by the scenery but his silence was caused by fear. He hated heights.

"Those are *toetoe,*" said Amiria, pointing to the graceful, pale yellow, feathery plumes of grass along the river flat.

"And those are flax," Grayson said, chuckling, as they rode through ten foot stalks of waxy, sword-shaped leaves.

"Yes," she answered. "You see, I told you it would not take long for you to learn the plants of my country."

They stopped again, this time to admire the elongated, narrow island in the middle of the river. "The water is down now," Amiria told him, "but in winter the river floods. I have heard that at times even the island is underwater."

It was difficult for Grayson to believe that the river ever flooded. At the moment it seemed more like a stream, wending its way between scattered beds of small, smooth rocks.

"There is the landing," Amiria pointed. "And I have heard a guest house has been built nearby."

But the Pipiriki Guest House was still in the planning stage. In another year it would accommodate one hundred guests, now there was just a marker indicating where it would be built.

Grayson was not overjoyed with the idea of living in the open air. As much as he liked traveling, he also liked the comforts of home. They tied their horses to some scrub and walked along the rocky shore.

"This is the area I'm to survey," Grayson said. "Mathew wants to build a proper landing here. But where are we supposed to live while I'm working?"

"We will build a hut and I will make some mats for us to sleep on. A block of wood makes a good pillow."

Grayson rubbed his head and frowned.

"You can lie in my arms," Amiria said, reading his thoughts. "I am soft."

They both laughed and Grayson pulled Amiria to him. "The ground's soft too," he whispered. "Let's make love."

"We are not alone."

Grayson looked around. "How do you know?"

"I know," she answered. "I see eyes in the hills."

It was not long before a group of Wanganoui Maoris approached them. *"Haere mai!"* called Topine Te Mamaku, the chief of the tribe.

Amiria returned his welcome and then, speaking in her own tongue, asked if they would help them build a shelter.

"You cannot live near the water," said Te Mamaku. "The *taniwha* lives there."

Grayson was puzzled. *Taniwha* was a word he did not know.

"It is a great, ferocious beast that eats people," explained Amiria.

"The *taniwha's* home is there." The chief pointed to a cave. "You come to our *kainga,* there you will be safe."

Amiria thanked the chief for the invitation to his village. Then she turned to Grayson. "The chief has asked us to be their guests. I think we should," she said, her voice hardly above a whisper.

"Thank you," said Grayson to the chief. "We'd be honored to come with you."

Unseasonal summer rains made surveying almost impossible, and with each day Grayson became more and more restless. He hated living in the *kainga.* Though he could speak the language of the natives, he had little in common with any of them and their conversations were, therefore, of the most limited nature. The Maoris in this area seemed to live on dried and roasted fern root and a *hinau* berry—both plants Grayson hated. Occasionally they ate eels. It was not only their flavor —steamed in a *hangi*—that he found revolting, the mere thought of putting an eel in his mouth was enough to make him lose his appetite. He longed to be back in Auckland, where he could have a decent piece of pork and sleep in a real bed. But he didn't dare leave the Wanganui River until his work was done; he knew if he did, Mathew would dismiss him at once.

Amiria, too, was unhappy in her surroundings. She longed to see her son again and could not bear Grayson's discontent.

To make matters even worse, she missed Grayson's lovemaking. He would not take her unless they were alone, and they were never alone. They slept in a *whare* with six people, and although the others thought nothing of fornicating with family or friends watching, Grayson's upbringing would not allow him to display any form of affection toward Amiria in front of an audience. He wouldn't even kiss her in public.

It was not until the end of June that Amiria and Grayson were ready to start the long trek home. And it was only then, after more than five months, that they found themselves alone.

Three nights after they left the Wanganoui tribe they rested in a small grove of ferns. The ground was hard and dry, but Amiria made them a comfortable bed of leaves.

"You don't know how I've missed you," Grayson whispered as they lay in each other's arms.

Amiria did not reply. She was covering his body with kisses, tenderly showing this man how much she loved him.

"I've ached for you," he said as he began caressing her in return.

She nestled close to him, her flesh trembling as he ran his hands over her. He kissed her fingers one by one and then began tracing the length of her arm with his lips.

She moaned softly, happily, feeling she was on a cloud of love.

Their lips touched but they did not speak, each intoxicated with the other, each lost in the wondrous ecstasy of the moment.

The Southern Cross was carefully following events in the south of the island. Today's headline read: 58TH REGIMENT SOUNDS ALARM. And below it: Conflict on the Wanganui. Attack Planned.

Caroline stared at the words, reading them over and over. All she could think of was Grayson and Amiria in the center of war.

"When will the fighting stop?" she asked Nevil.

Nevil shrugged but did not answer. He was rubbing his

thigh, more concerned with his pain than with the unending skirmishes in the south.

"It's all because of Grey's land-purchase scheme, isn't it?" Caroline asked bitterly. "He revels in stealing land from the Maoris."

"Do you really know what you're talking about?" Nevil asked.

"I certainly do," she answered. "The government buys land for sixpence an acre and sells it by the pound."

"Not always."

"So the land commissioners buy it for a shilling and sell it for ten shillings to the New Zealand Company, and they sell it for as much as twenty-five pounds an acre to the settlers. You don't call that an unfair profit?" She paused to wait for his reaction. When he said nothing, she continued, "The only one around here who doesn't seem to be making a fortune is Pollack. From what I understand, he never charges more than six pounds—"

"Joel Pollack?"

"Yes, at least he's trying to be fair. That's why the land sharks hate him so."

"You give that Jew more credit than he's due."

"I don't care what his faith is. At least he's honest."

"You're naive, Caroline. That man's richer than any of us."

"I'm not naive. He's come by every penny he has honestly. I don't understand any of you people in the government. I can't believe you're all out to cheat the Maoris. If it weren't for the Maoris, we'd starve. They're the ones who bring us almost all our food. They build our houses and clear the land, they do all our menial jobs . . . and what do we pay them? Practically nothing. How can you condone it?"

Nevil stood up and walked over to the credenza in the corner of the room. He took out a bottle of laudanum and gulped some down.

"You're becoming addicted to that," Caroline said. Her tone had changed to one of concern. "Is your leg really hurting you so?"

Nevil looked at his wife with annoyance. It was not for her to tell him what to do.

There was a dark side to Nevil which Caroline hated, but even worse, she had no idea how to talk to him when one of these moods came over him. She waited a few moments until Nevil seemed calmer, then asked, "Would you like to go to the Fitzroy tonight? They're doing *The Two Gregories* and *Lovers' Quarrels.*"

The Fitzroy Theatre was in the Royal Hotel and had been started by George Buckingham, a minor professional from Australia. The productions were not of the finest quality, but at the time it was all that Auckland offered in theatre.

"Impossible," said Nevil. "I'm working tonight. Grey's leaving for Wellington in the morning . . . there's more trouble in the Hutt Valley. I'll be in charge until he returns."

Caroline had long since learned not to complain when Nevil went out evenings, but tonight she wanted him with her, she needed him. Barely realizing what words were coming from her mouth, she held out her arms and said, "Please come upstairs first."

"Try to understand, Caroline. I must go."

"I understand," she answered. But there were tears in her eyes, and she didn't understand. She kept thinking of Eliza's words, and again she doubted her husband.

The following morning, while Caroline was still drinking her tea, a pianoforte arrived. On it was a note from Nevil: *To play when I'm working. With all my love.*

Caroline was so excited and thrilled that she hated herself for her thoughts the evening before. She spent the entire morning playing the music she had learned as a child. When Nevil returned home for lunch, she rushed to him with open arms. "That's the most beautiful present I've ever had," she said.

"More beautiful than the necklace I gave you?"

A warm smile filled her face. "More useful," she said.

They kissed for a long time, then Nevil pushed Caroline ever so slightly from him. "I've another surprise for you."

"What?"

"Grayson and Amiria are on their way home."

"Oh, Nevil! How wonderful! How do you know?"

"I saw Mathew this morning."

"When will they be here?"

"Within a week, I'm sure."

Moisture clouded Caroline's eyes. "Does that mean we have to give Hone back?" she asked. In the months that Hone had been with her, she had begun to think of him as her own son.

"He's not ours, my dear. You know that." He pulled Caroline closer to him and kissed her forehead tenderly. "I've some free time, let's go upstairs. I'd rather take care of our own baby anyway."

They started to walk from the room when they heard a forceful knock on the front door.

"Do we have to answer it?" Caroline asked.

"Let me. Whoever it is, I'll tell him to come back later."

A messenger had arrived with an envelope for Nevil. He read the note quickly and stuffed it into his breast pocket. "I'm sorry, Caroline. I must get to Government House immediately. It's urgent. We'll be together later." And without another word, he left the house.

Caroline refused to let Nevil's departure upset her. She went upstairs to look in on Hone. He was sound asleep. She summoned Aroha. "Watch Hone," she said to the servant. "He'll be up soon. I'm going out for a walk." She put on her crimson redingote and left.

Caroline started towards Karangahape Road, to the Grey's home, but as the house came in sight, she altered her course. She wasn't in the mood to talk to Eliza. She wanted to be alone. How could she admit to anyone that she didn't want to give back her brother's son? She felt guilty for feeling as she did but couldn't control her emotions. If only she could have a baby of her own!

She found herself heading toward the Anglican church. It was not her church, but she felt much closer to Richard Churton than she did to anyone at the Methodist church. Perhaps, if she spoke to the minister, confessed her thoughts, he would absolve her of some of her guilt. But as she reached the large wooden structure, again she changed her mind. This was a problem she would have to work out herself. She couldn't confide in anyone, not even Mr. Churton.

She walked past the busy stores, hotels, and grog shops along Queen Street until she reached the courthouse. Beside it was the gaol, its gallows and stocks in open view. A group of raucous men were laughing wildly as they threw rubbish from the streets at two men locked in the stocks. Caroline turned away. She had always found this a cruel and distasteful sport.

With no definite goal in mind, she headed toward the waterfront. Lower Queen Street was a sea of mud. Her shoes were quickly covered with the waste of wet, mushy earth, and her hemline was soaked and black. The call of criers mingled with the shouts of hawkers, but Caroline barely heard the cacophony of voices. She was too absorbed by her thoughts.

Suddenly she awoke from her dazed state. There, on the busy wharf, was Nevil. He was standing with a burly sailor. Caroline stared hard. It wasn't just a sailor, it was that horrible ship's captain, Peter Nolan. She had thoroughly disliked Nolan when she'd sailed with him on the *Rosanna*. There had been something about him that she hadn't trusted. Now, she could not take her eyes from him. He had that same smirk on his ruddy face that she'd seen so often during his four months aboard his ship. She shifted her gaze to her husband. He, too, seemed to have a silly grin on his face. But Nevil was supposed to be at Government House. Why was he here at the waterfront? What was going on?

Caroline turned away. She could no longer look at the two men. She was confused, understanding nothing. Why had Nevil lied to her? If he had had business with Captain Nolan, why hadn't he just told her he was going to meet him? Was Nevil seeing another woman? Were both these men, and Grey, too, involved with Maori mistresses? Was that why Nevil and the Governor were such close friends? Did they constantly cover up for one another?

Caroline's head began to ache. All she wanted to do was run away, but to where? Instead, she went home and laid down.

By the time Nevil returned home, Caroline was feeling somewhat better. He handed her a large bouquet of flowers and kissed her hello. For the first time she knew, without question, that all his gifts were to appease his guilt.

She put down the flowers without bothering to get a vase and give them water. "Why did you lie to me?"

"What do you mean?"

"I saw you at the waterfront . . . with Captain Nolan."

Nevil's immediate reaction was panic. For a brief moment he felt trapped, cornered in a cage with no possible escape. He took a deep breath and tried to relax. Should he tell her the truth? No. She would never understand. And why should he confess to anything when an excuse was so much easier? His tone was defensive as he said simply, "I had business to discuss with him. What's wrong with that?"

"Then why did you tell me you were going to Government House?"

"I went to Government House, Caroline, and then I went to see Captain Nolan. I don't understand what point you're trying to make."

"Don't you?"

"No."

Caroline was trembling as she picked up the flowers. "These need water or they'll die," she said, and walked from the room.

They dined together that evening but said little. Caroline hadn't believed a word Nevil had uttered and he knew it. "Please, my dear," he said. "I don't know why you're making such a thing of a simple meeting between me and the captain. You sound as if you don't trust me. You should know by now how much I love you. There could never be another woman in my life."

He walked over to her and put his arms around her. "Come upstairs and let me prove it to you."

"Not tonight, Nevil. I want to be alone. I need time to think."

"About what?"

"About everything. About the way you're always out and the nights I spend alone."

"That's ridiculous, and you know it."

"Is it?" she said, and rose from the table. "I'm very tired. Good night."

Nevil followed Caroline upstairs. He had to prove to her that nothing was wrong, that there was no other woman in his life. He waited until he was sure she had undressed, then knocked on her door. "May I come in?"

"I'd like to go to sleep."

"Just for a moment," he said softly.

"All right. Come in."

Nevil sat down on the bed and caressed Caroline's face gently. "I love you," he whispered. He bent down and kissed her cheek, then lifted her into his arms. "Please don't push me away. I need you."

The warmth in his voice touched Caroline, and she felt her anger dissipate. "Are you certain?" she asked. More than anything she wanted to believe him, wanted to think she was wrong.

"I've never been more certain of anything," he said.

He undressed quickly and came into bed with her. His arms enfolded her and she again felt a momentary sense of security. Her tears wet his cheek and he lifted his hand to wipe her face. "Don't cry," he said. "Kiss me instead."

She returned his kiss, trying desperately to forget what she had seen, wanting above all to trust him but wondering if she ever would again.

He tried to arouse her but Caroline felt empty—those wonderful sensations she had once known just would not return. Every moment they were together was like playacting. She wanted so to believe him, to be a part of him again, but her body would not respond.

And yet, there was an urgency in their lovemaking tonight because Caroline needed to feel Nevil's closeness—it was her only way of trying to forget the day, her only way to persuade herself that she was wrong—and Nevil needed his wife, needed the tangible proof that she had accepted his story.

Chapter 13

THE DAY GRAYSON AND AMIRIA RETURNED TO AUCK-
land, the fifteenth of July, was one of the worst days in Caroline's life, and the cold, dreary weather matched her desolate
mood.

Her brother had been back in town less than an hour when
he and Amiria arrived at Caroline's home. Amiria's greeting
to Caroline was stinging: "It's so wonderful to be back.
Where's my baby?"

"It's good to have you back," replied Caroline, forcing herself to kiss Amiria hello. Caroline knew her voice was quivering, but she could not control it. Her entire body was trembling. She turned to her brother. "It's wonderful to see you
again. I hope this time you'll stay awhile."

"Can you get Hone now?" asked Amiria. "It's been so long
since I've held him. I've missed him so."

Caroline nodded—it was easier than answering. She walked
from the room just in time to avoid anyone seeing the tears in
her eyes.

Several minutes later she returned with Hone. She had carried the baby down the stairs, then let him stand and took his

hand. "Mama and Papa are here," she said. "Give them a big kiss hello."

Hone stood on the threshold of the sitting-room door. He looked like the mirror image of Grayson at the age of one, dressed in long, narrow brown trousers with a fancy frilled shirt and a short brown jacket—a Pakeha child in every way.

"He looks wonderful," said Grayson, holding out his arms to his little son. "He's grown so . . . I can't believe it. Come to Papa," Grayson called. "Give Papa a big kiss."

Hone did not move. In the six months he had been separated from his parents, he had forgotten who they were.

Amiria began walking slowly toward him. She spoke in Maori as she said, "Mama is home. Here my baby."

Hone clutched Caroline's skirt and hid his tiny head in its deep folds.

Amiria reached for her son and Hone began to cry. Caroline was his mama. Who was this lady dressed so differently from the people he knew? He was afraid of Amiria and continued to cry.

Caroline lifted him up. "Shh, my love. It's all right," she said softly, patting his back and comforting him.

She turned to Amiria, "Children have short memories," she said. "He'll get used to you. Just give him time."

"We told you to take care of him, Caroline," said Grayson. "Not to take him from us."

"That's absurd, Grayson, and you know it."

Caroline began putting Hone back down. "Mama, no," he cried, lifting his little arms to Caroline. "Up, up," he sobbed.

"How dare you have our child call you Mama!" Grayson spluttered out the words.

"I didn't tell him to call me Mama. You should know that Ma-ma and Da-da are almost every child's first words."

She handed Hone to his mother and Amiria began singing softly to her son. In a moment Hone stopped crying.

"I think we should go," the irate Grayson said to Amiria. "The faster we get Hone out of here, the better off he'll be."

Amiria nodded. She, too, was very upset by Hone's greeting.

"And the less you see of Hone, the better," Grayson told his sister. "I'll come for his things later," he added as he opened the front door.

"*Haerera,*" called Amiria as she left.

"Good-bye," said Caroline.

As the door closed, Caroline burst into tears. How could her brother have been so cruel? Couldn't he understand that she had grown to love Hone as if he were her own?

A long time later, Caroline wiped her eyes and went upstairs to wash her face. She had promised to be at the hospital by eleven o'clock and it was already close to noon. She knew Dr. Philson would be understanding and she didn't care that it was late. Still, she had a responsibility to be there and wouldn't let him down.

The quaint shingle-roofed building that was Auckland's first hospital was nearing completion, but it was already open for patients. A stone foundation formed the basis of the wooden structure which would eventually comprise four large wards of eight to ten beds and two smaller wards of five beds. The surgery was completed, as was the kitchen. The loft of three small rooms for the staff, however, was still under construction. There would also be a detached morgue, but this had not as yet been started.

Caroline stood outside the hospital for a moment to savor the spectacular view of Waitemata Harbour and the Coromandel Ranges.

"I was beginning to worry about you," Dr. Philson greeted her. He looked into her sad eyes and knew at once that something was wrong. "What is it?" he asked.

With a sense of great embarrassment, Caroline tried to tell the doctor why she was so upset.

"You would be less than human if you felt otherwise," he said.

His reply was comforting and Caroline slowly began to relax. "Thank you," she said, wiping her eyes. She pulled herself together. "I'm ready to work now." Her voice had a brave tone. "What would you like me to do today?"

"We need an inventory of everything that's arrived."

"I'll start at once," she said, and went inside.

Caroline was glad she had this work. It took her mind off her loneliness and problems, and today, especially, it was particularly helpful. By the time she was ready to go home at four o'clock, she had come to terms with losing Hone. She was sure that her brother eventually would let her see the child again—it would just take time.

But the rest of Caroline's day was no better than the beginning. Upon her return home, she found a letter from Geoffrey. She opened it quickly but digested the words slowly, barely comprehending the cursive writing, not wanting to believe what she read:

> *My dear Caroline,*
>
> *It has been many months since you have heard from me. Every moment of my life since I returned to this land I once called home has been filled.*
>
> *When I came here, it was to see my family. But upon my arrival I met a charming woman, Lady Agnes Compton. Last week we were married.*
>
> *How I wish you were here, sitting by this quiet candlelight with us now. I know you two will like each other and become good friends. I feel certain that that shall happen in the not too distant future, for we are returning to New Zealand on the next ship.*

The tears were streaming down Caroline's face and her vision was so blurred it was impossible to read further. She was amazed by her reaction to Geoffrey's letter. She knew she should be delighted that he was married, she should be pleased that he had at last found a woman to love. But she wasn't. Somehow, she felt that now that he had a wife, her friendship with him would never be the same.

Long shadows filled the room but Caroline hardly noticed that dusk had fallen. A heaviness had come over her, a crushing weight seemed to be lying across her chest. But by the time Nevil returned home, her eyes were dry. Still, her sadness was clearly reflected in them.

"What's wrong?" Nevil asked even before looking into his wife's face. The mere fact that she was sitting in a darkened room was enough to make him know that something was not as it should be.

Caroline heaved a sigh, glad that she had what would sound like a perfect excuse; Nevil need not know how Geoffrey's letter had affected her. "Grayson and Amiria are back," she said. "They've taken Hone."

Nevil was wise enough not to make light of the situation, although inwardly he was pleased that the child was gone. He had always been adverse to bringing up a half-caste, convinced that it was demeaning for a person in his position to have the boy living with them.

In the days that followed, Caroline did all she could to keep busy, anything not to think of what she had lost. Work was her salvation but she couldn't be at the hospital at night. More and more, she found herself sitting at the keyboard, playing doleful melodies she had learned so long ago, but eventually she had to go to bed. Usually, she went alone. Nevil had unlimited excuses as to why he had to be out in the evenings and Caroline no longer challenged him. There seemed to be no point.

Late one afternoon Eliza Grey arrived at Caroline's door. "I must speak to you," she said.

"Do come in," Caroline said, pleased to have company. "Would you like some tea?"

"No, thank you. I just want to talk to you."

"What is it, Eliza?" Clearly this was not to be just a friendly chat.

"I had to tell you. Everyone in town knows but you."

"Knows what?"

"About Nevil."

"I know," Caroline said.

"You do!"

"Yes. He has a mistress and I'm certain she's a Maori. That's why he hated Hone here. Having a Maori child seemed to betray him . . . to announce his affair."

143

"It's not that, Caroline. Oh, darling, I'm so sorry," Eliza said, putting a comforting arm around her friend.

"What do you mean?"

"Nevil is having an affair, but not with a Maori mistress."

"Then with whom?"

"Eliza, how nice to see you," said Nevil, entering the room.

He walked over and kissed his wife. "Caroline, my dear, how are you today?" he said, as if nothing were wrong.

Caroline's entire body tensed. She hadn't heard her husband enter the house. She could not help but wonder if he had been privy to the conversation a moment ago. She steeled herself to speak in a controlled tone. "I'm fine, just fine," she said. But she was furious that he had entered at that minute. She had to learn what else Eliza knew.

Nevil poured each woman a glass of port and himself some whiskey, then sat down.

As upset as Caroline was by Nevil's behavior, she was glad that he was no longer mixing laudanum with his whiskey, that his limp had lessened. But she made no comment. With the way he'd been acting these days, the last thing she wanted was for him to be aware of the deep concern she still felt.

"We received a dispatch from the Governor today," Nevil began the conversation, looking at Eliza as he spoke. "There's full-scale war in the Hutt Valley."

Lower Hutt, as the Valley was called, was just to the north of Wellington. Ever since the New Zealand Company had brought out settlers in 1840, there had been trouble with the Maoris in the area over disputed land claims.

"It's that damn Colonel William Wakefield," said Caroline with disdain.

"Caroline, my dear, watch your language. Colonel Wakefield is the principal agent of the Company. What he does is in the interest of the settlers . . . our people."

"You know exactly how I feel, Nevil. If he wouldn't try to cheat the natives, there'd be no war."

Eliza felt extremely uncomfortable. Her mission here had been sufficiently difficult, she didn't now want to become involved in a family dispute. "It's getting late," she said. "Please forgive me, but I must leave."

"But you haven't finished your drink," said Nevil graciously.

"I know. I didn't realize the time." She turned to Caroline. "Perhaps we could have lunch tomorrow."

Caroline nodded. She was afraid to say any more.

The evening passed slowly, the hours seeming to drag on and on. Caroline was greatly relieved when Nevil said, "With the renewed fighting in the south, there's more work than ever. Grey wants me to dispatch a report to him in the morning. Don't wait up for me, my dear. I don't know how late I'll be."

Caroline did not sleep at all that night. She kept going over the names of all the prominent women in Auckland, wondering who her husband's mistress could possibly be.

By the time she met Eliza the following day, Eliza had thought better of what she was going to tell her friend.

"Please," said Caroline, "why are you keeping it from me? Tell me who she is."

"I really don't know a name," said Eliza. "I only know the gossip, and no names have been bandied about. What the other women are merely saying is that Nevil is disloyal . . . that you're not the only one in his life."

Caroline didn't really believe Eliza knew no more but she realized it would be pointless to try and press her for details.

In the weeks that followed, Caroline tried to find out who the other woman was, but her search was to no avail. She could not bring herself to ask anyone outright and no one seemed to want to offer the information.

Shortly before Christmas George Grey returned to Auckland. Caroline knew he was expected back but she was surprised to see him through the window of her home when she returned from the hospital late one afternoon. As she entered the house, the shouting in the living room startled her.

"Where're your brains?" Grey asked Nevil. The fury in his voice could not be mistaken.

Caroline stood near the doorway listening.

"Look who's talking," replied Nevil with indignation. "You think you're any better? Everyone in town knows about the great Governor of New Zealand, with his mission to bring two races together. Is that why you chose a Maori mistress? To practice what you preach?" he sneered.

"If you know what's good for you, you'll shut your mouth Nevil. To have a mistress is one thing . . . to have a man is quite another."

"Don't be so high and mighty, George. You know damn well, 'backside rules the seas'."

"May I remind you that you're not in the navy, you're in government . . . and that's a land job."

"So?"

"So, plenty. Have you forgotten that sodomy is a crime?"

"Don't be a fool, George. I'm not a homosexual and you know it. I've a wife and it was I who made her pregnant. I can attest to that and so will she."

"No bugger will work in my government," Grey replied.

"But George—"

"No buts," said Grey. "I'll arrange for you to be sent elsewhere. No one has to know more than they already do. But if you know what's good for you, you'll stick to women from here on."

Caroline leaned against the wall. She was in a cold sweat and afraid she would vomit, already tasting the bitter bile. No wonder Eliza had not told her the truth. How could she? She closed her eyes to try to obliterate the image of her husband and a man in each other's arms. All she could see was Peter Nolan. Suddenly it all became clear to her. That was why Nevil had gone down to the waterfront—to be with Captain Nolan. And that voice she had heard in Nevil's room one night a few months ago—it had been a man. Her husband had actually brought a man into their home, into his bed. That was why he wanted separate bedrooms, not as he had said, so that they could each get a better night's sleep.

"We'll talk about this tomorrow," said Grey.

Caroline overheard the words. The Governor was about to leave. She became panicky. The last thing she wanted was for Nevil to know that she had heard the conversation between him and Grey. But she felt paralyzed, unable to move.

"It won't happen again," said Nevil. "You don't have to send me away."

"I told you, we'd discuss this tomorrow. Good day, Nevil."

Caroline summoned every last ounce of strength and rushed back to the door. She opened it quickly and closed it with a bang. "I'm home," she called as brightly as she could and pretended to walk into the house. "So good to see you, Governor," she addressed Grey. "I hope you had a good voyage." She could feel the nervousness in her voice but her act was convincing, neither man even suspected that their conversation had not been a private one.

As soon as George Grey left the house, Caroline began to tremble. She was now alone with Nevil. What should she say? What could she say?

"You look positively white, Caroline. Are you ill?"

"Yes, yes," she answered, grateful for the excuse. "If you'll forgive me, I must lie down."

"Of course, my dear. Can I get you anything?"

"No, thank you. I'll be fine by morning, I'm sure. I just want to lie down."

"Shall I have a tray brought to your room?"

"I'm really not hungry. I just want to sleep." She turned towards the stairs. "Good night," she called, conscious that she was straining to speak in a less than hostile tone. She needed time to think. She could not let him know she suspected anything. Not yet.

Chapter 14

A HEAVY MIST GAVE DAWN AN EERIE QUALITY, A PRELUDE to a dismal day. Caroline felt numb. She had been standing at the window all night, staring into the darkness, wondering what had become of her life. In just a few short moments her entire world seemed to have been shattered. How could she pick up the pieces? And were they worth picking up?

The dew on the leaves began to sparkle as the morning sun cleared the air. Caroline turned from the window and looked down at the traveling dresser set she had ordered from England six months ago. It was a fine eighteen-piece silver-gilted cut crystal gentleman's toilette, a fitted case of cherry wood inlaid with brass and with a hidden compartment for a wood-framed mirror. A perfect gift for Nevil's thirty-fourth birthday, but she had no desire to give it to him.

She heard the chimes of the clock sound the hour of eight. She knew she should dress and go downstairs for breakfast but she felt paralyzed. She still had not determined how to confront Nevil. She was tormented by George Grey's words. She just couldn't believe what she had heard, and yet, there was no question that she had clearly understood every syllable the

Governor had uttered the evening before. She knew that boys at Harrow and Eaton had homosexual experiences, and Nevil was an Eaton boy. But now he was no longer an inquisitive student, he was the Colonial Secretary. How could he live such a life?

Caroline thought she heard a soft knock on her door. Her body stiffened but she did not speak.

"Caroline." The voice was hardly above a whisper. "Caroline, are you all right? May I come in?"

The words caused her to hold her breath as a feeling of terror engulfed her. The dreaded moment was upon her, but she wasn't ready to face her husband.

"Please let me come in. I'm worried about you. I want to talk to you."

"I'm fine," was all she could say.

She watched the door open slowly and wished she had turned the key in the lock. She gave Nevil a quick glance as he entered then her gaze dropped to the floor.

"What's wrong? What have I done to make you shut me out like this?"

"What have you done?" She heard her voice was out of control, high-pitched and verging on hysteria, but she couldn't help herself. She was trembling all over. "What have you done? How can you stand there so calmly and ask me that? You know exactly what you've done."

"If I knew, I wouldn't ask you," Nevil said defensively.

Caroline took a deep breath. She glared at her husband with icy eyes. Her composure had returned. She chose her words carefully. "I heard everything that was said between you and George last night."

Nevil's face blanched. "How could you have? I heard you come in."

"No, you didn't," she answered. "I came in and you *didn't* hear me. When I realized the conversation was just about over, I slipped out of the house and reentered."

"You what? You little sneak!"

"Don't you call me names, you . . . you—" She stopped herself.

"Caroline, let me explain."

"What's to explain? You'd rather go to bed with Captain Nolan than with me." Tears rushed to her eyes and she began to sob. "Oh, Nevil, how could you?"

"Please Caroline, it's not what you think."

"Don't make it worse, Nevil. You can't cover up what you've been doing. I know."

"I swear it will never happen again." He went over to her and put his arm on her shoulder.

"Don't touch me!" She jumped back, shuddering as she recoiled. "Don't ever put a hand on me again."

"Caroline listen to me. Sometimes things happen. Peter was lonely. He'd been at sea for six months and—"

"And you were there. But why? Why you?"

"I don't know. I don't understand, myself. Honestly, I don't. But it will never happen again. Never."

Caroline looked into Nevil's deep brown eyes. How could she still love this man, she wondered . . . this man who had committed an abomination, the worst of crimes. It was unnatural for two men to be together. It was against everything in the Bible, everything she had been taught.

"I need you, Caroline. Please give me another chance. You'll see. Things will be different from now on."

Caroline nodded slowly. These few minutes with Nevil had thoroughly exhausted her. She could not continue the conversation. She walked over to her dresser and picked up the traveling case. "Happy birthday," she said, handing him his gift.

He smiled, relieved that the discussion had been tabled yet believing he had not heard the last of it.

But he was wrong, for when Nevil left for Government House, Caroline decided that the only way she could continue her marriage was to bury the subject. There was no point in rehashing what had been said. Her husband knew how she felt, and she believed—wanted to believe—that nothing like that would ever happen again.

Nevil was in a cold sweat by the time he reached Government House. He dreaded seeing Grey again. He knew the

Governor had made up his mind—there was nothing to say that would make amends. His step was hesitant as he entered the large office.

"I'm glad you're here," Grey greeted Nevil. "I've just made arrangements to make you the new Commercial Agent for Fiji."

"Fiji!" The word immediately conjured up the erroneous picture of wild savages devouring human flesh.

"Yes," the Governor answered firmly. He was speaking in a matter of fact way, as if nothing had happened. "I need you there, Nevil. You're the only man I know whom I can count on to negotiate with Cakobau."

"Who's Cakobau?"

"He was the chief of the island of Bau, now he calls himself 'Tui Viti,' which means High Chief of Fiji, although he considers himself king of all the islands." Grey paused for a moment and then continued, "Ever since Cakobau came to power, our trade with those islands has been seriously affected. We need their Bêche-de-Mer and coconut oil . . . and our whalers must be able to sail those waters in safety. It's essential that we reestablish our trade there."

"But why me?"

"Because you're the one man who can talk to Cakobau. He's exiled our traders from Levuka and sent them to the northern island of Vanua Levu, to Solevu Bay. They've settled at Nawaido, a terrible place. The men and their families are dying like flies there. The natives on Vanua Levu are hostile. They think nothing of raiding our settlement for food."

"For food?"

"They seem to enjoy white meat," Grey said with a smirk.

Nevil could feel his stomach turn over at the thought of being eaten by some Fijian native.

"Furthermore," Grey continued, "our people can't survive on that island. The weather's unhealthy, there's no fresh water, and supplies are a serious problem . . . the reefs make it impossible for our ships to anchor. Levuka has clear streams, cool breezes, and a safe harbor. It's up to you to make Cakobau agree to let our people return to Levuka."

"Do I have a choice?"

"Not really. And Nevil, just be grateful that I'm giving you a second chance. Be smart. Remember, I could have sent you back to England in total disgrace."

"How long do I have to stay?"

"A year, two, three, however long it takes."

"And Caroline?"

"She can go with you . . . if she wants to, once she finds out why you're being sent away."

"She knows. She heard everything last night."

For a moment Grey was speechless, then he asked what she had said.

Nevil shrugged his shoulders. "Nothing much. I promised her it wouldn't happen again."

"See to it you keep that promise."

"Yes, sir," Nevil said with rare formality. "May I leave now?"

"There's a ship leaving for Tonga on the fifteenth of September. I'll arrange for it to stop somewhere in Fiji . . . you'll have to make your own arrangements from there."

"Yes, sir."

"Good day, Nevil."

"Good day, sir."

Nevil left the Governor's office a broken man. He could not believe that George Grey, once such a close friend, could exile him to the Fijian Islands. As he walked away from Government House he wondered what Caroline would say. Did she love him enough to sail with him to the Cannibal Islands—as they were often called—to islands in the middle of the South Pacific, weeks away from civilization? The little he had read about the Fijians was just enough to let him know that they were a fierce warring people with greed for human flesh and a savage thirst for blood.

The announcement of Nevil's new post did not come as a surprise to Caroline, but the knowledge that they were being exiled to the Fijian Islands was hardly an attractive thought.

She had heard stories of those islands, and the prospect of moving there was frightening.

She listened carefully as Nevil explained that approximately three hundred islands comprised the group known as the Fijis. He told her there were two large islands and a number of smaller ones which were just tiny dots extending over forty thousand square miles of the South Pacific.

"They're not tiny dots," she said sarcastically. "From what I've heard, they're nothing but a flotsam of island scraps . . . hundreds of bits of nothings thousands of miles from anywhere and as many years behind in civilization."

"I've no choice, Caroline. We'll have to make the best of it." He understood her anger and spoke as gently as he could, trying in every way he knew to pique her curiosity, persuading her that it would be interesting to live amongst the Melanesians, so different from the Polynesian Maoris whom she knew.

Caroline was not convinced. The only positive thing she could see about the move was that Nevil would have no contact with Peter Nolan. Maybe now he would be able to adhere to his new resolve.

They were to leave for Fiji in just four weeks. It was a tense time for both of them, and they argued incessantly. Nevil believed they should rent their home while they were away. He insisted that this was the only means to ensure its safety. Caroline did not agree. The idea of strangers living in her home and using her things did not appeal to her. She didn't understand why they just couldn't lock the door, barricade the windows, and leave. Certainly, she could impose upon Eliza Grey to check the house from time to time. As always, Nevil was stubborn and refused to listen to her arguments. He insisted that he was the man of the house and knew best.

And so, when Nevil finally told Caroline he had agreed to rent their home to the new Acting Colonial Secretary, she conceded. At least the man was given the title of *Acting* Secretary, which made her feel there was hope that once conditions

were settled with Cakobau, she and Nevil would return to
Auckland.

The problem of packing was not an easy one, for Caroline
had no idea how long they would be gone. Though she knew
she had no time to tarry, she seemed unable to take out their
trunks and make decisions about what to take and what to
leave. Nevil had told her it was hot in Fiji, they had no winters there. But what if he were wrong? He knew how she
hated cold weather—was he just trying to please her so that
she would not be so resistant to making the trip? How could
she believe anything he said now?

It was easy to procrastinate, and rather than start organiz-
ing their things, Caroline decided to write to Grayson. It was
one of the most difficult letters she had ever had to compose.
She didn't know what reason to give him for their sudden
departure. She was certain he would eventually find out the
truth. Everyone knew; Eliza had said so. On the other hand,
maybe by the time Grayson returned, the town gossip would
be focused on a different scandal. Caroline decided, therefore,
to say simply that Nevil was needed in Fiji. She would write as
soon as they were settled and hoped it would not be too long
before they could all see each other again.

The days ahead passed slowly for Caroline, for she could
not bring herself to visit anyone. She had always hated the
women's vicious, idle talk, and especially now that she knew
she was the most important food on their wagging tongues.
And yet when it came to packing, time seemed to evaporate.
Caroline didn't know where the hours disappeared to and just
couldn't seem to get everything ready for the long voyage.

The night before they were to leave, Nevil came home from
the office early. "I have to work tonight," he said, "go over
last minute things with George."

Caroline looked directly at her husband. He averted her
cold stare, knowing she didn't believe a word he'd said.

"I'm really going to work, Caroline. You can come with me
if you want," he told her, but his tone was not convincing.

"Aren't you going to say anything?" he asked. He could not bear her silence.

"What's there to say?"

"You don't believe me, do you?"

"Don't I?"

"No."

"Whatever you say, Nevil."

"Caroline, stop it. I told you I must meet with George tonight. I have to know exactly what's expected of me. I'll be at Government House and no place else."

She did not answer. She gave her husband one last glance, shook her head, then turned and left the room.

Chapter 15

CAROLINE STOOD AT THE RAIL OF THE FORTY-TON *Aquila*, looking out at the vast ocean, wondering if the tiny vessel was really large enough to be safe on such a long voyage. Weeks of unremitting boredom had given her far too much time to think of the past. Thoughts reeled in her head as day after day the same questions plagued her: Were they really going far enough away for Nevil to change? Could distance make her forget what he'd done? Could a new home, new ties, new adventures, be synonymous with a new life? Could they really begin again? She tried to force herself to think of positive thoughts, to concentrate on happy moments she and Nevil had shared; but she was tortured by the past.

She was still staring out at the gently undulating waters, so lost in thought that she barely noticed the crimson sun sinking into the sea, when Nevil approached her.

"Beautiful, isn't it?" he said, a chewed cheroot on the side of his mouth. He took the small piece of bound tobacco that remained and flicked it over the side of the rail. "We'll be there soon," he said softly. His voice was warm and loving. More than anything, he wanted his wife back.

Caroline looked up at Nevil. "When?" she asked.

"That depends on the winds, but it shouldn't be more than a few days."

Caroline glanced at the slack sails and then out at the calm waters. "The balmy air is lovely," she said, "but I wish there were more wind. We've been out on this water long enough."

In the two weeks they had been at sea, this had been the tenor of their conversations, polite chitchat and little more.

The Reverend and Mrs. Blackburn walked over to them. "Isn't the sunset magnificent?" said Mrs. Blackburn. She was a short, heavyset woman with a kindly face.

Caroline smiled and nodded.

"I brought this for you," said the Reverend. He handed Caroline a book on ferns. "You should start a collection of ferns while you're in Fiji," he told her.

"My husband's more than just a missionary," interjected Mrs. Blackburn, "he's an amateur botanist."

"Yes, I know," said Caroline.

The Reverend continued, "Remember what I told you. Sea weed can be dried in the same manner as ferns. Observe and collect everything, one day you'll be pleased you did."

"I'll try," she answered, looking directly at the handsome man of the cloth. He was well-built and obviously spent a great deal of time outdoors. Caroline could not be certain why he reminded her of Geoffrey Rutledge.

"It will be fun collecting ferns, won't it, Nevil?" she said turning to her husband. But Nevil was no longer by her side. Caroline couldn't believe he would be so rude as to just walk away without a word.

"Did you see where Nevil went?" she asked them.

They both shook their heads.

"I was looking at the sunset," said Mrs. Blackburn.

"Don't worry," chuckled the Reverend, "he can't have gone far."

"Will you excuse me?" said Caroline. Before they had answered, she began walking toward the stern of the ship. As she turned a corner, she saw Nevil engaged in conversation with the ship's captain. She felt the blood drain from her head as all her dreams of tomorrow vanished. She leaned against a wall, almost unable to take another step. Why had she bothered to come? Nevil would never change.

Nevil caught sight of his wife and came over to her, a broad smile on his face. "The captain says we should arrive by the day after tomorrow." Then he realized how pale Caroline looked. "Are you all right?"

Caroline nodded.

When the captain greeted Caroline, she could not bring herself even to say hello. "Excuse me," she said, in as polite a tone as she could. "I think I'd like to lie down."

Nevil followed Caroline to their small cabin. "Can I do anything for you?"

"Just leave me alone!" she snapped.

"But Caroline, it's not what you think."

In disgust she turned from her husband, grabbed her night-gown from under her pillow, and said firmly, "Would you please leave, I want to undress."

Caroline refused to say a word to Nevil that night but the following morning she knew she could not postpone a confrontation. Nevil pleaded with her, telling her that there was nothing between him and the captain. They had been talking about where they would land in Fiji—it was as simple as that.

"Caroline, you're not being fair. Surely, I can have a conversation with a man without it being incriminating." He took out a cheroot and nervously lit it. "There's nothing more I can say, because there is nothing to say."

Caroline was confused. Certainly Nevil had the right to talk to another man, but still she didn't feel she could trust him. Yet what could she do? Where could she go? "I'm sorry," she said, forcing a tiny smile on her lips. "It's just that he's a captain."

Nevil put his arm around her shoulder. "Let's go to breakfast."

Two days later, at dawn, the *Aquila* landed in Fiji on the shores of Viti Levu, near Suva Point. The harbor, lined with palm trees and lush tropical vegetation, was a splendid sight.

The island looked like a paradise, and it was difficult to believe that the natives in the area had been at war for the past four years. But Nevil knew that the town of Suva, once the center of the Rewa people, had been burned to the ground three years before. And he knew that Cakobau and the Rewa chiefs had been warring ever since. The natives had rebuilt Suva, but it was now only a small village.

Caroline was delighted at last to be on solid ground. She wanted to spend a few days in Suva, where she had been told the natives were friendly. Nevil insisted that they leave at once for Levuka. He had come to Fiji to make peace with Cakobau and the more quickly he succeeded in contacting him, the sooner they could return to Auckland.

Reluctantly, Caroline agreed to go straight to the island of Ovalau, and within two hours they were sitting in a long canoe, heading for Levuka.

Caroline studied the two young boys who were paddling. Nevil had been right, the Fijians were very different from the Maoris. Their skin was much darker, their features broader, and they had marvelous manes of bushy hair. She later learned they took great pride in these fuzzy halos, spending much of their time brushing them with wooden combs whose prongs were like those of pitchforks. She also was told they treated their naturally jet-black locks with solutions of lime and clay to give them a shade of crimson or maroon.

The boys seemed friendly, but since neither of them spoke English, it was impossible to carry on a conversation.

"Are the natives of Levuka like these boys?" Caroline asked Nevil.

"I don't think they're as favorably disposed toward foreigners."

"I'm sorry the Blackburns aren't with us," Caroline said unexpectedly. "Having a clergyman here would make me feel better."

"Didn't they go on to Tonga?"

Caroline nodded.

"There's nothing to fear, my dear. Cakobau wouldn't dare

start anything with a representative of the British Crown. He'd be afraid of all-out war."

"He wasn't afraid of exiling our traders."

"Yes, but they weren't government officials. Besides, Cakobau doesn't live in Levuka, he lives in a fortress on the Island of Bau."

"Then why are we coming here?"

"So we can establish residence. He'll learn quickly enough that we're in Levuka and I'd rather have our meeting on this island than on his."

She wasn't certain she understood but she did not question Nevil further.

As they neared the island of Ovalau, Caroline was overcome by its beauty. Thickly wooded hills rolled down to a sandy shore, and there, tall palms and mangrove trees lined the waterfront. The greenery was interspersed with poincianas in bloom, trees whose flaming red flowers, known locally as flamboyants brightened the beach.

"Bula venaka! Bula venaka!" shouted seven young children, waving their arms excitedly as they greeted the visitors.

Caroline had tried to study some Fijian vocabulary during her weeks at sea but she had no idea how the language sounded. She did, however, understand the words and tried to repeat the greeting.

The two boys paddling the canoe could not help but laugh at her accent. Slowly, they repeated the words until she could pronounce them correctly.

The exuberant welcome immediately put Caroline at ease. She turned to Nevil and smiled with a warmth he had not seen since that gruesome night two months ago. He pressed his hand in hers, at last feeling that he had been forgiven.

Nevil was more adept at languages than his wife and as soon as they reached the beach began to converse with the youngsters. Slowly, he asked them where he could find a hotel.

The children tittered at his question, for there were fifty-two hotels lining the waterfront road of Levuka. They pointed down the beach and told Nevil to follow them.

As they walked along the unpaved road, Caroline was struck by the native homes—curious one-story houses framed with limbs of trees and thatched with plaited fibers of coconut husk. Across the top of each roof was a ridge pole, a design Caroline had never before seen. "That house is different from the others," she said to Nevil, pointing to a particularly handsome structure ornamented with coconut plait and with an external ridge pole very much longer than the ones on the other houses. Also, its roof was two or three times higher than its walls.

"Bure," said one of the children. *"Bure."*

"I think that means temple," said Nevil.

"What are those things hanging from the pole?" Caroline asked.

"Cowrie shells," Nevil answered.

"No, I mean those . . . dear God, Nevil! They're heads . . . human heads!"

"Those are their enemy."

"Oh, Nevil," she said, taking his hand. "Are we going to be all right?"

"You mustn't worry, Caroline. I promise everything will be just fine. The natives have no reason to harm either one of us."

By the time they reached the Royal Hotel in the center of town, dusk had fallen. The large, white two-story wooden building, typical of colonial structures, made Caroline feel she had been here before. She had seen hotels like this on her way to New Zealand, when she had docked in Calcutta and again in Sydney, and the familiarity of the architecture was reassuring.

As they climbed the three steps to the long porch, they were greeted by an army of ugly, oversized toads. Caroline clung to Nevil in fear.

"They won't hurt you. Relax."

But she couldn't relax—she hated the slimy, jumping creatures.

Straw mats made from pandanus leaves, with geometrical designs in brown and black, lined the floors of the lobby; otherwise, the hotel was English in its furnishings. A Fijian man stood behind the front desk, clad only in a brown-and-white figured *sulu*—a kind of sash at least ten feet long, made from the bark of a paper mulberry tree. The sash passed between his legs and was wound several times around his loins. One end was secured in front, so as to fall over his knees like a skirt, the other end fastened behind and was left to trail, almost touching the ground.

"*Bulu venaka,*" said the Fijian, and then spoke in English. "You are a trader?"

"No," replied Nevil. "I am the new Commercial Agent for Fiji. I represent the British Government."

"I am forbidden to give rooms to traders."

"I am not a trader."

The receptionist walked away from the counter without a word. Several minutes later he returned. "You sign here," he said. "Then you come with me."

Caroline and Nevil followed him to the back of the hotel to what they were both certain was the smallest room available.

"*Kaivavalagi* are not welcome here," the Fijian said.

"What does that mean?" Caroline asked in a whisper.

"I think it means Pakeha," Nevil answered. "You know, European."

As soon as the Fijian had left, Nevil opened the wooden shutters to try to air the room. He was concerned that there were no windows, because he had read that the problem of mosquitoes was a serious one. "We'll have to put our netting up carefully tonight," he said, "or we'll be bitten from head to toe."

"Nevil!" cried Caroline. "Look!" She pointed to a centipede slowly making its way toward the center of the room.

Nevil stepped on the insect, killing it with no trouble.

"Don't they ever clean these rooms?"

"Centipedes won't hurt you," he said understandingly. "They look worse than they are. It takes time to get used to living in the tropics, but you will."

Caroline hardly slept that night. The sound of toads, the scurry of rats across the bedroom floor, the buzzing of mosquitoes and flies, and other strange noises terrified her.

Throughout the night she watched small green lizards run across the walls of their room. Nevil assured her that they were harmless. He refused to kill even one, saying that they lived on mosquitoes and the less of those insects around the better, but his words did not comfort her. It was only when she began to listen to the symphony of chirping birds which unexpectedly filled the air that she relaxed, for their songs signaled that morning had come.

Caroline found her first day in Levuka so fascinating that she had no time to think of how far she was from everything she had known. She and Nevil breakfasted in the hotel dining room before seven. They were served by a young Fijian woman dressed only in a colorful *liku* of pounded paper mulberry bark. Caroline felt her face flush with embarrassment as the bare breasted woman came to serve her. This was a mode of attire entirely foreign to her. Nevil laughed at her reaction, and though they both spoke volumes to each other with their eyes, neither made a comment.

After breakfast, they walked along the waterfront to the home of the *Tui Levuka*, the Chief of Levuka. He was under Cakobau, who now claimed himself king of all the islands, but he was still the most important person in Levuka at the moment. As they approached the north end of Beach Street, just before crossing Levuka Creek, they were greeted by the *Tui Levuka's* spokesman. He explained to Nevil that he could not have an audience with the Chief without bringing *yaqona.*

Nevil shook his head, not understanding the word.

"You know *kava?*" asked the spokesman, using the also popular Tongan word.

"Oh, yes," said Nevil.

"What's *yaqona?*" asked Caroline.

"It's made from dried roots of that plant," said the spokesman, pointing to a shrub of a pepper plant. "We chew it and then mix it with water. You will drink some, it is good," he said, giggling as if he knew something he would not tell.

They walked back to a friend of the spokesman, bought a small bag of *yaqona,* then continued on to the chief's home.

The welcoming ceremony for Caroline and Nevil was held

under a canopy attached to the chief's house. There were ten people, all seated in a circle on either side of the chief. The first thing Nevil and Caroline did was to remove their shoes—no one entered the sacred ground of the chief's home with their feet covered. Then Nevil presented the *yaqona* to the chief and he and Caroline were invited to sit down.

Everyone began chewing pieces of *yaqona* root. As soon as it was masticated into pulp, they placed the remains into a large four-legged wooden bowl and let it steep in water. The strength of the resulting grog depended upon how long the *yaqona* was allowed to remain in the water and the amount of water that was used. The grayish liquid that resulted was strained through a cloth made of beaten paper mulberry bark and then wrung out by squeezing the cloth. While the *yaqona* grog was being made, everyone chanted to the traditional *meke*—dance—and clapped in measured tempo.

Caroline suddenly realized she was going to have to taste this dirty-looking water made from the pulp everyone had chewed. "I can't drink that," she whispered to Nevil.

"You have to," he said. "You can't insult these people. You don't know what they'll do."

The hand clapping became faster and faster as the grog was strained into a coconut-shell bowl. Then a cup bearer came forward and faced the chief. Holding the bowl with arms completely extended, he slowly lowered his body until his knees were fully bent and every muscle was taut. At the appropriate line of the chant, he straightened up, approached the chief, stooped again, and filled the *Tui Levuka's* bowl. The chief lifted the shell ceremoniously, invoked the Great Spirit to bless the liquid, then drained the bowl amid hand clapping and cries of *maca! maca!*—empty! As soon as he had finished, he spun the bowl to the mat and the bearer returned with a fresh supply.

Then a common bowl, filled to the rim, was passed around, according to rank, to each person present. Caroline was beside herself as she watched the ceremony. Not only was she going to have to drink the grog, she would have to drink it from the same cup as everyone else.

"I can't, Nevil."

"You have *to*," he said impatiently.

"But women don't usually drink with men . . . I've read that."

"You do when you're a guest."

Suddenly it was her turn. The cup bearer filled the small bowl and handed it to her. "None must be left," he whispered.

Caroline looked at the filthy liquid and felt ill. She held it to her lips and took the tiniest of tastes. It had a slightly cinnamon, peppery flavor, but if she had to describe it, she would have said it tasted like thick, muddy dishwater.

"Maca! Maca!" they all shouted, clapping their hands vigorously.

Caroline took a deep breath and emptied the cup. She thought she would vomit. Never again would she do this, no matter what Nevil said.

The clapping intensified and wide smiles filled the faces of all those present—their guest had pleased them, she would be accepted by all.

Within a few minutes Caroline began to feel light-headed. It was only then that she learned that when dried and mixed with water, *yaqona* forms a liquor that has much the same effect on a person as opium.

She could not believe that these people drank bowl after bowl of this intoxicating beverage, and she wondered how they could stand up after one of these ceremonies, which were apparently held daily.

By the time Caroline and Nevil returned to the hotel, all Caroline wanted to do was sleep. She was light-headed and dizzy and felt as if she were floating above the floor. She hated the sense of losing control. A rush of warmth came over her, and in her euphoric state, she thought it was funny that everyone was so mad as to drink grog in this unbearable heat. Then the opiate's action began to sedate her. "Never again," she slurred, lying down on the bed. She was asleep before Nevil could answer.

Caroline's resolve did not last long. She soon learned that if she was going to live in Fiji, she was going to have to learn to drink grog at least several times a week, if not more. Every time she went anywhere with Nevil, the meeting began with a *yaqona* ceremony.

They had been in Levuka almost six weeks when Nevil told Caroline about the pigeon post. "Pigeons go back and forth between here and Suva," he said. "That's how mail is sent."

"Does it really get there?" Caroline asked.

"Apparently. From what I've learned, the pigeons are very reliable. They fly to Suva in less than thirty minutes. I'm sending a letter to Cakobau. From Suva it will be sent by boat to Bau . . . the islands are just fifteen or twenty minutes apart. I'm going to ask Cakobau for a meeting and hope I can persuade him to allow the traders to return here."

"How do the pigeons know where to go?"

"They've been trained," he said. "I'm walking over to the pigeon loft to send it. You stay here—it's too hot to go out in the heat of the sun. I'll be back soon."

"I'll write to Grayson while you're gone," she said, glad to have the time alone.

Less than five minutes after Nevil left, Caroline heard a knock on her door. "Come in," she called, expecting a servant finally had come to clean the room.

As the door opened, she saw two fierce-looking men with clubs in hand. Terrified at the sight of them, she could not scream. Before she knew it, there was a wet gag in her mouth. It tasted like grog. They spoke to her in muffled voices; she did not understand a word. The next thing she knew she was being carried out the back door of the hotel and into the bushes. The men tied her hands tightly behind her back then pushed her forward, leading her toward Mission Hill. Slowly, she climbed the two hundred steps built into the side of the mountain, terrified by what was happening. Insects buzzed around her but she couldn't brush them away. She wished they would take the gag out of her mouth, tell her what was happening. Where were they taking her? Why had they kidnapped her? What had she done?

Chapter 16

As Caroline walked slowly up the mountain, she found herself climbing into thick mist. Perspiration poured from every part of her body and she wasn't certain whether it was from the excessive humidity or just fear. Then she realized that part of the reason she was sweating was the grog, for this had happened to her before.

It was difficult to believe that the sky was so blue in the town below, for as she ascended the steep climb, the cloud that hung over the mountain's peak became thicker and thicker. Nevil had told her that the line of the equator ran across the top of the mountain. She had said she had wanted to climb to the line but this was not how she'd planned to go.

Her thoughts were confused and she had trouble concentrating. She kept trying to think of Nevil's words—the natives wouldn't dare harm a government official or his wife. Then why were these men forcing her to come with them? What did they want with her? What were they going to do to her?

She was at the top of the mountain now but the mist was too thick to see where they were heading. Just as she thought she was regaining her sense of awareness, her captors stopped, took off her gag, and ordered her to drink from a pouch. She tasted the grog immediately but it was very much stronger than any she had had before. She began to feel weak and unsteady on her feet. She wanted to stop and rest. She was exhausted and felt she couldn't take another step. Mercilessly, the two men shoved her forward and forced her on.

She thought she saw Nevil then realized she must be hallucinating. Her thoughts rambled. The heat combined with the grog intensified her hallucinations. She had visions of her father standing on the pulpit and she could clearly hear him giving his last sermon: "For we wrestle not against flesh and blood, but against powers, against the rulers of the darkness of this world, against spiritual wickedness in high places." She wanted to call out to him but the gag imprisoned her words. If only she could draw on her faith with her father's strength. But all she could ask herself was, Why me, O Lord? Why me?

She tried unsuccessfully to speak through the dirty cloth, tried to say "I can't take another step." Then she fell to the ground.

The men stopped and mumbled something to each other. The older man removed her gag.

Then the younger of the two addressed her. *"Vaka singa,"* he began, and she understood he was calling her the one with hair like the sun. "You will walk now. You will rest at my village." His English was well-learned, yet he mouthed his words slowly, carefully enunciating each syllable.

"You speak English!" she said with complete surprise.

"I do."

"Then tell me where you're taking me, and why."

"I have told you where. Why is for my chief to explain."

Caroline stood up and began forging forward, wondering with each step how she was managing to move her legs. Her vision seemed blurred and again she began to have the sensation of floating above the ground. Several minutes later she stopped again. "Who are you?" she asked.

"We are the *Lovoni,* mountain people. Now walk."

Caroline continued down the mountain, afraid to stop again. Suddenly there was a clearing. They had arrived at

their compound—a large fenced-in area built into the side of
the mountain.

"You will change your clothes before you are brought to
our *Tui Lovoni,*" Caroline was told.

She looked down at her crisp, pink cotton gown and
touched the deep folds in her skirt. "Why?"

"Our *Tui Lovoni* does not like *Kaivavalagi* dress. You will
put on our clothes."

Her throat tightened as a heavily tattooed woman approached her. Caroline had already learned, that in Fiji genuine tattooing was found only on women, the absence of it
punished by the gods after death, but this woman seemed to
have more tattooing than most. Or was it that she had never
really studied a woman as closely as she studied this one? The
woman was bare-breasted and dressed only in a fringed *liku,*
tied around her waist. Caroline's hands became clammy as she
realized that this was what her captors expected her to wear.
There was no way that she would expose her breasts, not for
anyone. Now that her hands were free, it would be she who
tied the *liku,* and she would tie it around her chest and nowhere else.

She let the woman lead her to a small house at the far side
of the compound. Caroline felt utterly shamed and humiliated
when her clothes were taken from her. She would have given
anything to have been able to stop the woman who was now
oiling her entire body with what she assumed, by the smell,
was a coconut oil. Then she was given a handsomely deco-
rated brown and beige *liku.* Defiantly, she tied it around her
chest.

"*Seengah! Seengah!*" said the woman. Then in English, she
repeated, "No! No!"

"*Eeo. Eeo,*" said Caroline. "Yes. Yes."

The woman began jabbering so quickly that Caroline
couldn't understand a word. In the end, Caroline made it
clear that nothing could persuade her to wear the *liku* in the
traditional way.

Next the woman tried to comb Caroline's hair. There was

no way that the soft, silky blond strands would stand on end and resemble the coiffures of the Fijians.

The woman motioned and Caroline followed her. The chief's house was a fair distance away, but not far enough for Caroline. Her head was beginning to clear but still she was not ready to face the chief.

The sun was setting, and as Caroline moved slowly forward, she wondered what Nevil had done when he found her gone. Had he started to look for her at once? Or was he angry that she had gone from the room without leaving him a note? Would he suspect that she had been carried away by the mountain people? How could he? Who would he go to once he realized that she wasn't coming back? Would he find her in time?

Before she could ask herself another question, she was at the chief's house. It was an imposing structure, by far the largest in the settlement, and Caroline judged it to be at least one hundred feet long and nearly half as wide.

"Sinandrah," said the *Tui Lovoni.*

"How do you do," answered Caroline. She would not give him the satisfaction of letting him know that she had learned to speak even a word of his language. "Why have you brought me here?"

"There are many reasons," began the chief. "But first I must thank our Great Spirit for bringing you here safely."

He turned to a tall hulky man standing to his left and addressed him in a rapid tongue. Caroline didn't understand a word. The next thing she knew, the man was beating the *lali* —a large drum, hollowed out of a tree, that looked like a canoe. Within minutes seven men stood around her. Another *yaqona* ceremony was about to begin.

Caroline choked at the thought of having to drink more of the grog in this heat. She didn't want to lose control of her senses but she didn't dare insult the chief, and so she partook in the ceremony, being as careful as she could not to display her disgust. Throughout, she waited patiently to find out what was wanted of her, why she was here.

When the ceremony was finished, however, the chief did

not inform her as to the reasons for her capture. "There is time," he said simply. "Much time. First we eat. Tonight we have a grand *solevu*," he said, a wide grin of anticipation on his face.

"*Solevu?*" questioned Caroline.

"A feast, you would call it, or a get-together," he translated.

The man standing near the chief again began beating the *lali*. The chief stepped into the open air and Caroline followed. As if from nowhere, there suddenly appeared some sixty naked warriors. Their bodies were painted in black, red, and yellow, each trying to appear more savage than the next, and as Caroline watched them walk single file to the center of the compound, she became more and more terrified. The men were quickly joined by innumerable women and children. Within minutes she saw that in the front of the procession eighteen men were carrying three dead natives, each lashed on a long pole.

Caroline was mesmerized by the sight. There was a gruesome fascination in what she was witnessing, for though she wouldn't admit it to herself, deep inside she knew the fate of these dead men. They were bound with rope to poles about twelve feet long. It took three men at each end of the pole to carry the heavy weights. The men walked with a limping gait, bending their left knees almost to the ground in exact time with the victory war song they were singing.

The warriors proceeded to a large hut, used only on public occasions, and threw the dead bodies from their shoulders with savage triumphal cries.

The chief took Caroline by the arm, turning her so that she faced him. "The glory of our people is not so much in killing our enemy as in eating them," he said with great relish. "It is part of our religion," he continued. "The bodies are given us by the gods, not merely to be killed, but to be eaten."

Caroline's free hand automatically clutched her stomach. She swallowed hard, hoping to keep down the bile. The last thing she wanted was to vomit in front of the chief.

"Sit," said the chief.

Without a word Caroline dropped to the ground, seating herself on the large root of a coconut tree. She was grateful to be sitting. Her stomach was easier to control in that position.

The Lovoni priest made a short speech, of which Caroline barely understood a word, then continued to utter guttural sounds and shake himself throughout the entire ceremony.

About a hundred dancers appeared, making violent and distended motions with their limbs, prostrating themselves on the ground upon their backs, and springing again instantly to their places, all the while chanting war songs and yelling at the top of their voices while the *lali* beat out their rhythm.

Then a warrior walked over to one of the dead and ceremoniously cut off his head.

Caroline vomited at the sickening sight.

"You do not understand our ways," said the chief, smirking at her reaction.

A fire was set to the severed head, and within minutes the hair was burned off and the flesh so singed that the bones were easily scraped perfectly white.

Then the entrails and vitals were cut out and cleansed for cooking.

It was the most revolting scene Caroline had ever witnessed. Yet, paralyzed, immobile, she continued to watch. She wanted to vomit again but her stomach was empty. Only bitter bile reached her mouth.

A *lobu* or oven was then made in the earth—it was much the same as the Maoris' *hangi*—and Caroline wondered if the Maoris ate their enemy in the same way.

She wanted to turn away but couldn't help herself. Something made her continue watching the warriors as they dissected the three bodies. Then they wrapped the parts with banana leaves, to prevent the flesh from falling off the bones in the event of overbaking, and threw the pieces upon the fire.

One head rolled a few feet away from the fire and a young warrior grabbed it and stealthily went behind a tree, where he began eating the raw brains. As soon as he was discovered, he was compelled to give up his booty and return it to the fire.

The process of cutting and cleaning lasted about two hours,

and then it took another four hours before the food was ready. The natives seemed to revel in the smell of the burning flesh. Caroline thought it a repulsive odor. Not only did it continue to make her ill, it made her absolutely certain that she would never eat meat again—any meat.

It was well after midnight before the chief's slaves were ready to open the oven and serve dinner. The chief, as would be expected, was given the choice parts of the bodies—the tongues and the livers. Then he was given a head—an unspeakably hideous head, staring with dull, wide-open eyes. He took a handsomely carved four-pronged fork and began digging out the meat from the skull. Then he took a three-pronged fork and began eating a liver.

A slave walked over to Caroline and handed her an arm. She looked at the grotesque limb and shook her head. "I'm not hungry," she said.

"We need to fatten you up," said the chief, laughing at his little joke.

"You're not going to eat me too!"

"Not if you do what I say." He paused. "Perhaps you would like some of our victims' teeth . . . they make beautiful necklaces."

Caroline shook her head, the thought disgusting her. "Please tell me why I'm here. What have I done?"

"Tomorrow we talk," said the chief. "It is late. Tonight we sleep."

When the gruesome festivities ended, Caroline was taken to a small hut. She had eaten nothing but hunger was not on her mind. She could only think, and wonder, if she would ever see Nevil again.

"Here," pointed the woman who led her. In the corner of the hut was an immense platform, about three feet off the floor, covered with eight layers of cream-colored mats Caroline recognized as being made of *voi voi*—a native flax—and fringed with tufts of red and blue wool. At one end of the mat was what looked like a miniature bamboo stool.

"What's that for?" Caroline asked.

"Head," answered the woman.

"Head?"

"Eeo," said the woman. "No move hair."

"Ah," answered Caroline, understanding that the uncomfortable looking thing was a headrest, sufficiently high off the ground to keep from ruffling a Fijian's headdress when sleeping. Without even trying it, Caroline knew she would not find it comfortable. She longed for her soft down pillow.

It was close to noon the following day before the chief sent for Caroline. Fearfully, she crossed the compound to his house. She knew, at last, the time had come. Her fate was about to be decided. If only Nevil would come.

As she walked across the grass, she wondered how she could have ever cared about Nevil's infidelities. What difference did it make if he had an encounter with a sea captain? As long as her husband loved her, nothing else was important. More than anything she wanted Nevil by her side. Now. He would know what to do, he would get her out of this horrendous situation.

But Nevil didn't know what to do. When he realized that Caroline had not just gone for a walk, he became frantic. He didn't know whom to approach for help, because he didn't have even the vaguest idea of what had happened to his wife.

Finally, at sunset, he went to the *Tui Levuka's* home. Before he could ask a single question, he was subjected to the greeting of a grog ceremony.

Each minute seemed to take an hour as he waited for everyone to drink their grog. He took one bowl but refused more. The last thing he wanted was for his brain to be dulled. Grog affected him much as laudanum had. It had been difficult enough for him to stop that, he had no intention of becoming addicted to anything else, especially now, when he needed to think clearly.

"My wife's disappeared," he began. "She's gone. Someone's taken her away."

"Vaka singa is gone?" asked the chief.

"Yes, the one with hair like the sun is gone," answered Nevil.

"And what can I do?" asked the *Tui Levuka*.

Nevil was irritated by the way the chief took his time in formally asking questions. "You can tell me where to start looking for her."

The chief lifted another bowl of grog to his lips, drained the vessel, then tossed it into the middle of the room for a refill. "How can you be certain someone has taken her?"

"Because Caroline wouldn't just leave. Where would she go? I've looked all over town, she's nowhere."

"Lost, perhaps."

"That's impossible," said Nevil, his frustration mirrored in his tone. "Levuka's too small a town for anyone to get lost."

"She may have wandered down the beach, toward Nasova."

"If she were going for a walk she would have left me a note. I know my wife, she wouldn't just leave."

"Neenee toma tah!" Nevil heard the chief's spokesman say.

"Yes, I am an angry man," Nevil repeated the phrase. "I want my wife back." He turned back to the chief. "Whoever has taken her will be punished. I will see to it that my government shows no leniency."

The *Tui Levuka* was silent for a long time. He drank another bowl of grog, then pulled on his long black beard, deep in thought. Finally, he spoke: "Cakobau has banished traders from Levuka. He may be behind this. By taking your wife, he knows you will meet his demands."

"But I'm not a trader."

"Yes, but you are the Commercial Agent for Fiji . . . you are in charge of trade for your government."

"But Cakobau is in Bau . . . how could he have arranged this?"

"The Lovoni want to rule the island of Ovalau. Cakobau is their high chief . . . you would, I think, call him King. If he has promised the *Tui Lovoni* that he will be Chief of Ovalau, there is nothing that man wouldn't do. Cakobau would like to oust me, too, but I am loved by my people. They will do nothing to harm me."

"Where does the *Tui Lovoni* live?" asked Nevil, feeling at last that he was learning something.

"They are mountain people, they live on the other side." He hesitated for a moment and then added, "Tomorrow I can send men to look for her."

"Tomorrow! Why not now?"

"The sun is setting. Dark will soon be upon us. My men will not go into the mountains in the dark."

"But they could kill her if we wait."

"No. They want her alive. They have no power to talk to you if she is dead." He turned to his spokesman and nodded once.

"Follow me," said the spokesman.

The meeting was over.

Frustrated and angry, Nevil returned to the hotel. He knew it was pointless to begin the search alone. He didn't know the terrain and he was unarmed. Like it or not, he would have to wait until sunrise.

For the first time in months his old thigh wound began to ache. Hoping to obliterate the pain as well as to relax, he took several shots of whiskey and went to bed.

Caroline listened patiently as the Lovoni chief explained why she had been captured. "We need arms. Ovalau is our island. I am its chief. We must raid Levuka and capture the man who calls himself *Tui Levuka*. He must die. Only then will I rule as *Tui Ovalau*."

"And you expect my husband to get you arms?"

"Yes. Arms in return for you."

"But if the *Tui Levuka* finds out that Nevil's supplying you with weapons, his men will kill. . . ."

"I hope not," said the Lovoni chief with a smirk on his face. "You see, if he dies, so do you."

"Me? Why?"

"Because it is our custom to strangle widows."

Caroline's hand reached for her neck. As she thought of her fate, she began to tremble. She knew what this man did with dead people. There seemed to be nothing that gave these people more joy than eating human flesh.

"You would then be buried with your husband's bones," he added.

"What do you want me to do?" she asked at last.

"Soon, I will ask you to write to your husband, to tell him my demands and to ask when the weapons can be delivered. Once they are in my hands, you will be freed."

"But that can take several months. He has no weapons here."

"Then I advise you to write as soon as I request the letter." His tone of supercilious sweetness disappeared, his voice cold and harsh: "You will not leave here until we have what we want."

"When are you going to contact my husband?" Caroline asked, no longer able to hide the fear she felt.

"We will wait for the new moon."

"When's that?"

The chief thought for a moment. "In a fortnight . . . no, in two."

"A month! But why so long?"

"We must give him time to worry about the one with the hair like the sun. Then we can be certain he will do what we ask."

"Please, please let me go to him. I will get you anything you want. Just let me go."

Her hysteria made the chief laugh—it was the reaction he had hoped for and it convinced him that the longer he held his prisoner captive, the more amenable her husband would be to his demands.

"Nevil will find me here, I know he will!" Caroline screamed.

"You are not staying here," the chief said. He turned to his spokesman and mumbled something.

"Where are you taking me?" she cried.

Before Caroline could utter another word, a slave had stuffed a cloth soaked in grog into her mouth. At the same time, another slave bound her hands behind her back.

In answer to the terror in her eyes, the chief said simply, "I am having you taken to a place away from my compound, where I know no one will look for you. For now, my people will not hurt you. You will be brought back here at the new moon to write that letter to your husband, then I will decide what shall be done with you."

Chapter 17

DURING THE NEXT TWO WEEKS, TIME STOOD STILL. THE only way Caroline could differentiate one day from the next was that night had come and gone. She tried to keep track of time but this was almost impossible because the only liquid she was given to drink was grog. She actually grew to like the opiate, finding that if she absorbed enough of it, it not only lessened her fears, but calmed her, and at moments, even in her frightened state, she still felt euphoric.

Naronga, the woman who guarded her, was a remarkably handsome Fijian with comely features. She was a kind person and did all she could to make her prisoner comfortable. But every time she began picking the lice out of her head and then cracking the vermin between her teeth, Caroline thought she would be sick. She now knew this disgusting practice was common throughout Fiji but she still couldn't bear to watch it. Yet she understood that this was their way, and it did not make her like Naronga less—for the woman was good to Caroline and sympathetic to her plight. Naronga's speech had a soft lilt and when Caroline was awake, she enjoyed talking to her. But not even Naronga could make the wretched situation tolerable.

By the third day Caroline was so bitten by mosquitoes and other insects that she didn't know where to scratch first. And when she did scratch, she drew blood, attracting even more insects to her.

Each afternoon two slaves would bring food. It was during one of these visits that Caroline learned that several men sent by the *Tui Levuka* were looking for her. For a moment she felt a surge of hope, then realized it was useless. No one would be able to find her in these woods. Yet there was still some comfort in knowing that Nevil was searching for her.

One afternoon, while Caroline was listening to Naronga, an idea came to her. Naronga had been married to the chief of the nearby island of Batiki. Her husband had been killed in battle and as was the custom, she was to be buried alive with his corpse. She had fled to Ovalau and come to her uncle, the *Tui Lovoni*. The chief had granted her his protection because she was with child.

"I am going to have a baby," said Caroline. "Please help me to escape. Please let me go back to my husband."

"If only I could," said Naronga, "but I owe my uncle my life. I cannot go against his orders."

Caroline could see that she had touched Naronga, but the plea hadn't been strong enough. "Please—"

Naronga held up her hand to silence Caroline. "We will talk another time," she promised, and walked from the hut.

Though nothing more was said, Caroline knew she'd failed. Naronga would do nothing to help plan an escape.

Exactly twenty-six days later, two tall warriors, clubs in hand, arrived at Caroline's small hut. "It is time to leave," said one, taking Caroline by the arm and leading her outside.

"Are you taking me to your chief?" asked Caroline.

The men did not reply, they merely led her forward.

"Naronga . . . isn't Naronga coming with me?"

Still there was no reply.

Caroline looked around. At least she could say good-bye to

her. "Please," her voice pleaded. "Naronga has been good to me, made me comfortable. I want to thank her. Where is she?" Fear crept over Caroline. What had they done to the woman? Who were these men? "Did *Tui Lovoni* send you to get me?"

"Silence!" ordered the man who had spoken before.

Caroline walked on without uttering another sound. The men were leading her up the mountain. The direction was wrong. This wasn't the way she had come when she had been brought here. All she could think of was that she'd been captured by yet another tribe.

It was a long, slow climb to the top of the mountain, and every few minutes the men stopped to look around, to make certain they weren't being followed. Once they reached the thick cloud that hung almost constantly over the mountain's summit, the men seemed to relax.

"We won't be seen now," whispered one.

"*Carloo*, the Great Spirit, is watching over us," said the other, addressing his remark to Caroline.

"Please tell me! Where are you taking me?"

A noise in the thicket made all three freeze. The man who had spoken last put his hand over Caroline's mouth to silence her. She nodded that she understood and he released his grip. The other man moved stealthily, trying to follow the sound.

"It must have been an animal," he whispered when he returned several minutes later.

"Not a word," said the other, speaking softly into Caroline's ear. He gave her a gentle push and the three continued up the mountain.

Caroline did not know what to think. If these were the *Tui Lovoni's* men, why were they so fearful?

What seemed a very long time later, they reached the summit of the mountain and began their descent. Suddenly they were out of the cloud. The sun was shining brilliantly. Before her was deep blue water, turning turquoise as it met the sea. And there were the reefs she had seen from Levuka. She was certain they were the same reefs, they had to be.

"Your husband is waiting for you," said one of the men. He

was smiling broadly, pleased that his mission had been successfully accomplished.

Tears streamed down Caroline's face. Though she was tired and weak, she found the strength to begin running down the mountain.

"You must go more slowly," said the man. "The ground can be slippery. You must walk carefully or you will fall."

Caroline slowed her pace but only slightly. And then she saw Nevil coming up the mountain to meet her.

"Oh, Nevil! Nevil!" she cried as she rushed to his arms. "I never thought I'd see you again. How did you find me?"

He silenced her with his lips and she realized how much he loved her, knowing clearly that his infidelity had nothing to do with his feelings for her. It was an embrace that neither would ever forget, a moment of love they shared deeper than any emotion either of them had ever felt.

Cakobau's message had been clear—he wanted the Commercial Agent out of Levuka immediately—and Nevil knew that if he didn't leave at once there would be further reprisals, with his wife as the target.

Four days later, therefore, Caroline and Nevil left Levuka. They were taken in a long canoe back to the island of Viti Levu, only this time, instead of going to Suva they traveled up the Rewa River, past Rewa—which itself was a group of villages merging into one another and strung for a mile and a half along the river bank—and on to Wainibokasi Landing.

The Rewa River carved its way through mangrove swamps. Small villages dotted its shores. Caroline was fascinated by the way the roots of the mangrove dropped down from tall branches, arching gracefully into the river below.

"Life will be easier here," Nevil told his wife. "The Rewa chiefs, from the high chief down, are our friends. Cakobau had his half brother, who was a Rewa chief, killed last year and then proceeded to destroy most of the settlements on the Rewa delta. Now the Rewa people want revenge."

"I don't understand, Nevil. If we stay with the Rewa people, how do you ever expect to negotiate with Cakobau?"

"It will take time, but I'll find a way."

There were no hotels in Wainibokasi, but it was not difficult to enlist the help of several Fijian young men to build Caroline and Nevil a shelter, a small thatched hut which would temporarily meet their needs. Two weeks ago Caroline would have objected to living in so primitive a fashion, but she was so grateful to be alive and among friends that she didn't complain.

Time passed slowly for Caroline, one day melding into the next. Natives worked at a leisurely pace in the intense heat, never rushing to complete anything. Caroline found life boring and tedious—she had read the few books she'd brought with her over and over; she was tired of collecting ferns, certain she had a specimen of everything around, and there was little else to do. Nevil, too, found each day more frustrating than the next. He wanted to contact Cakobau again, to have an audience with him and complete his mission, but making these arrangements was not an easy task, and as the weeks turned into months and a year passed, it was clear that Nevil had still achieved nothing.

The summer hurricane season, punctuated by a severe tornado, had played havoc with the Rewa delta area, and now the natives were busying themselves rebuilding their villages. Somehow, Caroline's house had not been touched, so she didn't even have this problem to help alleviate her endless hours of boredom.

From time to time Nevil would take her by boat to Suva, where he had business to conduct. On these days Caroline would usually visit the Bêche-de-Mer fishermen. She found it fascinating to watch them gathering the sea slugs so plentiful on the reefs of Fiji. The black and dark-red slimy creatures that looked like large leeches were sold to merchants from all over the world and were in such great demand among the wealthy classes of China that the profits were extremely attractive.

Caroline never tired of watching the curing process. The slugs were collected and then taken into an open shed with a thatched roof. Here, they were put in large iron pots similar to the try-pots used by whalers. Then they were parboiled in salt water for about ten minutes. The process was repeated and they were removed to a smoke house for curing. Four days later, the properly cured slugs looked like strips of long shoe leather.

"What do the Chinese do with them?" Caroline asked the Fijian in charge of the smoke house.

"Make soup," he answered, and went back to his work.

Later that afternoon, as they were returning home, Nevil explained to Caroline that the Chinese believed Beche-de-Mer had great restorative properties. But nothing he said could convince her that eating the dried, smoked slugs was appealing.

When they arrived at their small village, they were told that a letter had arrived for them. It was from Grayson.

Caroline was so excited she could hardly break the seal on the envelope. "He must have gotten my letter," she said. "Mail does reach here . . . even in the middle of nowhere." She began reading the letter, smiling with delight. "Amiria's had another baby, Nevil. A little boy. They've named him Turi." She looked at Nevil with a longing in her eyes. "How I wish we could go back. Do you think we'll have to stay much longer?"

Nevil shrugged his shoulders noncommittally. He, too, wanted to return to Auckland, but somehow, no matter how he tried, he couldn't succeed in meeting with Cakobau and settling the problems of Levuka.

"Grayson says he's thinking of giving up surveying," Caroline said a few minutes later. "I wonder what he's planning to do?"

"Knowing your brother," Nevil answered, "he's already got something definite in mind."

"I suppose," said Caroline, more interested in the rest of the letter than her husband's comment.

"Do you know tonight's Christmas Eve?" asked Nevil as a pleasant aroma of steaming pig wafted through their hut.

"Would you believe me if I told you I really forgot?" asked Caroline. "At least it will be better than last Christmas," she said, remembering the horrors of her days as prisoner.

For the most part the Rewa people had been converted to Christianity, and in their own way they celebrated the appropriate holidays.

They walked outside to the square in the middle of the village and watched several natives preparing for the feast. But the heat of the day had still not lifted, and most of the men, women, and children were lazily sitting around smoking. Caroline always found it interesting to watch the Fijians make their small cigarettes, folding leaf tobacco in a slip of dead banana leaf.

"I can't believe it's good for children to smoke," she said. "When I was a little girl, I was told cigarettes stunt growth."

"The Fijians are so tall, they probably don't care."

"Oh, Nevil, that's silly. I'm certain they just don't know. How long have they been smoking? Twenty or thirty years, not more."

"That's true. But I don't think we should be the ones to tell them."

Someone began beating the *lali* and then several men gathered to form a small orchestra. They began the entertainment by playing songs on conch shell, bamboo nose-flutes, Pandean pipes, and a Jew's harp made of a strip of bamboo. Within minutes the entire village was at hand, clapping vigorously, singing and dancing.

The performance was an impressive one, and for the moment, made Caroline less homesick.

The *lobu* was not opened until midnight, and the festive meal, which lasted until almost dawn, included pig, a fine boar, and a variety of fish, as well as turtle, kumara, steamed bananas, and banana bread. Grog, as always, was plentiful, and Caroline and Nevil drank so much that by the time they returned to their hut they were both in a stupor.

It was well after noon when Caroline awoke. Looking at Nevil sleeping peacefully, she silently thanked God that her husband was by her side. In her year in Fiji, Nevil had been wonderful to her, understanding her loneliness and boredom. "I love you," she whispered, not really wanting to awaken him.

He stirred and mumbled "I love you, too," then turned over and went back to sleep.

As much as Caroline hated life on this South Pacific island, she feared returning to Auckland, dreading that once they were back, Nevil would return to his old ways.

The year that followed was fruitless and frustrating. Nevil was constantly in touch with Cakobau's messenger to Bau, but Cakobau wasn't ready to receive Nevil. The High Chief refused to allow Nevil to come to Bau for the island was sacred, and every time Cakobau promised to meet Nevil, the High Chief's plans changed. And during all this time, guerilla warfare in the Rewa delta mounted—Cakobau's warriors fighting to gain control of the area.

The scarcity of food became a serious problem, and Nevil was not immune to the war—if his village had little food, there was no way he could arrange to obtain more.

Last September, Cakobau had burned Rewa for the third time, and Nevil feared that at any moment the chief could decide to march farther up the Rewa River and conquer the entire delta. With this in mind Nevil constantly urged Caroline to return to New Zealand, but she refused to leave him. She was not afraid of the powerful *Tui Viti* for she knew that warring tribes always sent word to their enemy to warn the women and children to stay inside before the battle began. Furthermore, as difficult as life was in Fiji, she was still happier here than she had been in Auckland.

Mail kept arriving from Governor Grey. He was impatient to see trade resumed with Levuka, but there was little Nevil could do. Finally, in January 1851, Nevil's break came. The great *Tui Viti*, Chief of all Fiji, was coming to discuss terms with Nevil. In just one day they were to meet at Laucala, the settlement at the mouth of the Rewa River.

Caroline had never seen Nevil so overjoyed.

"He won't disappoint me, Caroline. Not this time, not when he's planning the meeting for tomorrow. If all goes well, we can sail for home as soon as the next ship arrives."

"How can you be so confident that your meeting will be a success?" Caroline asked.

"I'm certain it will be . . . without question. I know for a fact that Cakobau wants our traders back on Levuka. He just wants to be persuaded, that's all, so that it doesn't look as if he made a mistake. He needs our merchandise and munitions. He misses them. You'll see, it will be an easy matter to convince him to let our people return."

The following morning Caroline and Nevil went to Laucala. They arrived before eight o'clock, and as they reached the shore, they could see the Bau fleet riding at anchor less than seventy yards away. There must have been one hundred outrigger war canoes, their tall triangular sails of yellow matting taut against the breeze.

"Why did he bring his whole army?" asked Caroline, her fear transparent.

"I'm not certain," said Nevil. "Look," he pointed, "that must be Cakobau's canoe."

Coming slowly forward, towering over the other canoes in the regatta, was a double canoe at least one hundred feet long.

A low, hooting blast from a conch shell was heard, announcing the arrival of the chief. And then there was silence as Cakobau's canoe pulled up to the landing and the great *Tui Viti* disembarked. Everyone on shore prostrated themselves before the chief, it being forbidden to look the *Tui Viti* in the face.

For a moment Nevil bowed his head out of courtesy, then he approached the chief. Cakobau was a tall man with a full white beard and slightly slanting eyes. Nevil's first thought was that he looked more like an Egyptian pharaoh than a Fijian chief. "How do you do," said Nevil. His voice sounded steady but inwardly he did not feel the strength he exhibited. "I am Sir Nevil Holbrooke, and this is my wife, Lady Holbrooke."

Caroline nodded politely, not knowing whether or not to extend her hand.

The chief stared at Nevil just long enough to make the foreigner feel uncomfortable, then handed him a whale's tooth reddened with tumeric. Nevil knew it to be a Fijian token of respect and thanked the chief.

"Where and when may we talk?" Nevil asked.

"Later," Cakobau replied. "Now is the time to prepare for our feast." He paused for a moment. "Let me explain," he began. "My name, Cakobau, means Bau is destroyed. I saved that island from the hands of rebel invaders. Now I am here to claim the Rewa as mine. Today is the ceremony of *soro,* atonement to the chief. It is time for the people here to humble themselves before me. Tomorrow, you and I shall speak."

Nevil made no comment, but his face was tense. He turned back to Caroline, wondering if he would ever succeed in convincing this arrogant man to do anything.

"Must we stay for this?" Caroline whispered. "I have a feeling they're going to be cooking people."

Nevil patted her shoulder understandingly. "Don't worry, the Rewa people aren't cannibals anymore."

"Yes, but Cakobau and the others from Bau are famous for their love of human flesh."

Before she could speak further, a score of men were being led off one of the canoes. Their hands were roped behind their backs and it was at once obvious that they were prisoners.

Caroline and Nevil stepped back as they watched the procession. After the prisoners, came seven young women carrying baskets of nothing but earth.

"That must be a token of the land they've given to their conqueror," whispered Nevil.

Next came an unending line of men carrying small offerings; warriors with wooden spears and clubs oiled and hung with hibiscus flowers; older men dragging leafy hampers of taro, breadfruit, and yams; and men with smaller bundles of salt, arrowroot, and tobacco. Then came eight young boys, each holding a green drinking coconut, followed by the final procession of men carrying a dozen cooked pigs.

It was apparent to Nevil that Caroline had been right, there were too many people present to be fed by twelve pigs. There would have to be more to the feast than that.

The ceremony began with the usual drinking of *yaqona* grog and thanking the Great Spirit for watching over them. Then the prisoners were made to crawl on their chests and stomachs toward the chief. Caroline shuddered at the sight.

"You do not understand our ways," said Cakobau as he saw her cringe. "It is only proper that my enemy prostrate themselves before me. I defeated their army. They were rebels, now they are mine," he said gleefully.

He turned back to the line of men crawling toward him. One obstinate prisoner refused to move. Cakobau shouted something to his priest, and the old priest immediately went to the prisoner and hit him with his staff, ordering him forward.

"Never! Never!" the prisoner cried in Fijian.

The priest did not need to wait for further orders. Precedence for this kind of behavior had long ago been set. Two warriors emerged as if from nowhere and handed the priest a bale of dried coconut leaves. They then helped the old man bind the prisoner's shoulders to the bale so that the leaves jutted out some feet on either side.

The crowd began to cheer as the priest ceremoniously lighted the dried leaves.

Caroline put her hands over her eyes—she could not watch. Nevil cradled her head on his shoulder and stared down at the ground. He knew there was nothing either one of them could do.

The horror of watching a man being burned alive was surpassed only by the horrendous sight of onlookers cheering on every moment of the barbaric event. Even more shocking to Caroline, the women seemed to be cheering the loudest and with the greatest enthusiasm.

"That should teach you to stay on my side," jeered Cakobau.

Nevil, as before, remained silent.

Even after the man had burned to death, the applauding did not cease. The nineteen prisoners who remained were ordered to their feet. At a single command of Cakobau, his warriors began stoning the men. Then, as if ordered by a silent signal, the warriors rushed upon the prisoners and clubbed them to death.

Caroline buried her head throughout the horrifying ritual. Nevil, too, kept his eyes averted from the scene. He held his wife close to him, trying to give her as much support as he could, attempting in every way he knew how to protect her, wanting desperately to take her away from this so-called ceremony, but he knew he couldn't leave.

"You do not understand," said Cakobau, seeing the reaction of the foreigners. "Do you *Kaivavalagi* not yet know, after being here for several years, that the glory of war is not in killing our prisoners, but in eating them? That is why our gods give us prisoners."

"You will be punished by *our* God," said Nevil emphatically. "It's a sin to take another's life."

"Silence!" ordered Cakobau. "If you wish to discuss your traders returning to Levuka, you will not criticize our ways."

The *soro* proceeded much as the ceremony Caroline had witnessed when she was prisoner of the Lovoni. The horrors of that nightmare had been washed away by Nevil's love. Now the memory of those days returned, more gruesome than before. Even though Caroline was awake, vivid, almost paralyzing images of her days in captivity flashed before her eyes —it was worse than being in a nightmare. She shook her head, trying to rid her mind of the grotesque thoughts, yet she could not. She wanted to close her eyes, to hide from what was going on in front of her, but that was even worse. When her eyes were closed, the images were even sharper. "Can we leave?" she finally whispered to Nevil.

"No!" Cakobau replied. Her voice had carried farther than she realized. "You will not be so disrespectful."

The long evening passed slowly, and when at last it was over, Caroline again was grateful for the intoxicating effects of all the grog she had consumed. By the time she reached her hut, she could barely see where she was going. Nevil helped her undress. Almost immediately she fell into a deep, drugged sleep, a sleep free of dreams.

The following morning, Nevil left the hut at least two hours before Caroline awoke. She was surprised at how late it was but pleased that the conference was already underway. Silently, she prayed that Nevil and Cakobau would conclude all arrangements in one session. All she wanted was to go back to New Zealand, to return to the land of civilized people.

She was still engaged in prayer, earnestly beseeching God to free them from this barbaric island, when Nevil entered.

"I've done it! Our traders can return to Levuka!" He threw his arms around his wife and kissed her excitedly. "We can leave, Caroline. We can go home."

Caroline was almost speechless. She couldn't believe her ears. "My prayers were answered," was all she could say. And then, through tears of joy, she asked, "When?"

"I'll take a canoe to Suva today and see when the next ship is expected in port. We'll be on it, I promise."

"Oh, Nevil, I love you," she said, holding him tightly. "I never thought we'd get out of here alive." She wiped her eyes before continuing. "May I go with you?"

Nevil hesitated, thinking it best that he go alone.

"Please," she pleaded. "I don't want to be here without you, not with Cakobau and his men still around."

Nevil knew that no one would bring harm to her, but her fear was so great that he didn't have the heart to refuse her. "Dress quickly," he said, smiling. "I'll make arrangements for a canoe."

"Thank you, darling," she called as he left. "I'll be ready before you return."

She took a clean *liku* and tied it around her chest, and as she did so the delightful thought came to mind that soon she would again be wearing her beautiful gowns, with petticoats and chemises, fancy shoes and bonnets. Even the tight-fitting corsets she had so hated would now be a pleasure to wear. "Oh, how wonderful it will be to return," she said aloud, reveling in the happy moment.

Chapter 18

WARM WINDS AND SUNNY SKIES FOLLOWED THE *Amity* from Fiji to New Zealand, and during her two weeks at sea, Caroline glowed with an inner happiness and deep feelings of contentment. When she saw Nevil talking to Captain Bell, it did not concern her in the least. She was secure in the knowledge that her husband loved her.

This time when the ship sailed into the Bay of Islands, there were no feelings of fear, no anxieties about what tomorrow might bring. This time she was able to enjoy fully the magnificent panorama of the bay, the glistening emerald water dotted as if with verdant jewels.

And when the ship sailed on to Auckland, her contentment became charged with excitement, joyful anticipation of their homecoming.

The house on O'Connell Street seemed larger than Caroline remembered, like a mansion compared to the tiny thatched hut she and Nevil had called their home.

"I can hardly wait to go inside," she said as she ran up the three steps to the verandah. She stopped abruptly and turned back to Nevil. "Is that Acting Secretary and his wife still here?" she asked, a mildly sarcastic tone in her voice. She had never wanted them living in *her* home and she certainly didn't want them there now.

"Didn't I tell you?" answered Nevil. "The Harpers returned to England last year. Grey told me in one of his dispatches. I thought you knew."

Caroline sighed with relief and smiled as she unlatched the front door. "Oh, Nevil!" she exclaimed, looking into the dark house. "We're home."

Before he could say a word, she rushed around, opening the shutters and the windows, letting the bright sunlight stream into all the rooms. The air was dank and musty, but the odor didn't bother her in the least. Anything was better than the putrid smell of burning human flesh.

"I can hardly wait to see Grayson and Amiria and the babies. Not that Hone is a baby anymore, but you know what I mean."

"Take it easy, my dear. There'll be plenty of time to see everyone. Let's go upstairs and unpack before we do anything."

"Upstairs?" she said, a mischievous gleam in her eyes.

"Later," he answered warmly. "As soon as I unpack a few things, I must go over to Government House. I have to see Grey and be reinstated as Colonial Secretary."

"I'm disappointed," said Caroline, mounting the stairs. But she had happiness written all over her face—nothing could dampen her spirits now that she was home.

At two o'clock that afternoon Caroline had finally finished unpacking. She could hardly wait to surprise Grayson with her arrival. She ran nearly all the way, barely realizing how out of breath she was. She knocked on the door, scarcely able to contain her excitement, wanting to rush inside and throw her arms around her brother.

"Yes," said the elderly matron who answered the door.

Caroline sized up the woman quickly. By her elegant dress, it was apparent she was the lady of the house and not a servant.

"I'm looking for Grayson Wickham," Caroline said. "I'm his sister. This is the address I was given."

"Mr. Wickham has moved to Dunedin," the woman explained.

"Dunedin! Where's that?"

"It's a new town in the South Island." She turned from the door and went over to the small intarsia table which stood against the far wall of her entrance hall. She took an envelope from the drawer and returned to Caroline. "He said you'd come and asked me to give you this."

In one brief moment all Caroline's happiness seemed to have been shattered like broken glass, her heart pierced by sharp slivers of pain. How far was Dunedin? Would she ever see her brother again? But she asked no questions, she merely thanked the woman as graciously as possible and left.

Caroline walked slowly toward a nearby lamppost, leaned against the sturdy pole for support, and took a long deep breath. Only then did she have the courage to open the red wax seal and begin to read Grayson's words. A film of tears quickly blurred her vision as she realized how far Dunedin really was—eight hundred and forty-five miles by land from Auckland, plus six to eight hours—depending upon the winds —by boat across Cook's Strait. "I'll never see him again," she said aloud. She began to weep, barely able to continue reading.

Dunedin's still just a rustic village, with a population of only about eight hundred, but one day it will be a most prosperous city. Already it's being called the little Edinburgh at the Antipodes. The harbor is spacious, the water deep; I am convinced it will become a major port. And the hills that encircle the city have majesty and beauty such as nothing I've ever seen. There are those who call the town a disgusting hole, too bad for convicts and without one redeeming quality. But these are people with no foresight. I can envision Dunedin ten years from now and I can't imagine living elsewhere.

Amiria is not too happy here because there are few Maoris in the area. She, like the rest of her people, doesn't like the cold weather, but I can't plan my life on the elements. I hated working for Felton Mathew, and when I had an opportunity to work at Tiger Beer, I couldn't turn it down.

You must come to visit us and see Hone. He has grown into a most handsome lad, with blue-gray eyes and shiny black hair. He's a real Pakeha now and I want to begin calling him John. Amiria objects terribly, so I only use the name when she's not around. Turi, unfortunately, is *her* son. He'll never be one of us, but one out of two isn't bad, so I can't complain.

Caroline was furious at how Grayson described his family. She folded the letter and put it back into the envelope without finishing it. She was aghast at what a bigot her brother had become. She couldn't understand why he had children with a Maori woman if this was the way he felt.

Yet, as she walked towards home, she could not help but wonder what Grayson was doing now.

Grayson stood in the office of Buck Freedman, his sandy hair tousled as if he'd been out in the wind.

"There's a big future for you here," said Buck. "I'm not a well man, as you know."

Grayson nodded.

"And I have no sons," Buck continued. "You're a bright young man, Grayson, and you learn quickly. One day soon I'd like you to take over Tiger Beer." The short portly man leaned back in his chair, pausing for effect. "What would really make me happy, is to see you marry my daughter . . . then Tiger Beer would be yours."

"Margery Joy is lovely," said Grayson. A life of wealth and opulence flashed before his eyes, then he thought of Buck's daughter—not only was she Jewish, but she was a sickly girl with sallow coloring and dull, mousy-brown hair. She was hardly the type Grayson would have chosen on his own to be his wife. But the prospect of owning Tiger Beer did a lot to compensate for a homely woman. "It would be a privilege to be her husband," he said barely a moment later.

"There's just one thing," Buck said, his voice suddenly more gruff than usual, and very firm. "You'll have to give up your woman. My daughter must have a loyal, devoted husband."

"That will be no problem," answered Grayson without hesitation. Then he thought of Hone. John was his son, not Amiria's. He wanted to tell Buck about Hone, to ask him if he could keep this son, but he thought better of it. He would let Hone go now. Once he was married, he was certain he could persuade Margery to let him send for the youngster.

"Then you'll speak to that woman at once?"

"Tonight," said Grayson.

"Margery Joy must never know of our arrangement," Buck added. "I'll invite you to dinner and expect you to handle things from there. You're to court her for a suitable time, then propose. If she ever finds out about this conversation, you'll get nothing."

"Of course," Grayson replied.

"Once you know my daughter, I'm certain you'll grow to love her as I do. She may not be the most glamorous young lady in Dunedin, but she's a wonderful girl, she'll make a fine wife." He rose, indicating that the meeting was over. Grayson left the office and went back to work.

Caroline did not finish her brother's letter until she returned home. As she read his closing words, she felt a dull ache within her. She sensed that he was going to send Amiria away and she promised herself that when Amiria returned to the north, their friendship would not be hampered by Grayson's unforgivable behavior.

By the time Nevil returned home, Caroline was busying herself with preparations for dinner. As her horrible experiences in Fiji faded into the past, she'd slowly begun to eat meat again. As she stood in the kitchen at the back of the house, she wished that the haughty Mathilda were back. Caroline had sent a note to the cook at once, but as yet the woman had not replied.

Nevil kissed his wife on the back of her neck. "It's all settled," he said enthusiastically. "Grey's reinstated me. Everything will be as before."

"That's wonderful," said Caroline.

"What's wrong?" Nevil could see by the look on Caroline's face and the sadness in her voice that something had happened.

"Grayson's gone . . . to Dunedin. Oh, Nevil, I'll never see him now that he's so far." She did not relate the details of the letter to her husband, for although she was furious at her brother, her sense of loyalty was greater than her anger.

"Perhaps we'll go there one day," said Nevil understandingly, and then returned to discussing Grey and the events of the day.

The first day back had not been easy for Caroline, but as the weeks passed, she quickly organized her household staff and began living as she had before. She contacted Dr. Philson and resumed her work at the hospital.

More than seven months later, while she was taking an inventory of the hospital linens, she saw a young woman being carried into a nearby ward. She recognized her at once. "Amiria!" Caroline gasped.

Amiria was covered with blood. It was obvious she had been in a serious accident. "What happened?" Caroline asked the young man who had brought Amiria into the hospital.

"A horse went wild," he said. "No one saw exactly what happened . . . all I can tell you is that she was trampled."

"Amiria," Caroline said softly, walking beside the man.

Amiria didn't answer. She just looked at Caroline but didn't try to speak.

"Is Grayson with you?"

Amiria closed her eyes at the sound of his name and Caroline knew that her fears had been well-founded.

Many days passed before Amiria told Caroline what had happened in Dunedin. "I do have the children," she said, "but

I am afraid Grayson will try to take Hone from me. He loves him, you know, he really does."

"He can't do that," Caroline said, adamantly. "You're his mother."

"I know. But Hone is so like his father . . . he is not one of us."

"When can I see the children?" Caroline asked.

"As soon as I am able to return home."

A week later, when Amiria was back with her people, Caroline went to the Orakei *pa*. As soon as she saw Hone, she understood her brother's description—the boy didn't look as if he had any Maori blood. And as Caroline watched him, she saw that most of his time was spent alone. He was not happy with the other children.

"You must learn our stick games," Amiria told her eldest son. "They teach quickness in hand and eye."

"I don't want to play that game," Hone said petulantly. "I don't like it. I want to read. Papa told me that reading teaches more than anything else."

The argument between mother and son continued, and Caroline could see that even at Hone's young age—the boy was not yet six years old—it was obvious that a serious conflict was developing between mother and son, a conflict that would ultimately be very difficult to resolve.

Turi, however, was the antithesis of his brother. The image of his mother, he played happily with the other children in the *pa* and made no effort to speak English. When Hone spoke to him in his father's tongue, Turi answered in Maori. Obviously, there was the same underlying conflict between brothers as there was between Hone and his mother.

Caroline returned home exhausted. Seeing Hone had been an enormous strain—she loved this child she had once thought of as her own and had no idea how to help. She wanted to discuss the problem with Nevil but feared he wouldn't understand her concern, for even when Hone had lived with them, Nevil had thought of the child as a mixed breed rather than a human being. Yet she valued her husband's opinion, and was determined to broach the subject as soon as Nevil had eaten dinner and was relaxed.

Dinner that evening, however, was a rushed affair. "I have to go back to my office," said Nevil as they finished their bread pudding dessert.

"Oh, Nevil, must you? I have so much I want to talk to you about tonight."

"I can't help it," said Nevil. "The Governor's moving to Wellington and he has a great deal to discuss with me."

"But look outside . . . it's almost a gale out there. You can't leave the house in this weather."

Caroline gazed into the flames of the dining room fireplace, barely listening to Nevil as he continued.

"Grey's speaking tomorrow at a public meeting. He wants to go over the contents of his speech."

Caroline nodded.

"I'll be home early, my dear," he said, and without waiting for his tea, he left.

But Nevil didn't return early, and Caroline, unable to sleep, couldn't help but wonder why the meeting of the two men had gone on until dawn.

She was exhausted the following morning but still agreed to accompany Nevil to the meeting. Her husband could not have been more solicitous and this, too, bothered Caroline. As she sat in the crowded room, Eliza Grey by her side, her thoughts drifted back to the past, to the horrendous moment when she had learned the truth about her husband's proclivities. Yet when the Governor rose to speak, his voice was so dynamic, his personality so mesmerizing, that she found herself drawn back to the present, listening to his words:

". . . now across this land lies the mantle of peace. It has not been cast without sacrifices, but these sacrifices shall be worthwhile. For this is my vision: We shall make these islands a nation where, for the first time in the history of the world, two peoples of differing skins, of conflicting cultures, can live and work together with harmony and equality . . ."

"He really believes that," whispered Eliza Grey bitterly.

". . . each race giving the other strength. And for all men, white or brown, I see a future of equal opportunity; to land; to education; to a say in the affairs of the nation. And in all the world, this land shall be unique. A country fit for God Himself."

"What did you say?" Caroline whispered to Eliza.

"I said, he really believes in two peoples living together. I haven't told you about his new one. Her name's Makere. He calls her his secretary . . . that's the biggest joke."

Caroline felt most uncomfortable, not knowing what to say. It saddened her to see her closest friend so unhappy, but there was little anyone could do to change the Governor's ways. "I hear you're leaving for Wellington soon," she said, trying to talk above the noise of the clapping audience.

"Within the next few months," Eliza answered.

"I'll miss you," said Caroline.

Then Nevil rose to give the concluding speech of the morning, and Caroline turned her head to face the dais.

"The Governor's vision is a vision for which I will work with all my strength, and one for which each and every one of you must be prepared to sacrifice everything, even life itself."

Again the audience began clapping loudly. This time it was Eliza who raised her voice to be heard: "I'm glad you two are happy Caroline. At least it's nice to know things have worked out well with you both."

But that evening, when Nevil told his wife he again had to work late, Caroline began to wonder if Eliza's words had been said to smooth things over, if she knew more than she cared to divulge. Caroline decided that she could not live with suspicion. Tomorrow she would confront Nevil.

She awoke with a start. It was after ten. As soon as she realized the time, she jumped out of bed and dressed as quickly as possible, not even taking time for a morning cup of tea. She had promised Dr. Philson that she would pick up some supplies from the *Victoria* by nine o'clock. There was a shortage of medicine at the hospital, and it was much more efficient to collect the package directly from the captain than to wait for the brig to be unloaded and have the precious parcel sent in the usual way.

The weather had cleared and the port was bustling with traders by the time Caroline arrived. She felt totally confused as she looked around, wondering how she would ever find the *Victoria* with so many ships at anchor. Captain Isaac Burgess, the harbormaster, would certainly know where she should go.

She was walking toward the captain's office when she suddenly stopped short. Standing not twenty feet in front of her was Captain Peter Nolan. There was no mistaking that ruddy face and curly red hair. Dear God! she exclaimed softly, for now she knew where Nevil had been these past few nights.

"Lady Holbrooke," Nolan called with an enthusiastic wave. It was the same tone of voice and the same gesture Caroline remembered him to have used when years ago she saw him greet that Maori chief.

"How do you do," said Caroline coldly. She continued walking, stepping up her pace.

The captain called out again. Caroline paid no attention to him and continued walking.

Her marriage was over and she knew it. She had thought in Fiji that she was no longer concerned what Nevil did, as long as his love and affection for her were constant. Now she knew she cared very much. She wondered if it was the fact that his lover was a man that bothered her. Would she have reacted the same way to a mate of the opposite sex? Was the crux of the problem that she couldn't, wouldn't, live with a man who was hers only part-time? Or was there more to it than that?

The hours passed slowly, and although Caroline went through the motions of working and did everything expected of her, all she could think of was Nevil.

Dr. Philson at once sensed Caroline's disturbed state, but when he tried to address the matter, she shrugged it off. She was grateful to him for suggesting that she leave the hospital early, for more than anything, she wanted to be alone. No one could understand how troubled she was, nor could anyone help her paste back the pieces of her broken dreams. At that moment her life seemed over—she could not envision a future in New Zealand alone.

When Nevil arrived home that evening, she did not give

him time to pour himself a drink before she spoke. "You've been seeing Peter Nolan again, haven't you?"

For a moment Nevil was silent. His mouth tensed in a line of cruel arrogance as he said, "Of course I've seen Captain Nolan. The government has business dealings with him, and when he's in port it's my responsibility to see that things are handled correctly."

"That's not what I meant."

"What did you mean?"

"Nevil, stop it. You know exactly what I meant. You've been seeing him. Sleeping with him," she said, blurting out the words without shame.

The silence that punctuated the air was almost unbearable. Caroline wanted to cry but tears would not come to wash away her anger. "Nevil, I can't live with you like this. As much as I love you, I can't . . . I won't share you with anyone."

"You're making too much of this. Your anger is all out of proportion—"

"Out of proportion! How would you feel if I had a lover?"

"Don't be ridiculous."

"Why? What's the difference? Because it's me, not you?"

Nevil walked over to the table where the liquor stood and poured himself a straight gin. At a loss for words, he was stalling for time.

"I want a divorce," she said.

"On what grounds?"

"Adultery."

"Who'd believe you?"

"Will you give me a divorce? Or would you rather me open your conduct to the public?"

Avoiding a direct response, Nevil said haughtily, "Divorce is only possible through a Private Act of Parliament. Do you plan to petition the British Government yourself?"

"I'm certain an attorney can do that for me."

"Have you any idea how much that costs?"

"No. But I don't care."

"At least eight hundred pounds," he answered. "And, even

if you had the money, which you don't, the chances of anyone in England taking you seriously are very remote."

"Then I'll just leave you," she said, realizing that Nevil was right—she didn't have the money and he did have position. No one would take her word over his, not now, with the gossip of the past more than three years old and Nevil reinstated.

"You're making a mistake, Caroline. We may not have a perfect marriage but it's better than most. And I do love you."

"Your professions of love are meaningless." Now it was she who walked over to pour herself a drink. She took a long sip of port and then said, "I'll pack my things at once and leave tomorrow. I hope you'll think over my request and let me begin life anew."

"I'll never give you a divorce, Caroline. I told you, I love you. I don't want you to leave. It's not in either of our interests."

"Why? Because you need a wife for your position?"

"We both need spouses for our positions. And you're the wife I want."

"Well, you're not the husband I want. I'm leaving in the morning."

"Where are you going?"

"I haven't decided. But I'll keep you informed. One way or another, you'll know my whereabouts."

Nevil went over to Caroline and gently began stroking her face. "Please don't leave me," he said.

Caroline tried not to recoil from his touch but couldn't help herself. "The dream is over, Nevil. It's ended. The stars that were in my eyes have been blotted out. There's nothing left."

"If I promise never to see Peter again?"

"You can't keep that promise," she said. A wave of sadness suddenly washed over her anger. "I wish I could believe you, but I know in this instance your word is meaningless. You can't help yourself."

Nevil sensed there was no point in saying more. Caroline was right. When he saw Peter Nolan, something came over him. He loved the man differently from the way he loved

Caroline, but he still loved Peter. There was no way Nevil could harness his uncontrollable urge to be near Peter, and though he didn't understand it, there was no question that she was right.

"I'll always love you, Caroline. If you must leave, then do, but don't go away being angry. Let's part as friends. If you ever need anything, you can always turn to me."

"Thank you," she said softly, but she knew that though she still loved him, even if she were in dire straits she would never again ask Nevil Holbrooke for anything.

Chapter 19

ONE-HUNDRED-AND-FORTY-MILE-AN-HOUR WINDS SWEPT across the waters, mercilessly tossing the brigantine *Deborah* in the angry sea. The gale, which had begun in the early part of the evening, was now a violent hurricane, and waves, seemingly mountain high, lashed against the sides of the small ship, a deluge of water swamping the decks.

The storm terrified Caroline. The deafening roar of the wind and waters, the creaking of the vessel—for she was certain every timber in the ship was cracking and coming to pieces—the shouting of men, the crash of falling things, all created a picture of impending doom. Then, at three in the morning, there was a thunderous noise, a crash far louder than the rest as the maintop gallant mast broke and the long timber pole and sail were swept overboard.

The dark night intensified Caroline's fears, and the horrors of seasickness made her wonder if she would ever see land again. She prayed for daylight, prayed she would touch ground again, but most of all she prayed she would not be buried in the trough of the sea.

By morning the storm had ceased, and now it was just bitter

cold and wet; heavy hailstones replaced the torrents of rain; sheets of ice carpeted the upper deck. Caroline knew they were heading south, that Dunedin was not more than sixteen hundred miles from Antarctica, which she knew to be a continent covered with an ice cap, but she had never expected temperatures to drop so low in this part of the world.

The agony of Caroline's second week at sea was something she would long remember. She yearned for a hot, perfumed tub and dry clothes, and perhaps some of the Fijians' *yaqona* grog to warm her bones. But these were dreams of other days, of the life she had left behind.

Three days later, when the *Deborah* sailed into Otago Harbour, the sun was shining, the sky without a cloud. The ground sparkled with white frost and the snow on the surrounding wooded slopes dazzled in the sun.

With her carpetbag in hand, Caroline left the ship, her excitement at the prospect of seeing her brother making her forget her fears of starting life anew. She had no difficulty finding his house at the top of High Street, for it was one of the largest homes in town. She approached the weatherboard dwelling with an easy gait and knocked on the door enthusiastically.

Caroline was taken by surprise when a sallow-faced woman heavy with child opened the door. She said hello but for a moment Caroline was speechless. Amiria had said Grayson had sent her away; she hadn't mentioned that there was another woman in his life.

"Is Grayson Wickham at home?" Caroline asked at last.

"I'm sorry, he's not. But he'll be back shortly. I'm Mrs. Wickham, perhaps I can help you."

"Mrs. Wickham!" Caroline said with such obvious shock and surprise that a moment later she wanted to bite her tongue. "I'm Caroline, his sister."

Margery Wickham invited her visitor into the house and offered her tea. But Caroline could see that the woman was not well and so declined the offer.

"Grayson didn't tell me you were coming," Margery began the conversation.

"He didn't know."

"What a pleasant surprise . . ."

As Margery continued talking, Caroline believed she understood why her brother had married her. She had a sweetness about her and a warmth that was extraordinary. Although Caroline had just met her, she felt completely at ease in her presence.

"You will stay with us?" Margery said, still not knowing why or for how long Caroline had come.

Before she could answer, Grayson appeared. "Caroline!" he exclaimed. His excitement at seeing her made Caroline beam. As he hugged her tightly and kissed her cheek, she felt loved and at peace—coming here had been the right thing to do. Her fears of tomorrow vanished, and at last she felt as if she had come home.

"What are you doing in Dunedin?" Grayson asked minutes later, then added, "Where's Nevil?"

"I've left him," Caroline answered timidly.

"You've what?"

"I've left him."

"For the love of Jesus, why?"

"Please don't ask me, Grayson. Just believe me when I tell you it was the only way."

"But—"

"I've asked him for a divorce," Caroline explained before her brother could question her further, "but he won't give me one. I hope he'll reconsider."

"And just what do you expect to do here?" His loving manner had changed abruptly to one of hostility and open anger.

"If I could live with you, just until I find some work and some place to go—"

"Impossible."

"It's all right with me," said Margery to her husband. "I'm certain Caroline won't be a problem."

"You won't find work here," said Grayson, avoiding his wife's remark.

"Why not?" asked Caroline.

"Because divorced women are tainted, you know that."

"No one has to know I want a divorce. I can use my maiden name and pretend I've never been married."

"Lies are found out, my dear sister," Grayson said with uncompromising bluntness.

"It can't hurt to try," said Margery. "Caroline, you must be tired after your long journey. Do let me give you some tea. As a matter of fact, everyone will feel better after a cup of tea," she added. "We can continue this discussion later."

As soon as Margery left the room, Grayson turned to his sister with fury in his eyes. "How can you do this to me, Caroline? Having a divorced sister can spoil my plans. Do you think Margery's father will let me take over his company with a sister who's a marked woman? Don't you see, I want more than just Tiger Beer, I want to control the brewery business in this part of the country."

"Why should my being here stop you?"

"Why? Because in no time at all you'll have a reputation of being free and easy. And that could well be the ruination of me."

"That's ridiculous. Why must I be free and easy just because I've left Nevil?"

"What else can you become? Any man who sees you will expect to take you to bed."

"That doesn't mean I have to go."

"Don't be so naive, Caroline. You'll have no choice."

Caroline stared at the burning wood in the fireplace, trying to hold back her tears. What had Grayson become? Did he have no compassion in his soul?

When Margery returned to the room, the tone of the conversation lightened, but Caroline knew she could count on her brother for nothing. She drank her tea politely, feeling she would choke on every sip, then asked, "Is there a hotel in town?"

"I won't hear of your going to a hotel," said Margery. "You must stay with us."

"The Commercial Hotel is just down the road," said Grayson, again ignoring his wife. "I'll walk you over there, Caroline."

"That's all right. I'm certain I can find it if you just tell me which way to go." She wanted to get away from Grayson as quickly as possible. She could feel her composure disintegrating and was afraid that at any moment she would break down and weep.

Caroline's reception in Dunedin had hardly been what she had expected, and in the days that followed, she quickly discovered that no one was going to receive her with open arms. Margery, alone, tried to befriend her, actually arranging for her to work for Mr. Archibald Brown, the most successful draper in town. Caroline never learned how furious Grayson was that Margery had encouraged his sister to stay.

Selling yard goods was not the most glamorous job, but it did afford Caroline the opportunity of meeting and making friends with the women of Dunedin, and though she worked hard and for only three pence per day, at least it was a start. But the position was short-lived. Just two weeks after she began to work, Mrs. Brown came into the shop. She did not bother to greet Caroline and by the expression on the well-dressed woman's face, Caroline knew at once that there was going to be trouble.

Charlotte Brown pulled her husband into the back room and in a loud, angry voice, ordered, "Get rid of her today. Sack her. Tell her whatever you want, but get her out of here now."

Caroline could not hear Mr. Brown's words. He was a soft-spoken man and she was certain that no matter how his wife provoked him, he would always maintain his calm.

"Because you don't need a loose woman working for you," Caroline heard Mrs. Brown say. "You should hear the stories in town . . . she'll ruin your business."

Unable to bear listening another moment, Caroline walked to the back of the shop. "I'll leave," she said simply. "It was kind of you to take me in. I don't want to cause any trouble."

Mr. Brown glared at his wife and then turned to Caroline. "Malicious gossip is not what runs my business," he said gently. "You're a good worker, Caroline, there's no reason for you to go."

Although he meant well, he could not fight against the Scottish mores of Dunedin, for it was a town almost entirely populated by Scots. By the end of the following week, there had been such a drop in sales that he knew his wife had been correct. Caroline had been labeled a tainted woman and they were ostracizing his drapery business.

"I'm sorry," he said to Caroline. "I really would have liked to keep you."

"I understand," she said. Quietly taking her warm woolen mantle, she bid him good-bye.

She walked toward the newly opened public library—books had always given her solace; maybe if she read for a while she would feel better. As soon as she walked into the quiet room, however, the silence deepened with hostility. Every hint of activity stopped. Every face looked at her with stern disapproval. Shaken, she turned and left.

There and then, she decided that Dunedin was no place for her to live. She had to go where she would not be known. She would wear black, tell everyone she was a widow, that her husband had died at sea. She would change her name, not even use her maiden name; no one would know who she was. As she walked aimlessly through the muddy streets of town, she wondered if she should return to England, to a land she knew and understood. But then she thought of the few pounds she had remaining, and realized that she did not have sufficient money for the passage. Briefly, she considered writing to Nevil—he had said he would help her—but she knew she wouldn't, couldn't.

She returned to her hotel room and wept until she fell into a troubled sleep.

The next morning Caroline picked up a copy of *The Otago News,* hoping to find the date of sailing of a ship leaving for some destination to which she could afford to travel. It seemed a mad way to choose, but she had no idea where to go or what to do. A small article caught her eye: the Canterbury Association was advertising for someone to work in their store in Christchurch. For the first time in days, she felt a glimmer of hope—she would go to the address mentioned, use an assumed name, and pray that no one recognized her. The advertisement didn't ask for references, which meant the company was desperate. They just had to engage her, it was her only hope. All at once the heavy pall of doom that had been smothering her lifted. Christchurch would be her salvation— she was certain of it.

Caroline was delighted to learn that the *Susanna* was leaving for Christchurch in just four days. She immediately made a reservation on the barque and began packing her things. As she was folding a brown twill skirt, she began wondering whether or not to tell her brother of her plans. Grayson had been so appalling to her, yet Margery had been so kind, how could she not say good-bye? She was debating the question when a knock on her hotel door disturbed her thoughts. Surprised that she had a visitor and in no mood for company, she answered the knock reluctantly.

Standing on the threshold was a young boy, not more than ten years old. "Lady Holbrooke?" he asked.

Caroline nodded, taken aback at being called by her titled name.

"This is for you," said the young lad, holding out an envelope.

"Thank you," she said, and handed him a halfpenny.

She recognized the handwriting at once. It was from Grayson. She had not expected word from her brother, not after the way he had acted. Her initial impulse was to tear up the note unopened, but curiosity overcame her anger and she broke the seal.

Tears came to her eyes as she read Grayson's words. Always delicate, Margery had not lived through childbirth. The baby, too, had died. Caroline couldn't believe what she was reading. She had seen Margery only yesterday. It was true that her sister-in-law hadn't looked well, but she certainly hadn't looked as if death were at hand.

"Please come to me as soon as you can, I need you."

Caroline read Grayson's last sentence over and over. It was so unlike her brother to say that he needed anyone. She had been hurt by the way he had received her, angry at his insinuations of what she would become, but he was still her next of kin, her only close relative. She could not desert him now. Without a moment's hesitation, she grabbed her mantle and headed for Grayson's home.

Much to Caroline's chagrin there were at least twenty people at Grayson's house when she arrived. They had all come back with him from the funeral to begin the Jewish people's traditional eight days of mourning.

Again Caroline felt the pain of being an outsider. How could Grayson hurt her like this? Had he been afraid of inviting her to his wife's funeral, fearing in some way that his own sister might taint the religious services? But Caroline didn't even try to express her feelings. She simply paid her respects, offered her condolences to the appropriate guests, and prepared to leave.

"Please stay, Caroline," said Grayson, taking her by the arm. "I must speak to you."

"I don't think there's much to say. Your feelings couldn't be more transparent."

He led her into his library so that they could be alone. "I've made a mistake," he said once the door was closed.

"It's all right. I'm not angry now. Hurt, yes, but not angry."

"I had no right to let you go to a hotel. Will you come back here?"

"I'm leaving for Christchurch at the end of the week."

"Why?"

"I've a job there and I won't be known. As you said, I won't have a reputation . . . I can start again."

"Caroline, please listen to me. It's only now that I've lost Margery that I realize how much I really loved her."

There were tears in his eyes as he spoke, and Caroline could sense that his grief was genuine.

"I was wrong to cast you aside," he continued, "wrong to

worry about gossip in town. You're all I have now, I need you here."

"There's no way I can stay. Much as I might like to, there's been too much damage. Everyone in town can point a finger at me . . . and they do. No one will hire me. . . ."

"I'll see to it that someone does. I'll arrange a proper position for you."

"I don't want work that way. I'm not a charity case."

"Then live here without working. I've plenty of money to support us both."

There was a note of desperation in his voice, but Caroline refused to waiver. She had resolved to move away, to make it on her own, and that was precisely what she was going to do.

"If you don't want to live with me, I'll have a home built for you. Anything you want, just don't leave."

"I must go, Grayson. But Christchurch's not far, I'll visit you as often as you like."

"Not far! It's almost two hundred miles away . . . and there are no roads."

"We'll see each other, I promise." Caroline heard the words coming from her mouth but she couldn't believe what she was saying. Never before had she had the courage to stand up to her brother. In fact, she had always done anything he had asked. But this time it was different. The hurt had been too great—the wound would heal, but the scar would always remain.

"Will you at least spend a month with me?"

"I can't, I start my new job next week. I'll write to you though, and we'll see each other soon." She leaned over and kissed him on the cheek. "Take care, Grayson, and God bless."

A feeling of desolation came over Grayson as he watched his sister leave. He had given up Amiria and his two children for position and now he knew how much he had loved all three; he had married Margery Joy for money and she had died before he was able to realize how much he'd grown to love her. And only now, when it was again too late, did he recognize how important Caroline was to him and what a beautiful woman his baby sister had become. She had the poise and dignity of the finest Lady, and would not compromise her beliefs for anyone—not even her own brother. But even more, she had a strength he admired, and a bravery he had always thought was reserved for men alone. At last, fully aware of all he had done, he silently vowed to try to make those who were still alive forgive him; to do all in his power to make amends to those who meant most to him in the world.

Chapter 20

WISPY CLOUDS FRINGED WITH GOLD LAY ON A CRIMSON sky. The waters of Lyttelton Harbour were like a silent pool mirroring the Port Hills which enclosed the Bay. The splendor of the sight was incomparable, and Caroline could not resist coming here at sunset to enjoy the picturesque scene. As the sun moved toward the horizon, she was aware that night would soon cloak the area, for there was almost no twilight in the Canterbury district, only a curious half hour of strange, shadowy light. Preferring not to ride in the dark, she mounted her horse and headed back to Christchurch.

In the eight months since she had been in Christchurch, she had come to love the irregular, straggling town. Adopting the surname of Reed—for this was her grandmother's maiden name—Caroline was known to all as the Widow Reed. She dressed in black and played the role as if she were a born actress. And though she spent most of her free hours alone, she never felt lonely.

When she first came to town, she had lived in a tiny cob cottage on Cashel Street. The cob was made of clay. Chopped-up tussock grass and manure mixed with water and salt to a porridgelike consistency; this was rammed between wooden slabs which were removed after the clay had hardened; it was then smoothed over with a clay finish, and whitewashed on the inside. Now she had a comfortable wooden house on Peterborough Street, just five minutes from the Avon River which flowed peacefully through the heart of the town. It was only a three-room house, uncarpeted and furnished in the most simple style, but she had managed to make cheerful yellow printed curtains in the kitchen, and enjoyed eating there; the living room, a pleasant blending of fabrics in tones of beiges and browns, was warm and inviting.

She looked at the future with optimism and felt a deep sense of pride in her achievement, for only this morning she had been elevated from shop girl to supervisor of the Canterbury Association Store, a position hitherto reserved for men. This had not only meant a raise in salary, but the added responsibility had made her confident that she was accepted by the community.

Caroline had left the store late and was surprised to find Alice Silver waiting on the small verandah of her home, her very first visitor since her arrival in Canterbury.

Alice, a young woman with the warmest of dispositions, had tried to befriend Caroline for many months; Caroline had been careful not to let anyone intrude on her privacy. She was desperately afraid that someone might find out who she really was.

"We're having a going-away party tonight for Tom," Alice said, after greeting Caroline. "We all insist that you come."

Tom Hughes had been the manager of the Canterbury Store but due to his wife's poor health had decided to return home to England.

"It's only fitting that you're there," Alice continued, before Caroline could say a word. "After all, you are taking over his position."

"Thank you," said Caroline appreciatively, "but I can't."

"You must."

"I'd like to," said Caroline, "but it's impossible."

"Why?"

"I'm still in mourning," Caroline said softly. She smoothed the folds of her black wool skirt, emphasizing that she had not yet given up wearing her widow's weeds. "I'm certain you can understand," she said somberly.

"Caroline, you can't live in the past," Alice told her firmly. "Your husband wouldn't have wanted you to spend your life alone."

"Next time."

"We all insist you come tonight," Alice said understandingly. "You don't have to stay long, but you'll offend Tom if you don't say good-bye to him."

A whisper of a smile brightened Caroline's face.

"Then you'll come," Alice said quickly, seeing Caroline weaken and not giving her a chance to reconsider.

"I'll be there. What time?"

"Eight o'clock . . . at the store." She squeezed Caroline's arm affectionately. "You won't be sorry, it will be a nice evening. And going out will be good for you, I promise."

As soon as Alice left, Caroline went inside to change. She took out her black moire gown and a white lace chemisette—a short bodice top that fitted around the neck to fill in the low-cut dress. She looked at the clock on the small kauri night table next to her bed. If she hurried, she had just enough time to bathe.

Soaking in the warm rose-scented water didn't relax Caroline. She was afraid of going to the party, afraid someone might be there from out of town, that some stranger might recognize her, yet she knew she couldn't live the life of a hermit forever. Steeling herself to cope with her anxieties, she stepped out of the bath, dried herself, and began to dress.

The Canterbury Association Store was a large, one-story wooden building, its walls plastered with old pages of English periodicals—Queen Victoria's coronation was the most recent number. A black horsehair sofa was pushed against one wall and several cane chairs were lined up on the opposite side of the room.

The store was crowded with guests by the time Caroline

arrived, and her initial impulse was to turn and leave. Then Tom Hughes came over to her, and she began to relax.

A middle-aged man with a short-cropped beard and thinning black hair, Tom had always reminded Caroline of her mother's brother. From the first moment they met, they'd liked one another.

"I've someone I'd like you to meet," said Tom after greeting Caroline with a warm hello and a friendly kiss.

Caroline followed Tom across the room and watched him tap the back of a tall, broad-shouldered man. "G.R.," said Tom with his usual enthusiasm. "I want you to meet the most beautiful woman in town."

As the dark-haired man turned around, Caroline gasped.

"This is Geoffrey Rutledge," said Tom. "The most successful sheep farmer in the High Country." Tom turned to Geoffrey, "And this is the Widow Reed . . . but I'm certain she won't mind you calling her Caroline."

The uncomfortable moment seemed to last forever. Caroline was speechless. She put out her hand automatically, staring into Geoffrey's deep blue eyes, praying he wouldn't give her away.

"Hello," said Geoffrey. His low voice was warm, almost too warm, and his handshake lasted just a little too long, but he did not betray her.

"Geoffrey's not the only man here," said Tom as he took Caroline's arm. "I want you to meet Jock Milsom . . . he's the manager of Lake Coleridge Station."

Caroline barely noticed that Jock was a splendid man of sturdy build. Had you asked her later that night to describe him, she wouldn't have been able to remember that he had chestnut hair, nor could she have recalled that his personality sparkled. She greeted him cordially and even talked to him, but had no idea what she said. All her thoughts were of Geoffrey. What was he doing here? He was a painter, an artist, not a sheep farmer. What had made him buy a High Country farm? Was he still married? And if so, where was his wife?

"I hope I'll see you again," said Jock.

"Yes, of course," Caroline answered politely, and turned to mingle with the other guests.

The evening dragged on and on. No matter how Caroline tried, she could not find Geoffrey alone. More than anything she wanted to talk to him, to learn the answers to all her questions, but no opportunity presented itself. Finally, as the party drew to a close, Caroline went over to Geoffrey and said softly, "I'm manager of the store. I'll be here early tomorrow morning. I hope you'll come."

Geoffrey nodded, and by the look in his eyes, she knew he would not disappoint her.

Caroline barely slept that night—thoughts of her past haunted her. She kept remembering Nevil aboard the *Rosanna*, and the morning she had met Geoffrey. And then her days with the Weatherbys came to mind, and that afternoon under the Pohutukawa talking to Geoffrey when Bradley had disappeared. She could almost hear Geoffrey's words when he said he was returning to England, and she could again feel the burning tears that had come when she read he'd married Lady Agnes Compton.

It was almost dawn by the time she fell into a troubled sleep, confused by the uncertainties that lay ahead.

At half past seven she awoke with a start. She had promised to be at the store early and that meant she should have been there at least thirty minutes ago. She jumped out of bed and grabbed her black wool skirt and matching blouse. Within minutes she was dressed, out of the house, and running down the narrow dirt road toward the center of town.

Geoffrey and Jock were waiting at the store when she arrived.

"You're late," Geoffrey teased. "I would have thought of you as someone who was always prompt."

"I'm sorry," answered Caroline, and just by these few words and the look in her eyes, Geoffrey could tell that she was disappointed he was not alone.

"We're going to load up today," Jock said, sensing nothing of the tension between the two.

Caroline opened the store as casually as she could. She was puzzled by the fact that Geoffrey hadn't come alone. Surely he, too, had questions to ask. If nothing else, she thought, he must be wondering why she was using the name Reed.

"I'll need ten two-hundred pound sacks of flour," began Geoffrey, carefully checking his list, "and twelve seventy-two pound bags of sugar."

"Why so much?" asked Caroline. She had never filled an order for a High Country farm and had trouble comprehending how anyone could plan such an extensive shopping list.

"It sounds a lot, but it goes quickly up there," Geoffrey told her. "We only come in once a year, twice at the most." He looked back down at his list and continued, "Six twenty-five-pound bags of oatmeal, one sack of rice, and two sacks of salt."

Caroline wrote down his order and then turned to Jock. "And what will you have?"

"Just what Geoffrey's ordered will be fine, only I want an extra two cases of strawberry jam." He chuckled. "The cook thinks jam's a staple."

"It will be ready in about an hour," said Caroline. "Is that all right?"

Geoffrey took out his gold pocket watch to check the time. "Just fine," he answered. "That means we can pack our wagons and be ready to leave before noon. You know, it's a hard week's ride back to the Wilberforce, and who can tell how long it will take to cross the river? One good rain can hold us up for another week."

Caroline gazed at him, looking directly into those deep cornflower-blue eyes which always reminded her of flowers in an English country garden. If only they could be alone for a moment, just long enough for her to find out if he was still married. Maybe Agnes had died. The thought made her smile, and she felt a twinge of guilt at secretly wishing that his wife were no longer part of his life.

The two men left the store, and for a short while Caroline

was alone. Then the hectic hours of the day began and she had
little time to think.

When Geoffrey and Jock returned, it was close to noon.
They were accompanied by their teamsters, the drivers who
would help them load their wagons. Again there was no way
for Caroline to be alone with Geoffrey. But as he was leaving,
he turned to her and, speaking barely above a whisper, said,
"I'll be back in town before the end of the month. We'll talk
then."

A rush of warmth coursed through Caroline's veins. So
Geoffrey did want to be alone with her, he did have questions
he wanted answered. She leaned against the wall and closed
her eyes, imagining how it would be. A kiss hello, and then
she would be in his arms. . . .

"Can I get some service here?" a sheep farmer said gruffly.
"Ain't got all day, ya know."

It was a well-known fact that the shearing of sheep in the
High Country began the day after Boxing Day and lasted
about three weeks. Caroline had learned that during this pe-
riod, business in the store was always quiet. She also knew
that until the shearing was completed Geoffrey couldn't come
to town.

The days passed slowly as Caroline awaited his return. For
the first time in her life, she did not celebrate Christmas and
refused to partake in any of the festivities welcoming in 1852.
But on the twentieth of January, when she awoke, the holiday
mood of the three previous weeks seemed to come over her.
She had a feeling it would be a special day.

As she started to dress, she decided the time had come to
give up wearing black—she had played the part of the mourning widow long enough. She stood before her armoire for a
long time, trying to decide which walking dress was most
becoming. At last she chose a rose moire gown striped with
pale green and white satin, and overlaid with serpentine
stripes in a carnation and ribbon motif. She combed her hair
carefully, pulling it behind her ears a little less severely than
usual, and instead of knotting it tightly in the back, let it hang

down in loose ringlets. By the time she was ready to go to the store, she was completely satisfied with her appearance.

She was about to leave when a messenger knocked on her front door. "I've a letter for the Widow Reed," the young boy said. "I've been asked to wait for a reply," he added as he handed her the envelope.

Caroline recognized her brother's handwriting and knew at once that his news couldn't be good. She had received a letter from Grayson just the other day, why would he write again so soon? As a rule she heard from him at very irregular intervals, and knowing her brother, she was certain that two letters in one week could only mean that something was wrong. Her hands were trembling as she broke open the seal. Hesitant, she took the single sheet of folded paper from the envelope. As she began to read, she felt the blood drain from her head and she leaned against the door frame to keep her balance.

I wish I were with you to tell you this in person, but there was no way I could leave Dunedin at this time.

Apparently, when Nevil heard that the *Rosanna* had crashed against the rocks of Cape Reigna, he became extremely despondent. Then, when news came that the ship had sunk and there were no survivors, he went berserk. The following morning his body was found hanging from the door frame of his bedroom.

My dearest sister, I know that even though you left Nevil, you still loved him. Please come and spend a few weeks with me. You should not be alone at this time. My messenger will escort you back so that you will not have to make the voyage by yourself. . . .

"Please tell Mr. Wickham that I can't leave now. I'll write to him in a few days," she said, and without giving the boy a chance to answer her, she closed the door.

She was in a complete daze as she walked into the sitting room and sat down. She could barely focus her eyes, overwhelmed with grief, consumed with guilt. She had loved Nevil and now he was gone. If she had stayed with him, comforted him, maybe he'd still be alive today.

She looked down at her brightly colored dress and a new surge of guilt enveloped her. Until today she had been in mourning, almost as if she had wished Nevil dead. Until today she had played the part of a grieving wife. Now that she had cast off her widow's weeds, her husband was indeed dead.

In fury, she ripped the front of her gown, blaming herself for Nevil's tragic fate. She stared at the fringes of her new cotton-pieced scatter rug in front of the sofa, and then the tears came. For a long time she sat and sobbed, desperately wishing she could push back time.

The chimes of the clock sounded—it was eleven o'clock. She couldn't indulge herself any longer, she didn't dare stay home today. No one must know her reaction to the Colonial Secretary's death. There was no way she could admit to the lies she had told since coming to Christchurch. She had said her husband had perished when his ship rammed against rocks in a storm. It was as if she had predicted what happened, for when Peter Nolan's ship crashed, Nevil had died along with the captain.

An emptiness came over Caroline, and she dried her tears. Crying could not ease her pain; nothing could wash away her grief. She rose slowly and walked to her room. Black was all she wanted to wear today for black alone personified her mood.

The store was crowded when Caroline arrived, but everyone was so busy discussing the news of the Colonial Secretary's suicide that no one had taken notice of her earlier absence. It pained Caroline to listen to the malicious gossip that was circulating, to hear people maligning Nevil.

"He was a weak man," said one woman.

"It doesn't surprise me in the least," said another.

"Do you know, I heard he had a boyfriend," tittered a third. "His poor wife, they say she ran away . . . returned to England. . . ."

Caroline could not bear to listen to the slanderous talk another minute. "Mavis," she said to one of the three women who worked with her. "I'm feeling under the weather today . . . that's why I was so late. Would you mind taking over? I must go home and lie down."

"Certainly," said Mavis, delighting in the fact that Caroline thought enough of her to leave her in charge. "You go home and rest . . . take a few days off, I'll tend to everything."

Chapter 21

GEOFFREY RUTLEDGE HAD BEEN IN TOWN FOR TWO DAYS.
He had gone into the store time and time again on every
pretext he could invent, until he could think of nothing else to
buy. He wanted to ask about Caroline, but knowing she was
hiding her identity, he felt he should conceal the fact that he
had known her for many years. Finally, on the third day, he
could contain himself no longer. He walked up to Mavis and
asked outright, "Why hasn't Mrs. Reed been here for the last
few days?"

Mavis was a slight redheaded girl of Irish stock. Her speech
was high-pitched and she seemed to precede every sentence
with an irritating childish giggle. "She's home sick," she told
Geoffrey. "She said she was under the weather—you know
what that means."

Geoffrey didn't know what that meant but he was certain
that Nevil's death, which he had heard about almost as soon
as he arrived, was responsible for Caroline's absence. What he
couldn't understand was why she was posing as a widow, and
if she had left Nevil, then why was she taking his suicide so
badly?

"Could you tell me where she lives?" he asked Mavis, and added quickly, "A mutual friend has asked me to deliver a message."

He knocked on her door and waited patiently. It reminded him of that day in Auckland when he had come to say good-bye and she had not answered. He was just lifting his hand to knock again when Caroline opened the door. Her eyes were bloodshot and she looked as if she had not slept in days.

"Are you all right?" he greeted her, without even a hello.

Caroline tried to smile but instead burst into tears. "Oh, Geoffrey, I'm so glad you're here," she sobbed, gulping for breath.

They went into the sitting room and Caroline tried to talk, but words wouldn't come. All the questions she had wanted to ask seemed to have disappeared.

Geoffrey waited quietly, putting an arm around her to comfort her and help ease her grief.

At last, when she had no more tears, she began to recount all that happened. Geoffrey let her speak, not interrupting, though there was so much more he wanted to know.

"Now tell me about you," said Caroline. "What made you come here and go into sheep farming? Are you still painting? "Are you—" She wanted to say still married and was glad when Geoffrey interrupted.

"One question at a time," he said, and chuckled. "I never told you that my father was the Earl of Pembroke," he began.

"You mean you're a viscount?" she asked.

He nodded and continued. "We never got on well. He wanted me to stay in England, live the life of the landed gentry. It just wasn't for me. When I returned to England, I finally persuaded him that I had to live my life, not his. And so, he gave me my share of the inheritance and I returned and bought Wilberforce Station. I'm happy up in the mountains. Being close to nature has always been important to me."

"Are you still painting?" Caroline asked again.

"When I have time." He paused for a moment. "Agnes also paints, but somehow both of us rarely seem to find enough hours in the day to take out our paints and canvases."

Caroline felt her hands turn cold and clammy. Since the moment she had seen Geoffrey six weeks ago, she had dreamed of being in his arms, spending the rest of her life with him, and now once again her dreams were evaporating into thin air. She knew she had to say something but words failed her.

"You'll like Agnes when you meet her. She's a fine woman."

Caroline nodded and tried to smile. "I'm glad you're happy," she said softly.

"She'll be here tomorrow," Geoffrey continued. "She's coming to town for her yearly shopping spree. Jock's bringing her in. You know, he thinks you're quite a woman. When we were driving back home a few weeks ago, he told me he thought you'd make him a perfect wife."

"That's ludicrous. He doesn't even know me."

"He knows more than you think."

"What do you mean by that?"

"I told him all about you."

"You didn't!"

"Well, not everything." He laughed. "I didn't tell him that you'd been married to Nevil."

Caroline sighed with relief. "Please don't," she added.

"You should know me better than that. I'd never hurt you, Caroline. I love you."

A long silence followed as the two gazed into each other's eyes, both longing to be closer to each other, neither daring to move.

"I love you too," whispered Caroline, hardly realizing the words had slipped from her mouth.

Geoffrey leaned over, took her in his arms, and kissed her gently. When she responded, he pressed her to him, unleashing the pent-up feelings of love he had felt for her from their first days together. He kissed her with passion, with an emotion more intense than anything she had ever experienced, and she returned his kisses with equal ardor.

"We met too late," he said a long time later.

Tears came to Caroline's eyes and all she could do was nod.

She had dreamed of his lips on hers, wanted his closeness more than anything else in the world, and now that they both knew they loved each other, there was little either could do.

The following morning, when Agnes came into the store, Caroline understood Geoffrey's attraction to her. She was tall and walked with a stately air, and when she smiled exuded a warmth that seemed to light up the delicate features of her face. Caroline liked her at once; even though Geoffrey was hers, Agnes was not a woman Caroline could resent.

While Agnes was ordering some items that she'd forgotten to list for Geoffrey, Jock took Caroline aside and began to describe Lake Coleridge Station to her. "It's one of the most beautiful places in the country," he said. "The lake is a magnificent teal blue, and the surrounding mountains are snow-capped much of the year. You'd like it there, Caroline, I know you would."

Geoffrey had told Caroline of Jock's intentions and she understood that this was his way of proposing, but she barely knew the man and couldn't imagine being his wife. Didn't love mean anything in this part of the world? Was the fact that he needed a wife in the High Country—any wife—his only consideration?

"I'm just the manager," Jock continued, "but the three men who own the run—Barker, Harman, and Davie—live in England, so I really think of the land as mine."

Caroline looked at him inquisitively, *run* was not a word with which she was familiar. The men she had served referred to their holdings as stations. "What's a run?" she asked hesitantly, not wanting to sound ignorant.

"The same as a station, or farm," answered Jock. "It's an Australian word, but many of us use it here. We've one hundred and twenty-five thousand acres," he said, bragging, "and twenty-two thousand sheep. It's not quite as large as Geoffrey's station, but it's enough for one man to handle."

Caroline liked the way Jock spoke—his personality sparkled and was endearing—but she certainly couldn't accept the proposal of a man she had only met once or twice before, especially when she was in love with another man.

"I know you'd be happy there," said Jock. He realized Caroline was not responding to him as he would have liked, and didn't want to do anything to push her away. "There's no way I can see you during the winter months," he continued. "The roads close when the snows come. But I'll be back with the first thaw, and we'll see each other then."

"Sorry to interrupt," said Geoffrey, "but we must start back." His eyes met Caroline's. "I'll see you next spring," he said softly. "As soon as I can cross the Wilberforce, I'll be back."

"I'll be here," said Caroline. I'll wait for you forever, she thought, but dared not speak the words.

Winter set in early. Throughout the long months that followed, Caroline could not come to a decision. She knew she could never be with Geoffrey, but did that mean she should marry Jock? The question tormented her. When she was alone at night, it was all she could think about. Jock was a charming man, a hard worker, obviously very kind, and according to Geoffrey, Jock was in love with her. Caroline wondered if she could ever reciprocate his feelings. She hated the lonely life she was leading and the idea of being married again was a pleasing one. Still, she couldn't make up her mind.

Though the winter had seemed endless, the first week of spring came too quickly. Before Caroline had fully realized it had come, she found herself talking to Jock.

"Is Geoffrey with you?" she asked.

Jock had sensed that Caroline was in love with his friend but he knew that no one could affect Geoffrey's devotion to Agnes. "He thought we'd like to be alone," he answered. "He'll be around later."

"Did you have a good winter?" she asked. The conversation was stilted because she was stalling for time. Any minute Jock was going to ask her to marry him, and she didn't know how to answer him.

"The winters are cold at Lake Coleridge, but the weather's

invigorating and work keeps everyone busy." There was a short lull in the conversation, then Jock asked, "Caroline, will you come back with me? I'll be a good husband to you, I promise. I know you've had a difficult time, Geoffrey's told me everything."

"But he promised—" And as he continued speaking, she wondered how much Jock really did know.

"He knows how much I love you. He wanted me to understand your fears. You'll have an easy life with me, a happy life. I'll always be there for you. Please say you'll be my wife."

At just that moment Geoffrey walked into the store. Caroline and Jock were standing in a corner, away from everyone. Geoffrey came over to them and kissed Caroline on the cheek —a warm, brotherly kiss which could be interpreted no other way.

"I've decided to marry Jock," said Caroline. It was a spur of the moment decision, and she wasn't quite certain what had made her say the words.

"I think that's wonderful," said Geoffrey with sincere enthusiasm.

Jock took Caroline's hand and pressed it in his. "Thank you," he said. "You won't be sorry, I promise."

Caroline left the store early that day to spend the afternoon and evening with Jock and Geoffrey. She fixed dinner and they all celebrated the betrothal. It was only after they left that she realized she and Jock had had almost no time alone. She went to bed wondering if Geoffrey had purposely stayed with them so as not to give her the slightest opportunity to change her mind. But why? Why did he want to see her married? She dismissed the question as a foolish one and blew out the flame of the gas lamp by the side of her bed. But sleep did not come. Caroline tossed and turned throughout the night, unable to reconcile her conflicting feelings, worrying that her decision had been unwise.

The following morning Geoffrey was waiting for Caroline as she came out of her house. "I thought I'd walk to the store with you," he said. "I wanted to be alone with you so that we could talk."

"Shall we go back inside?" Caroline asked. She, too, wanted to be alone with him, but not to discuss Jock.

"Is that a good idea? Won't you be late?"

"Does it matter?" she asked. "I can't be sacked for being out one day."

They went inside and Caroline prepared some tea. Then they sat down in the sitting room. At first neither spoke, they just savored each other's presence.

Finally, Geoffrey took Caroline's hand and said, "It's better this way. Living alone in Christchurch is no life for you. You'll be happy with Jock, I've known him for a long time . . . he's a fine man."

"Geoffrey, be honest with me. What's the real reason you want me married?" She hesitated and then, unable to control her thoughts, added, "You know it's you I love . . . and you said you loved me."

"I do. I fell in love with you almost the first moment we met. But I'm married, Caroline, and I wouldn't do anything in the world to hurt Agnes. She's a wonderful woman and a good wife."

"And that's why you want me to marry Jock?"

"Perhaps. It will be easier for both of us that way."

"I suppose. . . . I don't love him, Geoffrey."

"I know. But you'll learn to love him, I'm certain you will, and then you'll know that you made the right decision."

Tears came to Caroline's eyes. She didn't know why she was crying but she couldn't help herself. "Will I ever see you?"

"Of course you will. Whenever I come into Christchurch, I spend the first night at Lake Coleridge Station."

"And how often is that?"

"At least twice a year, sometimes even more."

Caroline wiped her eyes. "I think I should be going now. I haven't told anyone that I'm leaving."

They walked from the house hand in hand and headed toward the center of town.

"Did Jock tell you the wedding's tomorrow?" Geoffrey asked.

"Tomorrow! Why so soon?"

"Because we have to leave the following day. The spring rains are treacherous. Once you see the Wilberforce flooded, you'll understand. Also, November is one of our busiest months," he explained. "That's when we begin mustering."

"What's that?" Caroline asked.

"Mustering means rounding up the sheep. The musterers are the men who take out the dogs to round up the sheep from the tussock blocks." By the look on Caroline's face, he knew she didn't understand his last word. "A block is about four hundred acres," he said, and then continued, "First we tail all the lambs, then we take the rams and cut off their . . . and neuter them."

Caroline burst into laughter as she saw Geoffrey blush at his description.

Geoffrey continued quickly, "The neutered lambs are called wethers."

"We also have to mark the ewes and the wethers so that we can easily distinguish them," Jock said. He had been walking behind them for the last few minutes but had been unnoticed.

Caroline greeted him warmly, hoping he would not sense her anxieties.

"Once you're at the homestead," Jock continued, "you'll learn all there is to know about a sheep station. I think you'll find it interesting. And you'll soon see, it's a good life."

For the first time, Caroline noticed what a sensitive man Jock was. He understood more about her than she had realized. There and then she decided that Geoffrey was probably right, Jock Milsom was the kind of man she eventually could grow to love.

Caroline and Jock were married on October 30, 1853. It was a small wedding. Geoffrey was the only witness and the only guest, but that was the way Caroline wanted it. She had come to terms with the marriage but she wanted to make explanations to no one—she needed time to accept her new life.

That afternoon, instead of celebrating, Jock suggested that

Caroline shop for whatever she might want or need during the months ahead.

It was a difficult task for Caroline to imagine what her desires would be for an entire year. She knew she liked apricot jam and she had seen Jock order strawberry, but how much did she need for a whole year? And she loved sultanas but couldn't fathom how many boxes of those to order either.

"I know what I want," she said to Jock, "but I have no idea of quantities."

Geoffrey threw back his head in laughter. "Do you remember Agnes's first list? She ordered a pound of peppercorns. They'll last us at least another twenty years."

"Order two cases of jam and one of sultanas," said Jock, sensing his new wife's embarrassment. "If some is left over or there's not enough, you'll know better next year. And Caroline, you'll need warm clothes and a sheepskin coat—temperatures in the High Country drop much lower than they do here."

Geoffrey looked at his watch. "You don't have much time," he said. "It's already almost three o'clock, and the shops all close before six."

"I know, and I have to pack my things besides. What time are we leaving tomorrow?"

"As early as possible," said Jock. "If we could be on our way before seven, it would be good."

"Will you both come for dinner?" Caroline asked, then realized that Jock would expect to sleep with her tonight. She suddenly became very nervous, not knowing how she would handle the moment when it came time for bed.

"You have enough to do without worrying about cooking for us," said Jock. "We'll bring the wagons to the house at dawn and see you then."

Caroline was speechless. This man seemed to read her thoughts, to sense her every fear.

"We'll have our whole lives together," whispered Jock.

"There'll be time enough to get to know each other when we're at the homestead."

"Thank you, Jock," she said, looking into his eyes with gratitude. And for the first time she noticed their color was a vibrant blue-green, so very similar to the nearby sea.

Chapter 22

Caroline was standing outside, not far from the main house that had been named the Homestead, admiring the wild, primitive beauty of the glistening snow-clad Craigieburn Range in front of her. From her first days in New Zealand, she had heard people talk of the Southern Alps, and as she gazed at the majestic mountains, she found it incredible that so small an island should have such a spectacular chain.

Suddenly she jumped in fright as a great electric flash streaked across the darkening sky. Then a violent clap of thunder resounded, the exploding sound magnified by the surrounding mountains. She had never heard such an ear-splitting noise. The very ground on which she stood seemed to tremble, and she could hear the windows of the house rattling.

Several men ran to the far side of the Homestead grounds and rushed inside a large cob-and-slab house. Jock had told her that that was where the mustering gang stayed. Unlike the station hands who worked on a yearly basis, the musterers were transient workers, coming around when they were needed twice a year—in spring and in autumn. It's like a little village, Caroline thought as her gaze traveled to the large cook house where the shearers stayed when they came to work—there was always a significant influx of men at shearing time which accounted for the size of the cook house. The wool shed, a large corrugated-iron building with holding space for up to fifteen hundred sheep, was at the opposite side of the Homestead, as well as store rooms, the stables, the house where the sheep were killed, the cart shed, and the blacksmith. It was difficult to believe that these extensive grounds were only a small part of the station.

Suddenly the rain came, torrents of water pouring from the heavens.

"It's a nor'wester!" shouted Jock. "Get inside."

Already soaking wet, Caroline ran over the creaking wooden bridge—across the small stream that flowed through this corner of the property—and headed straight for the house. "I've never seen anything like it," she said once inside. "Does it always rain like this?"

"It certainly does," said Jock. "And worse. That's why we can't get into town at this time of year. The strong, hot, dry nor'west winds, and the rains they bring, thaw the snow—you'll soon see millions of tons of water thundering down from the mountains. It's that thick brown mud that creates an impassable barrier."

"And in winter the snows make us prisoners," she said.

"That's a little strong. Once you adjust to life up here, I hardly think you'll call yourself a prisoner. Most of us go into Christchurch only because we need supplies, and we're always glad to be back."

"Do you ever have visitors?" Caroline asked. Though she had just arrived, the isolation of station life was already beginning to make her feel uneasy.

"The vicar usually comes around once a month, and then we have a service for all the men. And when we're not too busy, and the weather permits, friends from surrounding stations get together of an evening."

Caroline stood in front of the fire, rubbing her hands together as she tried to warm herself. Though it was officially spring, she had the feeling she would never be warm again.

"You should change your clothes or you'll catch cold," said Jock, seeing how his wife was shivering. "Come, let's go into the bedroom."

Caroline avoided Jock's eyes as they walked to the back of the house. This was the first time since their wedding that they had been alone, and with the weather as bad as it was, she knew that Jock had time to take advantage of the situation. She had grown to like her husband but love was still not something she felt. She was in a quandary: She couldn't say no to him but wasn't certain she was ready to say yes.

Once in the bedroom, she turned her back to Jock and slipped off her clothes then put on a warm, woolen plaid dressing gown. "That's better," she said, hoping he would let her stay as dressed as she was.

"I've never really kissed you," he said as he took her in his arms and held her to him.

His lips were tender as he pressed them to hers. Caroline could feel his love. Not wanting to hurt him, knowing she must pretend, she responded to his kiss. His kindness and love unknowingly demanded a passion from her which she thought she could not wholly feel. Her thoughts drifted to Geoffrey and she was consumed by guilt. With some difficulty she brought her attention back to Jock and put her arms around him. This dear, kind man deserved everything she could give him, and she was determined to make him happy. She let him carry her to the bed and did not resist as he slowly took off her undergarments.

"I've never seen a more beautiful woman," he whispered, covering her face and neck with kisses as he spoke. "I so want to make you happy."

Caroline closed her eyes and as he touched her she felt a rising desire. His hands magically awakened her and her hesitancy vanished. At last, she wanted him almost as much as he wanted her. She began to revel in the pleasures he was giving her. It had been so different with Nevil—he had always been so demanding, expecting her to do whatever he desired at the moment. Jock was caring, considerate. He wanted her to be passive, to enjoy every moment of his lovemaking. There would be time enough for them to make love together in years to come.

Before the first light of dawn, Jock awakened Caroline. "We're starting the mustering today," he said. "Do you want to come?"

"What time is it?" she asked sleepily.

"Five o'clock."

"In the morning!"

"In the morning," he laughed. "The men always turn out an hour before daylight, so that they have time for a hearty breakfast. They usually eat a couple of mutton chops—they call them hockey sticks—and a slice of bread, and often they even have eggs and porridge then cut themselves some lunch."

"Cut some lunch?" Caroline questioned the expression.

"Yes. The cook doesn't bother with lunch. It's up to the men to cut their own bread, meat or cheese, whatever they want. . . ." Jock paused for a moment. "You'll get used to the language up here, it just takes time. Now come, we've a lot of riding to do. If we don't get started at once, we won't make the out-station by dark."

"What's an out-station?" Caroline asked as she got out of bed.

"It's our second homestead," he explained. "It's a hard day's ride from here, so we've built a cob cottage on the banks of the Harper River. It's a very simple house, but it's a place to keep warm and have a meal. We start our mustering from there and then work backward."

By the time Caroline and Jock finished their breakfast and walked outside, the ten musterers were waiting with their dogs, their packhorses, and their horses. The packman—or packy, as he was often called—was standing nearby. It was his job to take the packhorses out to the camp, unpack them, and have a meal ready for the musterers at the end of the day.

"Those are huntaway dogs," Jock explained to Caroline, pointing at three Border collies. "They chase the sheep either up or down the hill, depending on the season. In the spring they bring them in so that the lambs can be tailed and the long-haired sheep shorn, then they take them up to the top of the hills; in the autumn they hunt them down from the summits because it's too cold up there in the winter. Those are heading dogs," he continued, pointing to three plain Head collies. "They head the sheep and bring them back to their masters. And those two are handy dogs . . . musterers use them wherever they're needed."

"And who's that?" Caroline asked, looking at one dog that was barking loudly.

"That's Sam. He's our Sunday dog. He used to be our best huntaway, now he's getting old. He refuses to work if the going is hard or the weather too hot. But I can't part with him, he's been with me for nine years."

Jock introduced Caroline to the men and then they all mounted their horses and headed toward the Harper River. It was still dark, and Caroline stayed as close to Jock as she could, anxious about riding unfamiliar terrain lit only by the light of the moon and the stars. As the first pale streaks of dawn began to show in the east, she felt more at ease.

Now, in the light of day, Caroline could appreciate the vast landscape of purple mountains capped with sparkling white snow, swiftly running streams, and wide open spaces. There were no trees anywhere, just soft golden clumps of tussock grass blowing gently in the spring breeze, and spiky matagouri plants which Jock explained the sheep used as shelter during snowstorms.

As the noon sun warmed the air, Caroline realized that although they had been riding for more than seven hours, she had hardly seen any sheep. She had been lagging behind, more interested in the land itself than in keeping up with the others. Now, she galloped up to the front of the straggling group so that she could talk to Jock. "I thought you said you had twenty-two thousand sheep. Where are they?" she asked.

"The sheep blend in with the tussock," Jock answered, remembering for the first time in many years how he, too, had been surprised at not being able to see any sheep when he had first come to the High Country. "Look up there," he said. "There's a whole line tracking across the mountainside."

"Where?"

"See that track." He pointed to a deep ridge on the mountain. "The sheep carve a track, then they usually travel on the same ridge year after year. If you stare at it for a moment, you'll be able to see them."

"Ah, yes," she said. "But it certainly doesn't look as if there were thousands up there."

"We've a lot of land. They're spread out . . . we try not to have more than five hundred sheep on a block."

"And a block's four hundred acres," she said proudly, remembering Geoffrey's words.

"Right."

Caroline gazed up at the sheep. "Even with so few sheep on a block, I can't understand how they survive. There's no grass up there . . . the mountains are nothing but rock and shingle. What do they graze on?"

"See those patches of tussock?" he said. "They shelter smaller plants which the sheep eat. They also like the sweet native herbs that grow in the cracks of the shingle."

Soon, they stopped for lunch.

"Swing the billy, will you, Roy," Caroline heard one of the musterers call to the packman.

It was then that she learned the meaning of black billy tea. The packman built a small fire under a matagouri plant and hung an iron pot with a handle—a billy—from a branch. When the water began to boil, the billy began to swing, and Caroline understood how the expression "swing the billy" was coined. Then the packman removed the billy with a stick and set it on the ground. He added four heaping tablespoons of tea to the pot and let it settle for several minutes. The brew that resulted was not particularly strong, but it was very black, and Caroline found the flavor delicious.

The lunch break was a short respite in the day, for within forty-five minutes, the men mounted their horses and began riding toward their destination.

Caroline was already saddle sore and would have loved to pitch camp right there, but she didn't dare complain. She was an excellent horsewoman and knew Jock expected her to keep up with the others; what he didn't realize was that she had never ridden this many hours at a stretch. By the time they reached the Harper River, she was not only stiff and tender, she felt she might never walk again.

As the sun set, the temperature dropped considerably and she forgot her aching body, now concentrating only on keeping warm. Unfortunately, there was no way. The out-station was a rather primitive dwelling devoid of all comforts. The men built a fire, but the wind and cold found its way inside. Silently, Caroline vowed that this was the first and last time she would accompany Jock for a muster.

At two o'clock the following morning, Jock awakened Caroline. "It's breakfast time," he said.

"But it's still dark," she replied, not understanding why they were up so early.

She quickly learned the reason for such an early start: every man had to be on his beat by daylight to prevent the sheep wandering back to the country they'd already mustered. As the boundaries were all open, it was necessary to hunt the sheep as far ahead as possible before leaving their beats and descending to camp.

The night was clear and stars overhead indicated a cloudless sky. The wind had eased into a warm gentle breeze, but at this hour it was still very chilly. By the time the first rays of sun began to show above the ranges, the men had separated and were covering their beats, their dogs following close behind. They formed a rough diagonal line across the hill and began shouting to the dogs.

"Come out, Bess!" Caroline heard the lead musterer yell. And almost instantly the huntaway dog ran to chase the sheep.

"Stand, Bess!" the musterer shouted, and at the command the dog stopped in his tracks.

"Stand, Bess!" he called again, and this time Bess began to bark.

The sheep heard the bark, and started running away from the sound, following the tracks across the hillside at a furious pace.

"Wayleggo, Bess!" shouted the musterer, and Bess bounded back to the musterer's side.

"Come here, Tim!" the musterer called.

Caroline couldn't understand why that command made the heading dog race forward—away from his master. Jock explained that it was the accepted command for a heading dog to go get the sheep. The dog made a wide detour around his sheep without disturbing them. Within minutes he came out in front of them.

"Come out, Tim!" the musterer shouted, and the dog began to walk forward, quietly leading the sheep across the hillock.

"Tim's also a stopping dog," said Jock. "Once he's headed the sheep, he'll just lie and hold the mob until his master arrives."

"That's the most amazing sight I've ever seen," said Caroline. "The dogs are so well trained! It's incredible!"

"It is," he answered. "One tends to forget how impressive it is the first time you watch the mustering. But wait until you see thousands upon thousands of sheep running together. That's really something."

"How long does it take to get them all back?"

"About three weeks. Right now we're mustering the wethers. The ewes and lambs are all on low-country blocks. The tailing muster of the lambs was last week, while we were in Christchurch. The newborn lambs were separated from the ewes, tailed, and taken to lambing blocks . . . they won't be weaned until next March."

Three weeks, thought Caroline, and she remembered the cold of the night before. "Do we stay at the out-station the whole time?" she asked.

"No. As we head back, Roy pitches tents for us. Over the summer I hope to have another four campsites built, with huts at each station," he explained.

"Really three weeks, Jock?"

"I hope that's all it will be," he said. "We just have to hope that none of the streams flood too badly. That always delays us."

"Had I known we'd be out here that long, I'm not certain I'd have come."

"I'd have missed you." He smiled warmly, reached over and took her hand. "It's nice having you around."

Caroline felt secure at Jock's side. When she looked back at him and squeezed his hand in return, he sensed, for the first time, that she was falling in love with him.

The tender moment was fleeting. Almost at once they turned their attention back to the sheep and dogs. Watching mustering for a day or two would be interesting, Caroline thought, but after three weeks, she was certain she would be totally bored. But slowly, the spirit of the High Country began to reach her, become a part of her, and as each day passed, she found the life more and more fascinating. She began to love the serenity of the wilderness, the beauty of the mountains and streams, and though the men shouted, the dogs barked, and the sheep bleated, there was a peace unlike anything she had ever experienced.

It had been an exciting month, but a wet one. After the third day, wind and rain accompanied the group all the way. When at last they arrived back at the Homestead, Caroline was delighted. Once again she could sleep in a real bed, instead of a sleeping bag, bathe properly and put on clean, fresh clothes—she never could have imagined she would spend an entire month with only one change of clothing, a wet buckskin hat, and a yellow oilskin cape.

Her first impressions of the Homestead had been of a simple but cold four-room house which was larger but not very different from her home in Christchurch. Now, as she looked around the sitting room at the crude handmade kauri and stiff Victorian furniture, it seemed to have a much warmer, cozier feeling. The fireplace lent itself to the same treatment she had used before—it needed a mirror above it and a lace cloth on the mantel. With a few pictures on the walls and a feminine touch here and there, she was certain she could transform it into a beautiful, inviting home. She knew Jock would let her redecorate however she wished; she'd only have to ask him.

Caroline longed to spend time alone with Jock. But almost as soon as she'd returned, she learned that the real work was just beginning. Once the wethers were brought in they had to be eye-clipped, shorn, and taken back out to high-country blocks for the summer months. Then the ewes and hoggets—the yearling sheep—were shorn and transferred to the low-country lambing blocks. She was fascinated by the incredible speed at which the shearers worked, shearing at least two hundred sheep a day.

And still the work was not over. Once the sheep were shorn, the fleece had to be classified, scoured, dried, and put into bales which were then weighed, named with the station and numbered by class. Finally, teams of bullocks were hitched to wagons, ready to carry the large loads into Christchurch, where the bales were shipped to England. Wool brokers in London set the price on the fleece to be sold.

Caroline was thrilled when Jock told her she could accompany him to Christchurch. She looked forward to their three days there as the honeymoon they had not yet had time to take. However, upon their arrival in the growing town, she soon realized that Jock had come to work. Their time together was confined to the evening.

Caroline busied herself with shopping. Although she had only been at Lake Coleridge Station for a few months, she now had a much better knowledge of what she needed for High Country life. On her second day, she went into the drapers to buy some warm cloth. Agnes and Geoffrey had arrived only moments before.

As Caroline greeted Geoffrey, she felt a surge of excitement. It was a reaction she knew too well and, now that she was married, it made her feel guilty, but she could not legislate her emotions.

"It's good to see you again," said Geoffrey. "How was the mustering?"

"Nice seeing you," answered Caroline, avoiding Geoffrey's eyes. "Everything went well. Jock took me out with him. I loved every minute of it. And how are you both?" she asked, and then was sorry she had posed the question, for Agnes didn't look well; or, perhaps, it was just the sadness Caroline noticed in her eyes.

"We're both fine," said Geoffrey.

"Yes," added Agnes. "I'm always fine when spring comes. The winters are too cold for my liking."

"I feel the same way," said Caroline.

It was a brief conversation, for Geoffrey had an appointment and he wanted Agnes to accompany him. As they walked away, Caroline felt uneasy—something was not as it should be, she was certain of it, but couldn't figure out just what the problem was.

Chapter 23

DAY FOLLOWED DAY, WEEKS FLOWED ONE INTO THE other until only the change of season made Caroline cognizant of the passing years.

After Caroline's first experience with mustering, she began to learn the true meaning of a woman's place on a High Country station. She was in charge of the Homestead and that not only meant caring for the house and cooking—for the cook only prepared food for the station hands, and the transient workers—it also meant learning nursing skills so she could give first-aid to anyone who had an accident, making clothes for her husband and herself, and entertaining unexpected visitors throughout the spring and summer months.

Each year, at the end of summer, the older ewes were culled from the flock and taken on a three-day drive to Colgate, where they were sold for food at the Ewe Fair. Caroline looked forward to this time of year because Geoffrey always crossed the Wilberforce and spent his first night out and last night back at the Homestead. Although over the years she had grown to love Jock, she still enjoyed an evening with her old friend. Jock was wonderful to her and could not have been a kinder husband, but Geoffrey understood her as no one ever had. He always seemed to know just what she was thinking and was never at a loss for what to say.

She would never forget the day she received a letter from her brother just an hour before Geoffrey arrived. Jock was still rounding up the last of the ewes, so she and Geoffrey had time alone. They were sitting in the kitchen drinking a cup of tea when Geoffrey said, "What's worrying you, Caroline? I've rarely seen you look so distressed."

"It's Grayson. I don't understand what's happened to him."

Geoffrey let Caroline unfold her problem without saying a word: "I received a letter from him this afternoon. He says Hone's run away from Amiria. Hone insists he can't live with the Maoris, that he's not one of them. His people call him a *Kua Pakeha*—a Maori who's become a Pakeha—and he refuses to go back to his family's *pa*. Grayson doesn't want him in Dunedin . . . says he'll ruin all his plans."

She paused for a moment. "All my brother seems to care about is money. One brewery didn't satisfy him, he needed more. Now he has four. He wants to monopolize the entire beer business in the Otago region. He even has a number of hop farms. He just keeps expanding . . . nothing is enough for him. I would think Hone could be a great help to him. Wouldn't you?"

Geoffrey nodded but waited to voice his views. He sensed that most of all, Caroline needed to talk.

"It's because Hone's part Maori," she continued. "Grayson's afraid a son of mixed blood will hurt his image. I just can't believe he's become such a bigot. Margery was Jewish, and this was not particularly pleasing to him, but her father offered to give him the company, so he married her. It was only after she died that he realized what he'd lost." There was a long silence, then Caroline said, "What should I do, Geoffrey? Hone's just sixteen years old. He still needs a family. If he won't go back to Amiria, how will he live?"

Geoffrey took Caroline's hand and held it reassuringly. "Write to your brother and tell him you want Hone here. You loved the boy as a baby and your feelings haven't changed. You'd be good for him."

The tensions of the afternoon were suddenly released, and tears streamed down Caroline's cheeks. "But Jock? How can I ask Jock to take him in?"

"Why not? Jock's not Grayson. Jock's a compassionate man, you know that. I'm certain he'll accept Hone with open arms. And the boy can be a great help up here."

"What's wrong?" asked Jock, entering the kitchen and seeing his wife in tears. "Are you all right?"

Slowly Caroline related the story a second time.

"Where's the problem?" asked Jock. "I'll have a messenger take a letter to Dunedin at once. Tell Hone to come here," he said before Caroline had even broached that part of the subject.

Caroline went over to her husband and hugged him tightly. "Thank you," she whispered, now crying with joy. "You're very special, Jock. I love you so."

Caroline and the two men spent the rest of the afternoon in a happy frame of mind. They joked and talked and the hours went quickly by.

That evening Caroline prepared a special dinner, the main course being a Merino hogget. Hoggets were not usually killed for food but the young sheep were tastier than older ones, and Geoffrey's coming was always considered a special occasion.

"Do you remember the first time I cooked a Merino, Jock?". she said. "I couldn't believe that such a scraggy animal could be tasty."

They all laughed because nothing was as tender or more delicious than a well-prepared Merino.

"I wish I could go with you both," she said, changing the tenor of the conversation.

"There's nothing to see or do in Colgate," Geoffrey replied.

"And besides," added Jock, "you have soap to make. We're down to our last few bars."

"I know," said Caroline. "I'd do anything to get out of that chore. Last time I made our year's supply, I got that awful caustic soda all over my hands . . . the burns lasted for weeks. And you know how I hate the smell of boiling mutton fat."

Jock chuckled. "One day we'll be rich enough to order soap from England."

"At those prices!" interjected Geoffrey. "No matter how much money you had, Caroline, I don't think you'd waste it on soap. The whole thing doesn't take more than a few hours to make."

"I know," said Caroline. "It's not the soap . . . it's just that I'll miss you both."

When the men returned two weeks later, Geoffrey only stayed long enough to have a light lunch. He wanted to take advantage of the dry weather, hoping to cross the treacherous Wilberforce without incident.

Each time Geoffrey came to the Homestead, Caroline asked about Agnes. His answer was always the same: "She's fine, thank you, just fine." But today when Caroline asked the question, she did not believe the answer. It had been three years since she had seen Agnes. Why did the young woman no longer come to town?

"Will you bring Agnes for dinner after the muster?" she asked. "Spend the weekend with us?"

"Agnes won't cross the river if she can help it," Geoffrey answered without hesitation. "And I can't blame her. So many people have drowned there. . . . It's fine when it splits into two streams, gently meandering along its course, but one good rain and it's a killer river. Next summer, after the snows melt and the river's down, you'll both have to cross over and visit us. We've built on a new wing to the house and redone the old section. I'd love you to see it."

Jock promised they would come. Caroline just smiled. She couldn't say why, but she had a feeling the visit would never materialize. She was certain Geoffrey knew what she was thinking, but if he did, he made no comment. Geoffrey bid them both good-bye. Promising to see them in the spring, he rode away.

The following morning the autumn muster began. Caroline

disliked this muster because it was when the sheep were dipped and she was always asked to help. She had made herself a pair of black twill trousers for this work. They were hardly the most feminine outfit she had, but straddling a sheep's neck and pulling it across a floor by the head was far from a ladylike chore.

The sheep were dragged, one by one, onto a platform, then plunged into an antiseptic dip to cure them of bugs and mites which burrowed under their skin. The stench at dipping time was dreadful, and Caroline found the whole procedure revolting, but she had grown strong and never complained. She was, however, delighted that she was never asked to help when, following the dipping, the sheep were crutched—the fleece beneath their tails closely clipped. Then they were mustered back to the winter blocks.

As soon as the autumn muster was completed, the men were to hold their traditional dance in the corrugated-iron building where the sheep were held. It celebrated the onset of their holiday, for their was little work for musterers during the winter months. This year, however, the snows came earlier than usual and there was no time for festivities. The first winter storm was quickly followed by more snow, then rain and the ultimately hard frosts. On sunny blocks the stiff crust of snow would melt daily, a new iron-hard crust forming each night. This was devastating for the sheep. As soon as the sun was strong enough to thaw the crust, the sheep would sink into the soft snow which was often more than three feet deep. At night, bogged in the snow, they could easily be buried under a newly formed crust. Starvation was a major problem, as were the keas—large, dull-green mountain parrots with long powerful beaks and strong talons, believed to delight in attacking sheep. There were no wild animals in the High Country when the first stations were built, and it was the keas who were blamed whenever a sheep was found in a mangled bloody heap, its back stripped of flesh.

Jock rode out with several of the station hands to go snow raking. With the help of their dogs, who seemed to be able to sniff out sheep, the men raked away the snow wherever they suspected sheep had been buried in drifts.

Day after day the snow continued to fall in dense, fine clouds, covering the ground to a depth of four feet in the shallowest places. As Caroline watched the snow fall steadily, she knew that this year the process of snow raking would be longer and more tedious than usual, and she was certain that Jock and the men would be gone for days.

She had been sorry to see Jock leave but she didn't feel the loneliness of his departure as much as usual, for though she hadn't yet received an answer to her letter to Grayson, she was confident that any day Hone would arrive. But a week after Jock left, she would have given anything to have him by her side.

Caroline was standing in the kitchen, preparing some lunch, when suddenly the dishes began rattling. Only minutes later the roof of the wash house just behind the kitchen caved in. At the same time several windows shattered. Caroline didn't know which way to turn. Panicky, she ran to the bedroom and crawled under the bed. The whole house began to shake. "Jock! Jock!" she cried. But no one was there.

A long time later, when the trembling stopped, Caroline heard her name being called. Cautiously, she came out from under the bed and went back to the front of the house. Ron, one of the station hands, was waiting for her.

"You all right, Missus?" he asked.

"I think so," she answered, not really convinced that she was.

"That's the worst slip we've had since I've been up here," he said. He pulled at his long red beard, as if deep in thought. "Would you like me to stay awhile?" he asked hesitantly, not certain it was his place to make such a suggestion. "Help you clean the mess?"

"No, thanks. I'm all right," she answered. "But Ron, what about Jock and the men? How can we know if they're all right?"

"No need to worry, Missus," he said. "There's nothing to fall on them out there. They'll be just fine."

"Ron," Caroline said before he had time to leave, for she really wanted him to stay. "Is the earthquake over?"

"We may get another tremor or two. I wouldn't expect more than that."

In the eight and a half years Caroline had been at Lake Coleridge, she had never felt a quake. She wondered whether they came in cycles but didn't question Ron further.

"I'll be going now," he said. "If you need me, just give a call."

Though badly shaken, Caroline still felt it her duty to clean up the house and see to the damage. The cook house was in a shambles, its chimneys collapsed and most of the crockery broken. The other buildings had also been hit, but the damage was not as great.

By the time Caroline returned to the Homestead, all she wanted to do was weep. The thought of being alone that night terrified her. The windows were broken and a kea could fly in and attack her, she thought, knowing this was an illogical fear, yet she didn't dare close her eyes.

A terrible storm followed the quake. She prayed for Jock's safety, wishing above all that he would return quickly. For the first time in her adult life, she left the lamp burning all night, the idea of darkness enveloping her more than she could bear.

Though she had no memory of sleeping that night, she awoke to find it morning. Snow was falling lightly now and somehow a peace had returned. Caroline lay in bed much longer than usual, daydreaming of Jock, of his arms holding her, making her feel loved and secure. She didn't seem to have the strength to begin her daily chores. The house was chillier than usual with so many windows broken. She pulled the covers up to her neck, thankful that her bedroom had escaped the havoc of the quake.

A light rapping on her window jolted her back to the present. She put on a warm dressing gown and went to see what or who was tapping at the glass.

Soft gray eyes met hers. Caroline recognized Hone at once. She ran to the door and opened it excitedly. "Hone, I'm so glad you came," she said, throwing her arms around the youngster. "You'll never know how happy I am."

"Aunt Caroline?" he questioned hesitantly, for he hadn't seen her since he had been two.

Caroline smiled warmly. "Yes," she said, and ushered him into the house. "How on earth did you get here in that storm?"

"I wasn't in the storm," he answered. "I was a few miles down the road, at the Howdon place." Before Caroline could comment, he asked, "How did you know me, Aunt Caroline? It's been so long."

"I could never forget those eyes—they're exactly the color of your father's. How is Grayson? And your mother and brother? Tell me everything."

"I hardly know where to begin," said Hone, but then the words just came to him. "My mother is fine, she's living with our extended family. And Turi is grown now. He's not like me at all. He has never accepted my father. He believes the Maoris have no right to intermarry with Pakehas. He's always lecturing me on why his people should remain pure. He doesn't look at me as a brother . . . says I have deserted my own. That's not true, Aunt Caroline. It's just that . . . well, when I was a child, I lived like a Pakeha, he never did. My ways are different from his. We don't understand each other, I guess."

"And Amiria?" Caroline asked when the conversation lulled.

"My mother was so badly hurt by my father that she has gone back to her people in every way. She, too, hates me because my ways are not her ways."

"I don't think she hates you, Hone. No mother hates her child."

Caroline could clearly see the sadness Hone felt—it was reflected in his eyes. She wished she knew how to comfort him.

"My father," he continued, "cares about me, I know he does. And I think he cares about Turi, too, though he never talks about him. But his business is far more important to him than people. I think he wanted me to stay, but he was too afraid of what others might think."

"We want you, Hone, no matter what anyone thinks."

"I know," he answered. "I can still remember when I lived with you . . . not everything, but the way you hugged me and played with me. . . . You always loved me." He hesitated a moment, then added, "I won't stay long though."

"Why not?"

"I can't impose upon you. If I could just stay the winter, that would be wonderful. By then I'll have had time to decide where to go and what to do."

"Your being here won't be an imposition. Jock's looking forward to having the extra help." Caroline studied the boy for a moment. He was a strong, healthy lad with a warm personality. She knew that he would be a survivor. No matter what anyone did, he would rise above adversity.

"My father's been having a lot of trouble with the company," Hone continued, as if trying to justify Grayson's behavior. "Someone tried to sabotage his breweries by contaminating the wells he uses. Bad water is like a plague to a brewer."

"Who would do such a thing?"

"I'm not certain," he answered. "My father thinks it someone from C.B. . . . a man named Rodney Fletcher."

Colonial Brewery, known popularly as C.B. beer, was the only real competition Tiger Brewery had. Caroline was aware that over the years, Grayson had been trying to buy out C.B.

"While I was in Dunedin," Hone explained, "I heard it rumored that my father had tried to court Rachel Golden. Her father owns C.B., and Fletcher's the manager. They say Rachel was in love with father when she was very much younger but now she won't have anything to do with him. I suppose she believes father only wants her because of the brewery, and father thinks that's why Fletcher wants her." A serious look came over Hone's face. "I'm not certain she's right, though. I think father really cares for her—not that it matters if she won't even have dinner with him. Maybe that's why father doesn't want me there."

"Grayson hasn't had much success with women, has he?" Hone shook his head but did not reply.

"Let me show you your room," said Caroline, deciding that the conversation had become too heavy. "Then I'll take you around the grounds."

"Where's Jock?" Hone asked as they were walking to the back of the house.

"He's out with the sheep. He should be back soon. He'll be pleased that you're here," she said. "And I know you'll like him."

Jock returned to the Homestead two days later, and from the moment he met Hone, Caroline knew that the two would be good for each other. She also sensed that Hone would be like a son to Jock, the son he longed for but never had. A twinge of guilt came over her as she wondered why in all these years with Jock, she had never been able to conceive. After her miscarriage with Nevil, Dr. Philson had assured her she could still have a child. Now, more than ever before, she felt inadequate, blaming herself completely for her barren state, never once considering the possibility that Jock should share the responsibility.

Hone thrived that winter and both Caroline and Jock delighted in his company, but though her nephew loved the High Country, Caroline could see that he was restless. He was unaccustomed to the isolation of mountain life and no evening passed when he didn't mention his desire to go into town. Yet he worked hard and without thought of fatigue. In June he helped Jock muster the rams and put them out on the low-country paddocks with the ewes, then he took over the weekly job of rounding the ewes up to the rams—this was mating season and it was essential that ewes and rams get together. Whenever there was a bad storm, he accompanied Jock in the tedious, frustrating task of snow raking, and no matter how cruel the weather, he never uttered a complaint. Then, without stopping to rest, he would take on the chore of feeding hay to the sheep, as the snows covered their only food supply.

As the days passed, Jock not only learned to love Hone, as Caroline had predicted, but to depend upon him. But when

Jock offered him a salary of ten pounds a year, Hone was extremely upset.

"I won't take money from you," he told Jock.

"Why not?" asked Jock. "You've been working hard . . . you deserve a salary."

"I get room and board," replied Hone. "And you're my family," he added shyly.

"That has nothing to do with it," Jock answered, completely unaware that he was hurting this boy he loved. "I pay a musterer five pounds a year and you've been doing far more than twice the work of any one of them."

Hone pushed the question aside—they would discuss it at another time. Caroline knew he wouldn't allow the subject to come up again. Hone was a stubborn boy and if he decided he wouldn't take money, there was no way he could be persuaded to do so.

It had been a long, harsh winter, and when the first signs of spring came, everyone began talking of their forthcoming trip to Christchurch.

"When do we leave?" asked Hone.

"As soon as we finish the spring muster," Caroline told him. Even as she said these words, she knew in her heart that Hone would not return with them. His was a free spirit, not one to be confined for months at a time. She wondered if she should ask him his plans. But how could she tell him what she suspected? He might feel she was pushing him from her and that was the last thing she wanted to do.

Chapter 24

IN THE YEAR CAROLINE HAD BEEN AWAY, CHRISTCHURCH seemed to have blossomed in every direction. On Wakefield Square there was a new bookseller, stationer, clockmaker, and jeweller; down the street, a china shop had opened, and even a needlework shop. As Jock drove through town, Caroline was nearly speechless—she just couldn't believe that Christchurch, no longer a village, had grown into a sizable town.

"I wish we could spend more than just a few days here," she said, trying to drink in all the newness.

"I do too," said Jock, "but you know we can't. There's grass to be sown, and it's haymaking time."

"I know," she answered petulantly.

They drove up to the Mitre Hotel, and Caroline went in ahead to arrange for their rooms while Jock and Hone unloaded the wagon.

A few minutes later the men entered the hotel, and Caroline overheard Jock's words.

"As soon as we've unpacked a few things, I'll take you over to the Bank of New Zealand," he said to Hone.

"I won't take money from you, Jock. I told you that once and I meant it."

Caroline wanted to strangle her husband. How could he bring up the subject of money as soon as they arrived? He knew how Hone felt. Why didn't he understand that Hone couldn't be pushed? She could clearly see that if Jock kept pressuring him, Hone would run away.

"We'll go tomorrow," said Hone, tactfully avoiding an argument. "This afternoon I'd like to look around town . . . if it's all right with you, that is."

"Certainly," said Jock. "We'll meet you back here at dinner time."

"How could you, Jock?" asked Caroline as soon as they were alone in their room.

"How could I what?"

"Tell Hone you were going to take him to the bank. You know how he feels about accepting money from you."

"Don't be foolish, Caroline. He should be paid for what he does."

"You're wrong," she said emphatically. "You've never been so wrong."

Not wanting to discuss the matter further, Jock told his wife he was going for a walk. "I'll be back in time to change for dinner," he said quietly, and left the room.

It was their first argument, and Caroline was sorry she had raised her voice, but once again she had the sad premonition that Hone would not return with them to Lake Coleridge.

It was close to six o'clock when Hone knocked on Caroline's door. "You look lovely," he said, and kissed her hello. He couldn't remember seeing his aunt dressed in city clothes.

One of the things Caroline loved most about coming into town was the opportunity to dress as a Lady. Instead of wearing long merino undergarments and course woolen skirts, she now had on a fancy crinoline and a decolleté blue silk gown trimmed in black lace. She had been just ready to start her toilette when Hone arrived.

"Did you have a nice day?" she asked.

"Oh, wonderful, Aunt Caroline. I've the most exciting

news. Look!" he said, pulling out a newspaper from his pocket. "Read this! It's dated December 2, 1862 . . . just ten days ago."

Caroline took the paper and stared at the headlines:

GOLD! GREAT FIND! 100 POUNDS IN ONE DAY!

She did not need to read more. Hone's adventurous spirit would draw him to gold, she was certain of it.

"I can't go back with you," said Hone before Caroline could utter a word. "It's not that I'm not happy at the Homestead. It's just that I have to go . . . I have to make my own fortune."

"I understand," said Caroline, but she couldn't keep her voice from quivering, nor could she hold back her tears.

"I love you both," Hone said compassionately. "I really do, but I can't impose on you forever. I must make my own way."

"Where are you going?" asked Caroline; her eyes had been too clouded to read more than the headlines.

"To Skippers."

"Skippers?"

"It's south of here, in the mountains. I'll take a boat to Dunedin and then ride inland."

"Is it near Dunedin?" she asked, barely able to talk.

"The man I asked at the newspaper office told me it's about one hundred and twenty-five miles due west, but I can't be certain."

"Oh, Hone, I'll miss you so," she said, hugging him tightly. "Must you go?"

"I'll write Aunt Caroline, I promise. We won't lose touch."

When Jock returned to the hotel room, he was shocked to hear his wife attack him.

"It's your fault," she began without even a hello. "You had to bring up money again. You couldn't treat Hone as a son."

"Caroline, what's wrong with you? What's happened?"

"Hone's leaving."

"Why?"

"Why do you think? Because of you."

Jock went over to Caroline and started to put his arm around her shoulder.

"Don't you touch me."

"Caroline, please. There must be more to it than you've told me. Where does he say he's going?"

"To Skippers."

"To where?"

"Skippers. It's miles from here. I'll never see him."

"What's there?"

"Gold."

"So he's caught gold fever," said Jock, smiling. "There's nothing wrong with that. He's young and healthy and wants to make his fortune. Can't you see that's a good thing?"

Caroline began to sob. "I guess so," she said.

This time when Jock took his wife into his arms, she did not push him from her. She needed his love and affection, and inwardly she knew he was right.

Three days later Caroline and Jock took Hone to the *Miranda,* said their good-byes, then headed back to the Homestead.

The week's ride from Christchurch to Lake Coleridge seemed to them longer than usual. Though they sat side by side at the front of the wagon, they barely spoke. Caroline couldn't accept Hone's departure nor could she forgive Jock for his insistence that he bore none of the responsibility for the boy's actions.

Jock, however, wanted to make peace between them. He could not bear Caroline's indifference toward him. "Would you like to spend next weekend with Geoffrey and Agnes?" he asked.

"Cross the Wilberforce in spring? You must be mad."

"If the weather keeps up like this, we should have no trouble," Jock answered, at once sensing that he had lifted her spirits.

"I'd love to, if you really think we could."

"Don't you worry, I have a direct line upstairs." He smiled warmly as he spoke. "I'll order the sun to shine."

"Thank you, Jock. And I'm sorry I've been carrying on so. It's just that I love Hone. He always was like a son to me, and now more than ever. . . ."

"I know," Jock said. "The trip to Wilberforce Station will be good for you . . . for both of us."

"I wonder why Geoffrey hasn't taken his wool into Christchurch yet?" Caroline said. "He usually comes with us. I hope there's nothing wrong."

"The Wilberforce has been high. He probably plans to come in next week."

"And if he's already gone?"

"Then we'll stay with Agnes until he returns. She'll enjoy our company," he said. "At least she always used to."

"We're back in High Country," Caroline said, smiling for the first time in more than a week. "I love the tradition up here of white houses and red roofs. Just seeing them makes me know I'm home."

At last they were talking again, and by the time they returned to the Homestead, the rift between them had been bridged.

Two days later, when Caroline awoke, the sun was shining brilliantly.

"There's not a cloud in the sky," said Jock at breakfast. "Just as I promised, the weather is perfect. Pack up and we'll leave as soon as you're ready. I'm certain we'll have no trouble crossing today."

But just an hour later, when they were already on their way, the clear blue skies had clouded over and become a threatening gray. As they rode toward the river, Jock began to wonder if they were wise to attempt the crossing. If the rains came before they were on the other side, they would be in serious trouble. Few rivers could be swifter than the Wilberforce when it flooded, but his judgment was colored by his desire to please his wife and he decided to go on.

"We'll start our crossing below the Wilberforce, at the Rakaia," he told her, "that way, by the time we've reached the Wilberforce, we'll be halfway across."

As they reached the banks of the Rakaia, a light drizzle

began to fall. "Do you really think we should try to cross?" asked Caroline.

Detecting the disappointment in his wife's voice, he assured her that they would have no problem reaching the other side in safety.

"We're better off fording the river here than higher up," he said. "The current's not as dangerous."

Caroline gazed out at the rushing brown water. It must be almost a mile to the opposite shore, she thought. She looked up at the black sky and began to wonder if she shouldn't suggest turning back. But she had never been to Wilberforce Station, and for some reason she could not understand, she felt compelled to make the crossing.

Jock cautiously led his horse into the water, Caroline close behind. The Rakaia was filled with rocks and boulders, and from time to time the horses stumbled over the rough terrain. Halfway across the riverbed they met the treacherous Wilberforce, and as they did so a nor'wester greeted them, bringing with it a torrential rain.

"Let's go back!" shouted Caroline, trying to be heard over the powerful wind.

Jock didn't need to hear his wife's words to make the same decision. He started to turn his horse around when he heard a distant cry.

"It's Geoffrey!" shouted Caroline, terrified as she saw his horse stumble into the furious river. She couldn't believe how rapidly the muddy waters were swelling.

Jock, too, had seen Geoffrey, and without a moment's hesitation guided his horse toward his friend.

"Dear God! How will we ever get out of here!" she asked herself. She felt paralyzed as she watched her husband riding away from her.

Within seconds Geoffrey was swept off his saddle and became part of the rushing tide. The river was coming down with such force that his horse, unable to breast it, lost its footing. Caroline watched with horror as she realized there was no way Geoffrey could fight the tremendous pace of the racing waters. By some miracle a boulder stopped him from being carried too far downstream, and he crashed into the partially submerged rock. Caroline was terrified as she saw him go under. She thought he had drowned, having no way of knowing that he had only snapped several ribs and cracked his shoulder bone.

She knew she had to go to him and see if he were still alive. She strained to see him but pelting rain made it extremely difficult. She started riding slowly forward, too terrified to turn back alone. Then she saw Geoffrey's head above the water. He seemed to be swimming but he was only using one arm. She led her horse on. She had to keep both Jock and Geoffrey in sight.

"No!" she screamed with terror as she saw Jock being swept off the saddle of his horse. She couldn't tell what had happened, she only knew that her husband was being carried downstream.

Suddenly Geoffrey's voice reached her. "Go back Caroline! Turn back!" he shouted.

But Caroline couldn't move. Her gaze was glued to Geoffrey as she watched him swim toward Jock, using the current to carry him downstream.

Geoffrey was wracked with pain but nothing could stop him in his attempt to rescue Jock. Horrified, she watched her husband's body being thrown against a lethal boulder, his head bashed against the great rock. Only seconds later Geoffrey reached him, but it was too late. Jock was dead.

Dragging Jock's body behind him, Geoffrey made his way toward Caroline.

Caroline started to dismount from her horse.

"Don't get off!" ordered Geoffrey. "Your horse's footing is steadier than yours."

"Jock! Is Jock all right?" she asked as soon as Geoffrey was by her side. But she knew it was a futile question.

"I'm sorry," was all Geoffrey could reply.

Geoffrey's features were contorted by pain, yet somehow he managed to keep hold of Jock's arm, refusing to let his friend's broken body be carried out to sea. With the other hand he grabbed the mare's reins. "I'll lead him," he called to Caroline. "Just hold on tight."

Once back in the Rakaia the water was shallower, the current less furious. It took them more than two hours to ford the river, but by some miracle they reached the shore.

Geoffrey tethered the horse to a matagouri and Caroline fell to the ground and wept. Verging on hysteria, she was almost oblivious to the strong winds and driving rain.

"Ride back to the Homestead, Caroline, and have one of the hands bring me a horse." Geoffrey spoke firmly, hoping to make Caroline regain control.

"I won't leave you," she sobbed. "I can't go back alone."

Geoffrey studied the horse, trying to determine if the exhausted beast could carry all three of them. There was little choice, he decided. They would have to strain the animal and hope for the best.

By the time they reached the Homestead, Caroline was trembling with cold and in a state of near collapse. She sunk into the sofa, too tired to speak.

"You should change your clothes," suggested Geoffrey. "And I should too."

"Take anything you want," said Caroline, but she herself did not move.

Geoffrey was going to try to persuade her to take off her wet things but realized there was little point. And so, without asking, he helped her up from the sofa and led her into the bedroom. "I won't change until you do," he said, trying to sound lighthearted. "If I catch cold, it will be your fault."

His words did not impress Caroline.

He finally convinced her to take off her dress and put on a warm dressing gown, then went into the other room and changed. He knew he needed a doctor, but there would be time for that later. He found some laudanum and took a swig, hoping temporarily to ease his pain.

When he returned to the bedroom, he found Caroline sobbing, consumed with feelings of guilt. "Oh, Geoffrey, if only I could tell him how sorry I am. He'd be alive today if it hadn't been for me. He was only crossing the river to please me . . .

he knew I wanted to visit your homestead and he was trying to make up for Hone's leaving." A sudden expression of confusion came over her face. "But then you'd be dead," she said, still trembling, tortured by guilt and overcome with grief.

Geoffrey wasn't quite certain he had understood the meaning behind Caroline's words. He couldn't fathom why any of what had happened was her fault. He put his arm around her and quietly held her to him, hoping his closeness would comfort her, make her feel less alone.

"What will I do now?" she asked a long time later. "Where will I go?"

"When the river's down, you'll come to us," he said. "Agnes will enjoy having you around."

Caroline stared at Geoffrey disbelievingly. "Cross the Wilberforce! Never!"

"We'll wait till summer, when it's no more than a gentle stream—"

"No, Geoffrey," she said. She had regained a modicum of control and spoke somberly, choosing her words with care. "I couldn't live in your home. I couldn't even visit you, not now, not with Jock gone. You have your life, it's up to me to make mine, and I have to do that alone."

"But—"

"No buts, Geoffrey. You know I'm right. I'll stay here until I can make other arrangements. I've a great deal to think about, a new life to plan. It will take time and thought, but it's something I must do by myself."

"Can't I be of any help?"

She shook her head slowly. "No, but thanks. I appreciate your concern. One day I'll come to visit, I promise. But not now."

She began crying again as she realized how alone she really was. "I love you, Geoffrey," she sobbed. "I'll always love you. You're the dearest friend I have."

"Then come with me."

"I can't. Please don't ask. Let me do it my way, because that's how it has to be."

Geoffrey did not press her further, but when he left after the funeral the following morning, he wondered if he would ever see Caroline again.

Chapter 25

DROWNING WAS OFTEN CALLED THE "NEW ZEALAND Death," but knowing the grim statistics of the toll of the rivers did nothing to comfort Caroline. For the next few days she stayed in the Homestead, unable to function. Every cross and angry moment she had had with Jock emerged, as fresh in her memory as if the words had just been spoken. She tried to imagine life without Jock and every time she did, she began to cry, until there were no more tears. Desolation overwhelmed her and her feelings were only those of total despair.

Night after night her sleep was confined to short fitful dozes, and by the end of a week she was worn out with fatigue. But as the pain of her great loss slipped into the past, a new strength budded, infusing fresh hope into her soul and a conviction that she must renew the battle for life.

On the first of January 1863, she awoke to the realization that time was not her friend—if she continued to indulge in self pity, she would be trapped at Lake Coleridge until spring. She had concluded that without Jock, she had no desire to continue living in the High Country. With this decision firmly in mind, she had a compelling urgency to map out her future before the snows isolated her from the rest of the world, and knew she had to leave while the weather was still good.

Though she had come to no decisions concerning her future, she knew her present responsibilities: before she could leave Lake Coleridge, she had to write to Barker, Harman, and Davie, the owners of the station, and tell them of Jock's tragic death. She also had to appoint a temporary manager to fill Jock's place.

The days passed quickly as she busied herself with preparations for departure, but still she had no destination in mind. Then one day a letter arrived from Hone. His youthful enthusiasm about life at Skippers fired Caroline's imagination. Suddenly, it became clear to her that this was where she should go. She could open a store for the miners. Her experience in Christchurch made her feel confident she could succeed, and this new challenge helped to wash away her incapacitating grief.

Within two weeks Caroline was ready to leave Lake Coleridge. She had decided to go to Dunedin and spend a week with her brother before traveling into the hinterland. In Dunedin she could arrange for supplies to be shipped to her once she had established a location for her store, and hopefully, Grayson would oversee the first few shipments.

Her departure was delayed several days by one of the worst gales in memory, but when the torrential rains eased, Caroline said her good-byes and left.

As the High Country receded into the horizon, Caroline began to feel optimistic about the future and impatient to reach her destination. She had written to Hone to tell him of her plans, but knowing how irregular the mails could be, she didn't know whether he had received her letter. At first this worried her, since Hone might have moved on to other finds. But the more she thought about it, the more unlikely it seemed in view of his letter. And even if he had moved to another sight, she would have no trouble tracking him down. Someone would know where he was.

When Caroline arrived in Dunedin, the center of the Otago Province, she was astounded by how much it had changed.

Only months before Otago's population had been less than thirteen thousand. Now, with the number over thirty thousand, the Dunedin she remembered as a sleepy, wooden village, had been transformed into a thriving, brick metropolis with six times its previous population. It had become a bustling city, a center of banking and commerce. The gold rush had set Dunedin on the path to prosperity, and the city's commerce flourished beyond the settlers' wildest dreams.

Gold had galvanized the town and Caroline quickly realized that Grayson was taking full advantage of the boom. Not only had he increased his production of beer for the townsmen, he had managed to infiltrate the Otago hinterland so that more Tiger Beer was consumed on the goldfields than any other beer. Just two months ago he had completed the purchase of Well Park Brewery, and with the combined resources of the two companies, Tiger Beer became the leading brewery on the South Island.

Grayson had moved into new offices on the corner of Rattray Street. It was here that Caroline stood listening to her brother's wild dreams.

"I'll be the leading brewer in New Zealand, Caroline, you just wait and see. The day will come when everyone in the colony knows who I am."

"But are you happy? Success is only one part of life."

Grayson hesitated to answer his sister. Happiness was an emotion he had almost forgotten about. It had been so long since he had known what it meant to feel love. His days were filled with work, his nights spent in planning his future moves. He had almost completely obliterated his social life—he had thrown one love to the winds, his second had been taken from him; his third was unrequited. He would not open his heart again. "I'm very fulfilled," he said at last. "I enjoy what I do."

But Caroline sensed her brother's loneliness.

"I saw Hone last week," he said, changing the subject. "He's grown into a fine man. He's doing well and enjoys the mountain life. The lure of gold has infected him." He chuckled. "He may never come back."

"Is he still at Skippers?"

Grayson nodded. "They say the Shotover River—it runs through Skippers—is the richest in the world. I don't think the gold will ever run out there."

"I'm going to join him," said Caroline offhandedly.

"You're what!"

"After Jock died I knew I couldn't stay at the Homestead. Lake Coleridge was fine with a husband. It's no place to be alone."

"You can't go into the goldfields. It's rough country, and I don't mean the terrain. The riffraff that have invaded the area are the worst in the world. You can't imagine the hordes of lawless men there."

"Hone's there, he'll watch out for me."

"Hone can't take care of you and you know it. It's ridiculous to think he will when he's out prospecting all day."

"I can take care of myself, Grayson."

"I won't let you go, Caroline. It's my responsibility to care for you, not Hone's. You can come and live with me."

Caroline could not hold back a smile. How she would have loved to have heard these words when she first came to Dunedin years ago. Grayson looked at her as a fallen woman then —it was interesting to see how much he had changed. "Thanks, Grayson," she said, without bringing up the past. "But you can't stop me. I've decided to go and I'm going."

They talked for a long time, and finally Grayson, realizing that his stubborn sister could not be persuaded to do anything she didn't want to, suggested she at least let him take her to Skippers and help her get settled.

He was surprised when she conceded without reluctance. In fact, he detected that she was pleased by the idea of traveling inland with him, yet realized she would never give him the satisfaction either of telling him she appreciated his offer or of relating any of her fears. It was only much later, in a weak moment—when she asked if there would be other women out there—that Grayson's suspicions were confirmed.

"A number of ladies have left to join their husbands. You've nothing to be afraid of, Caroline, you won't be the only one."

"I'm not afraid," she snapped, then started to laugh, for she knew her brother saw through her bravado.

By the time they were ready to leave the following week, Caroline had outfitted herself with a pair of watertight, thigh-high boots and a prospecting pan, just in case she, too, was stricken with gold fever. She also purchased three scarlet blankets and a supply of stores to take with them on their journey.

It was only after they were on the road toward Queenstown that Grayson broached the subject of what Caroline would do once she got to her destination. "I own several hotels between Queenstown and Skippers," he said. "Would you like to take over managing one of them?"

"I don't think so," she answered. "I want to run a store. It's something I know how to do and do well."

"Then I'll talk to McHardy," he offered. "He'll do anything for me . . . he owes me one. I loaned him the money to get started. He'll be glad to let you work with him."

"I appreciate your help but that's not what I want. I want to open my own store."

"Then I guess that's what you'll do," he said. He reached over and squeezed her arm affectionately. "You've become quite a woman," he told her. "Your strength is really remarkable."

It took them just over a week to travel the one hundred and seventy-five miles to Queenstown, and although it had been a tiring trip, the moment Caroline saw the glorious clear waters of Lake Wakatipu, she felt reborn. The jagged summits that surrounded the lake presented a panorama of majestic beauty as impressive as anything she'd ever seen. Here and there, the mountaintops were capped with snow, a reminder of what winter would be like in this area.

"We'll leave for Skippers at dawn," said Grayson. "It's a hard trip, so we should get a good night's rest. We'll stop at the Greenstone Land Hotel, it's the most comfortable one in town."

Caroline agreed without an argument but didn't have an

inkling as to why this part of the trip should be any more difficult than the terrain they had already crossed.

By the time they were on the road the following morning, a long line of travelers proceeded them—men on foot, with their blankets on their backs, shovels and tin pans in hand, pannikins slung to their waists, walked cheerily along. Not quite five miles from Queenstown, Caroline and Grayson turned off the main road and headed up the steep pack trail that led to Skippers.

At the top of the hill Caroline stopped. She looked ahead at the winding trickle of stones that was called a road, then down at the deep ravine below. She was too terrified to dismount her horse, afraid she would fall over the cliff, but she was even more frightened to stay on the animal's back, certain it would lose its footing.

"Would you be more comfortable walking?" asked Grayson, seeing the look of panic on his sister's face.

"How far do we have to go?"

"About ten miles."

"And it's all like this?" she asked, pointing to the narrow path.

Grayson just nodded. He didn't have the heart to tell her that the road was worse ahead—steeper, more dangerous, and far more hair-raising.

Caroline looked out at the parched countryside, a mountainous land of prickly gorse, matagouri, and tussock grass. "I think I'll walk," she said, but she still wasn't certain how to dismount her horse. She looked at Grayson helplessly.

"Here, let me help you," he said, taking her hand.

Once she was on solid ground, she felt relieved. "I couldn't have done this without you," she admitted gratefully.

"I know." He smiled warmly. "That's why I came."

It was the longest ten miles Caroline had ever walked, and when they reached Shotover Point and she looked down at the rocks in the bed of the river, which she was certain was at least a thousand feet below, she thought she'd be sick.

But the worst was yet to come. In order to cross the Shotover, the miners had built what they called the "Flying

Fox." They had set up an aerial cable more than three hundred feet above the river and equally long across, and had attached an iron chair to the cable.

"I'm not going on that!" gasped Caroline as she watched a prospector climb onto the chair.

"It's the only way across," Grayson said gently. "It's really safe, you don't have to worry."

By now the prospector was halfway across the river. Caroline stared at the chair with horror. "What if the cable snaps!"

"It won't," said Grayson. "Thousands of people have crossed over on it. No one's been hurt."

Caroline had never experienced the terror she now felt, not even in Fiji when she was in danger of being eaten alive—that was nothing compared to her fear of heights. But she had no choice. She'd come this far and she wasn't going back. She waited in silence for the chair to return.

"I'll meet you on the other side," said Grayson, helping her into the chair.

Caroline didn't answer. She grabbed the arms of the chair as tightly as she could and closed her eyes. At least if she didn't have to look at the chasm below, it would be easier.

When Grayson finally joined her on the opposite shore, all she could say was, "I'm never going back. I'll die here, even if everyone leaves, but I'm not going on that thing, not ever again."

Life at Skippers was nothing like Caroline had expected. The area was crowded with men from all over the world—Chinese, Australians, Americans—but they all had one thing in common with New Zealanders: they were there to strike it rich. And there were many more women than she had expected. Dancing girls were imported at great expense. There were twenty-six hotels in the Skippers' area, and at least half of them had entertainment.

Hone was thrilled to see Caroline and insisted that she stay with him. The quarters were modest—a one room, log hut with a thatched roof—but big enough for the two of them.

As soon as Grayson saw that his sister was settled, he returned to Dunedin, promising to see her again before winter set in. He rode away, wondering how his sister had become such a pioneer, so hardworking and courageous, for as he watched the men panning in the river, he knew he could never adjust to such a strenuous life.

With Hone's assistance Caroline set up a store almost adjacent to the hut where they were living. It was not a typical store, for besides catering to every need of the women in the area, it also carried tea—great quantities were consumed on the goldfields—and various items for men: working shirts of blue or red check; moleskin and cord trousers; belts; and heavy, watertight thigh boots. Caroline called the store Everybody's Mart, and within just a few weeks it seemed as if everyone for miles around had heard of it and was shopping there.

Everybody's Mart prospered beyond anything Caroline could have anticipated. By the following spring she realized that ordering supplies through Grayson was not satisfactory. If she wanted the store to continue to grow, she had to go into Queenstown herself, not only to replenish her supplies but to increase her stock. The thought of the trip did not entice her, but by now she had grown accustomed to the rugged terrain and was no longer frightened by it.

"Before you go, you should spend one day panning," Hone told her.

"I can't leave the store," Caroline answered.

"Who are you going to leave in charge when you're away?"

"I've asked Elizabeth Collins to mind it for me."

Elizabeth was the wife of Tim Collins, who owned the Miners' Rest Hotel. She was a heavyset blond woman of the true pioneering breed. She was hardworking yet gentle and hospitable, and well-liked by all.

"Then ask Elizabeth to watch the store tomorrow," said Hone. "Just one day in the river and you'll find enough gold to pay for your trip and all your supplies . . . and buy yourself a present besides."

"I'll do it," said Caroline, for she'd wanted to try her hand at panning for some time but had been too busy.

The following morning at dawn Caroline and Hone set out for the banks of the Shotover River. Caroline had on her watertight boots and a long woolen skirt. She would have loved to have put on the trousers she had worn at dipping time at the homestead but Hone discouraged her, explaining that the men here wouldn't understand.

Once they were at the bed of the river Hone explained, "Just remember, gold is heavier than dirt. Let me show you."

He took a shovel of dirt from the riverbed and put it into his pan. Then he swirled the water and let the soil and stones carefully wash out over the rim of the pan. "The gold sinks to the bottom of the pan," he said as he continued the procedure. "You have to shake off the water, stones, and gravel." He added more water to the pan and continued with a circular movement, letting the gravel mix with the water and then carefully pouring off the mixture. Several minutes later the tin pan was dry and only pieces of gold remained.

"That's amazing!" said Caroline. "Let me try." She stepped into the river. Even through her boots she could feel the cold of the glacial water, but rather than minding it, she found it invigorating.

It took her a long time to master the slow, laborious process, but by the end of the day she had obtained several ounces of gold.

"Now, take that to the bank in Queenstown and see what you've earned . . . then you can buy yourself a piece of Greenstone."

For hundreds of years the Maori had journeyed to Lake Wakatipu in quest for greenstone, a soft jade which can be delicately sculptured into ornaments. *Tangiwai,* as greenstone from these waters was called, is the Maori word for teardrop, the greenstone being a beautiful transparent green which, when held up to the light, sometimes has a teardrop seemingly ingrained in the smooth stone.

Without even looking, Caroline knew she wanted a *heitiki,* a neck pendant. Though she was not overly superstitious, she secretly liked the idea of wearing a good-luck charm. The *heitiki* were skillfully sculpted female figures which originally were probably made as ornaments but now were believed to have the magical potency of amulets. Caroline felt a great sense of accomplishment as she walked back to the hut with Hone. "It's been a marvelous day," she said. "I wish I could do this again tomorrow."

"You can."

"No, I must get into town. My stock's so depleted, I've almost nothing left to sell."

"I'd like you to do me a favor when you're there," said Hone seriously.

"Certainly. What is it?"

"I've learned a great deal since I've come here," he began. "I see now that everyone has a right to live his own life. I've written a letter to Turi that I'd like you to mail. I want to make amends to my brother. He's a Maori and I'm not, but we're still brothers."

Caroline hugged her nephew. "I think that's wonderful," she said. "I wish you could make your father feel the same way."

"I think he does," said Hone. "I just don't think he knows how to tell Turi he wants to undo the past."

"Perhaps next time Grayson comes here, you can speak to him."

"I'll try," Hone answered. "I'll really try."

Chapter 26

THE FOLLOWING MORNING WHEN CAROLINE SET OUT FOR Queenstown alone, she did not feel lonely. Somehow at Skippers her life had taken on new meaning. She was living with her nephew—whom she adored—she had succeeded in achieving a reconciliation with her brother, and she was successful in her business. Though she had lost Jock, and missed him greatly, she had come to terms with her new life.

The two-day ride to town was a difficult one, but the weather was still warm and though the sky was gray, she felt as if the sun were shining brightly; her hopes were high, her spirit optimistic. She checked into the Greenstone Land Hotel at sunset and decided to take a stroll along the lake. She was only minutes from the hotel when she came upon two men resting on a bench near the shore.

"They say at least three men were killed," said one.

Caroline couldn't help but overhear the loud voice.

"Who were they?" asked the other.

"Two were Maoris . . . I'm not certain who the other was. From what I understand, the Maoris were leading a party of mountain climbers. There was an avalanche . . . they say the men must have slipped on a snow slide. They fell at least fifteen hundred feet."

Caroline walked up to the men. It was obvious at once that they were not prospectors, for they were well-dressed in dark suits of the latest Victorian fashion. She introduced herself and asked if they knew who the climbers were.

"We've no idea," said one, who Caroline later learned was John Gordon, proprietor of the Greenstone Land Hotel.

"None," said Tim Gordon, his younger brother.

"All we know," said John, "is that five men decided to climb Mount Earnslaw. Mad to try it at this time of year, before the snows melt."

"Where's that?" Caroline asked.

"Not too far from here," said Tim.

"Up the top of the lake," John said, pointing north along the shore of Lake Wakatipu. "Maybe ten miles beyond," he added.

"Don't know why they had to try it," said Tim. "That Irishman, what was his name? Oh, I remember, Green—he tried it last year. A man was killed then, too, and Green didn't reach the top. You'd think that would have been a lesson."

"You know you can't warn mountain climbers." John sneered cynically. "Those people are a special breed."

An uncomfortable feeling came over Caroline as she looked at the dark mountains that surrounded the lake. She shuddered as she thought of how terrible it would be to be trapped in the snows with no way to come down.

"Do you think they'll get the men back safely?" she asked.

John looked up at the overcast sky. "Not if it snows tonight," he said.

Caroline thanked the men, excused herself for intruding, then walked away.

That night she was restless and couldn't sleep. She kept thinking of the five men, worrying that the search party wouldn't reach them in time. It was foolish to be so concerned about men she had never met, but each time she closed her eyes, all she could envision were five men buried alive in an avalanche of snow.

There was no sign of spring the next morning, in fact, it looked as if winter had returned to stay. From her window Caroline could see nothing but a falling curtain of snow. The temperature had dropped considerably and a biting wind made the weather even more disagreeable.

Caroline had no time to stay in the hotel. She had a great deal to accomplish in a very few days and was determined that the elements were not going to delay her return.

She was having breakfast in the hotel dining room when the proprietor approached her.

"How much first aid do you know?" John Gordon asked. He had heard it said that she had cared for several miners at Skippers.

Caroline looked at the tall, bearded man for a moment, shrugged, then said, "Why do you ask?"

"Dr. Barker's gone to Dunedin. Won't be back for a few weeks. If they get those men down, they'll need medical attention."

"I worked for a doctor once," said Caroline. "And I worked in a hospital. But I don't know much."

"You know enough, Mrs. Milsom. Will you stay and help?"

Caroline didn't know how to answer. She had tended to the superficial wounds of several miners, and at the Homestead she had had occasion to bandage some of the musterers; she had even helped Dr. Weatherby years ago, but that hardly made her competent to care for men who were badly hurt.

"Another pair of hands is better than nothing," said John, sensing her lack of confidence.

"I'll stay if you think you need me," said Caroline. "When do you think they'll get them down?"

Now it was John who shrugged. "No idea, Missus. Not the slightest."

Late that afternoon several of the rescue party came into the hotel to have drinks at the bar.

"The snows were too bad to stay up there," Caroline heard one of the men tell John. "But we found an ice axe, so we're looking in the right place. If the weather clears up, we should have them out by tomorrow."

"Dead or alive!" snickered one of the others.

Caroline couldn't listen. These men were supposed to be a rescue party yet they seemed heartless. She walked back to her room and busied herself with making a list of what she needed to do the following day, then dashed off a note to Hone to explain her delay.

The hotel was having entertainment that evening—a magician had come from Dunedin and a singer was performing. Caroline was in no mood for festivities—she could not see celebrating when five men were dying.

That night she had a dream that Grayson was among the five. She awoke in a terrible sweat even though she knew, without question, that Grayson was safely at home in Dunedin. But then she kept asking herself: Was he at home? Was mountain climbing a new passion of his? Was he one of the five? Was he the one who had fallen? She had never been so pleased to see dawn break, and she was even more delighted when she saw the sun brightly shining. Spring had come again.

Two more days were to pass before news came that the men had been found. One had died of exposure and the other four were badly hurt, but with care it was believed they would live.

"The hospital's not finished yet," Tim Gordon told Caroline, "so my brother sent a message for the rescuers to bring the men here."

"Do you have everything I'll need?" she asked.

"Like what?"

"Bandages, alcohol to cleanse their wounds, laudanum—"

"We've got all that."

"Good," said Caroline. "I'll do my best but I'm not a doctor, you know that."

Tim nodded. "Like John said, you're all we got."

Several hours later the first of the rescued men was brought into the hotel. Caroline was called at once. She looked down at the young man; glassy eyes stared back at her. "Where does it hurt?" she asked.

There was no answer.

Caroline took his hand gently. It was cold and lifeless. "He's dead!" she gasped.

Tim pulled the covers over the boy's face.

"He couldn't have been more than eighteen," Caroline said. "How terrible!"

"There's another man in the next room," said Tim, wanting to get Caroline away from the dead boy as quickly as possible.

There were actually two men in the adjoining room. They both had frostbite and were suffering from exposure, but miraculously, there was nothing else wrong.

Caroline was exhausted by the time she turned to Tim and said, "There should be one more."

"This way," said Tim. "You're really doing a find job. Don't know how we would have managed without you."

Caroline smiled. "You'd have managed, but I'm glad I could help."

As she started to cross the threshold of the next room, she stopped in her tracks. She couldn't believe who was lying in front of her. She tiptoed across the room and stared at the sleeping face.

Her presence awakened the man. "Caroline?" he asked, thinking he was hallucinating.

"Geoffrey?" was all she could answer, still not believing her eyes.

"I tried to find you—" he said.

"Shh! Don't talk."

"The others . . . how are they?"

Caroline was hesitant. She didn't want to upset Geoffrey, but she couldn't lie. "Two of the men are fine," she said, "but the youngster . . ."

"David?"

"I don't know his name."

"Tell me," said Geoffrey, trying to sit up. "Will he be all right?"

"I'm sorry," said Caroline. "Please lie back, Geoffrey. You need all your strength."

Geoffrey's eyes closed. For a moment he was silent. "That was Richard's son," he said. "Oh, God! That poor man. He lost his wife last year . . . that's why he moved to the High Country . . . to start again. He took over Lake Coleridge . . . and David died on the mountain. . . ."

"Not now," said Caroline gently. "We'll talk later." She began cleaning the cuts on his face, feeling his pain almost as acutely as he did, wincing each time the alcohol burned his open wounds. Silently she thanked God that his cuts and bruises were all relatively minor. She had so many questions to ask but they'd have to wait—his eyes were closed, he wasn't strong enough to speak.

Several minutes passed before Geoffrey found the strength to ask, "What are you doing here?"

As she continued to tend him, she told him briefly how she had come to Skippers and exactly what she was doing there.

"Why didn't you let me know that's where you were? I would have come to you."

"You have your life, Geoffrey, I had to make mine."

Again Geoffrey closed his eyes, exhausted as much from the excitement of seeing Caroline as from being trapped for five days on the mountain.

"We'll talk later," she repeated again softly. Then she sat quietly by his side as he drifted off to sleep.

For the next three days Caroline refused to leave Geoffrey. Day and night she remained with him, just stroking his head gently or holding his hand. She had her meals brought to his room and though Tim and John tried to convince her to get some rest, she refused to leave.

On the fourth day Geoffrey awoke feeling much better. "Are you still here?" he said, his eyes sparkling with the pleasure of seeing Caroline.

Now it was she who could barely talk.

"You're exhausted," he said. "You should lie down."

"No, I'll be fine," she answered softly.

Geoffrey could see she was too tired to speak, and so he decided to carry the conversation. "I was in Dunedin before I came here," he began. "I spent two days with Grayson. I can't understand him."

"What do you mean?"

"I asked him about you . . . told him I was going climbing on Mount Earnslaw. . . . I can't believe he didn't tell me you were so nearby."

"What did he say?"

"That you were with Hone. But I thought that meant that you were both in Auckland." He took a deep breath before continuing. "Right after the climb I was planning to come to you." He paused for another moment, seemingly deep in thought. "I don't understand why Grayson was so evasive," he continued, "except that he said he hoped one day you and Hone would come back to him."

"That's true," said Caroline. "He's a very lonely man. But I couldn't live with him . . . and he doesn't need me, he needs a wife." Her voice was hoarse, her fatigue such that she could barely continue.

"Your brother certainly has changed."

Caroline tilted her head in a questioning motion.

"He's decided to make amends to Amiria," Geoffrey explained. "Really, I think it's more Turi who he longs to see. Anyway, he realizes, at last, that the only way back to Turi is to accept the boy on his terms. Now that Grayson's a wealthy man, he's decided to set up a school for young Maoris. It will be aimed at improving the lot of the Maori without insisting they assimilate with the Pakeha."

"How absolutely wonderful," said Caroline. Her voice was suddenly animated and she felt as awake as if she'd had a long night's sleep.

Geoffrey smiled. "Now that you're talking again, tell me why you didn't tell me you were here."

"I told you," she answered.

He ignored her response and continued, "I tried to find you, but nobody at the Homestead knew where you'd gone."

"I would have written eventually."

"I didn't want to wait," he admitted.

There was a long silence, then Geoffrey said, "When Agnes died—"

"Agnes died!"

"Yes, about three months after Jock."

"What happened?"

"She had been ill for a very long time. That's why she stopped coming to town with me. The last three years she was in a wheelchair. It was terrible to watch her become paralyzed and lose all her strength. She'd been such a vital woman. But there was no way to help her, nothing any of the doctors could do."

"I am sorry," Caroline said. "I know how much you cared about her."

Geoffrey took Caroline's hand and pressed it to his chest. "You know how I feel about you," he said, and pulled her to him. He kissed her lips tenderly, almost brotherly.

"Careful, you'll hurt yourself."

"There's nothing wrong with me that a few more days of rest and some good food won't make right."

"Are you hungry? Would you like me to get you something to eat?"

"No, just stay here and talk to me. Will you come home with me?"

"To Wilberforce Station?"

He smiled. "To Wilberforce Station."

She returned the look of love in his eyes and held his hand tightly.

"Oh, Caroline, I can't believe that at last we're both free."

"Are we?" she asked smiling happily, knowing they were now bound to each other.

ENJOY ALL OF THESE TITLES FROM PARADISE PRESS

LOVE'S FRANTIC FLIGHT by Joan Joseph. She escaped to a new world in search of the man she loved.

A DREAM OF FIRE by Drusilla Campbell. Her beauty warmed Scotland's green hills—and a warrior's fierce heart!

NOW IS THE HOUR by Joan Joseph. In New Zealand she found wild beauty, savage splendor, and her heart's hidden desire.

THIS RAGING FLOWER by Lynn Erickson. She was an exotic English blossom in a land barren of all but the wildest passions, the boldest men.

CONQUER THE MEMORIES by Janet Joyce. 1847: The Mexican-American War. A spirited English noblewoman braved the perils of battle and her own unbridled passions.

RED ROSES FOREVER by Amanda Jean Jarrett. 1875 - On the night of the first Kentucky Derby a fiery Southern beauty encounters romance and intrigue— and a lover with a startling secret.

OUTRAGEOUS DESIRE by Carla A. Neggers. Summer: 1874 - The rich and powerful of Saratoga Springs held little allure for this beautiful reformer. Then, who was this charming, handsome stranger who came to town with his outrageous behavior?

ENJOY ALL OF THESE TITLES
FROM PARADISE PRESS

ISLAND OF PROMISE by Madeleine Carr.
1779: Georgia in turmoil. A beautiful Savannah
heiress—imprisoned in an exotic house of pleasure—
was determined to escape and find her island lover.

PASSION'S HEIRS by Elizabeth Bright. In the rugged
wilderness of the new West, she was caught in a
whirlwind of danger and passion by a masked stranger
she met at a costume ball.

THE PASSION AND THE FURY by Amanda Jean
Jarrett. 1872 - On a vast plantation in South Carolina a
spirited Southern girl and the suddenly appearing
mystery man from the North face a strange and
dangerous destiny.

FORTUNE'S TIDE by Gene Lancour. A proud,
beautiful woman pays the price of passion over a man
with a fearsome secret.

THE SILVER MISTRESS by Chet Cunningham. Silver
City, Nevada 1870: A sensuous and resourceful woman
fights to save her silver mine.